REVIVAL

UNVEILED - BOOK 1

DEBBIE LYNN

ISBN paperback: 979-8-9886697-0-8

ISBN ebook: 979-8-9886697-2-2

Book Cover by MoorBooks Design

First edition 2023

Published by Watermeadow Press

To R, P, and B –
Without you, my heart wouldn't be whole.
Also, without you, this book would
have been finished a lot sooner.

ONE

"Tori," Grey called from the kitchen, "where are the blueberries?" Refrigerator drawers slammed, and he mumbled words I couldn't discern.

I stopped applying mascara and sighed. "On the shelf with the eggs."

He didn't reply.

In his silence, I made my way from the bathroom to the kitchen, one eye still bare, holding the mascara wand. "Find them?" I rounded the corner to the open kitchen.

He held up a bag of fresh fruit over his shoulder. "Weird place for blueberries. Instead of, you know, with the other fruit."

I was close enough to touch him now, and since he was wearing nothing but boxer briefs and bed-head, I couldn't help myself. I wrapped my arms around him from behind and buried my face in the muscles of his upper back.

Rather than respond, because I really had no reason for not putting the blueberries in the crisper, I nuzzled in closer and wiggled my hips. My skirt rose a little when I did so, making me feel even sexier.

He spun around in my arms, wiping a line of makeup across his stomach from the wand I was still holding.

I touched it with one finger, noticing the way the mascara moved over defined muscle lines and stopped near a small birthmark just above the edge of his boxer briefs. I bit my lower lip and peered up at him.

"I was going to make some pancakes, but that can wait." His voice was silky and low.

He was a head taller than me, but I reached my free hand up and tussled his hair. I loved his hair, curly on the top and just long enough for stray ringlets to fall onto his forehead, occasionally brushing the top of his plastic-framed glasses.

And he loved when I played with it. He responded with a soft moan and reached both hands to cup my butt and lift me up onto my tip-toes. He kissed my forehead and pulled back enough I could look into his hazel eyes.

I tossed the mascara wand onto the counter behind him and nodded, raising an eyebrow.

Grey lifted me off my feet.

I wrapped my legs around him, and we headed for the nearest surface, which was the kitchen island behind me.

He set me down on the counter and lifted my blouse over my head.

Freshly applied makeup smeared across the inside of the shirt. I didn't mind.

His tongue teased my ear, my neck, the space between my breasts. I tilted my head back and closed my eyes, letting myself get lost in the blissful feeling.

Suddenly, the bliss disappeared. My chest tightened, and my body felt hot. Not the type of hot that normally accompanied Grey's body touching mine, but a new, uncomfortable kind.

I took a deep breath, causing Grey to lift his head a few inches from my skin. "Everything okay?"

I tried to nod, but my head felt heavy. My whole body ached. "No," I choked out. "Something's wrong."

Grey stepped back and studied me, squinting his eyes despite wearing his glasses. "You look alright. What's going on?"

My head was too heavy to hold up. I maneuvered myself on the counter to lie against it, curled on my side. The coolness of the marble soothed my burning skin, but only barely.

As I closed my eyes, Grey's voice drifted from miles away, calling my name.

And then the world faded away.

I OPENED MY EYES one blink at a time. Lights above me burned, making my eyes water. I closed them and tried to focus my senses elsewhere. A cacophony of sounds assaulted me from all directions. My body tingled, like it had been asleep for a long time, which made little sense—it was very much awake a moment ago.

A voice called my name, but I couldn't make out who it belonged to, or where anyone was. The blinding light seeped through my closed eyelids. This couldn't be Heaven; it wasn't peaceful enough. I tried to turn my head, but a new heaviness stopped me. Even though I could only sense a bright fluorescence around me, I had a feeling this wasn't the other place either.

"Goodness, glory!" a familiar voice shouted nearby.

I winced at the noise and forced my eyes open, squinting through tears that formed instantly. My vision was blurry, so I couldn't see the speaker, and I couldn't quite put my finger on who it was.

"Tori," the voice said again, closer this time. Someone's fingers squeezed mine. "Victoria."

I blinked a few times against the lights and tried to focus in on the figure now leaning over me. Her near-black hair was very long. The woman's eyes were blue, like winter ice. I'd know those eyes anywhere.

"M... Marina?" I stuttered. Speaking made my throat hurt, and I groaned.

My sister looked around and motioned to someone I couldn't see, speaking to them so frantically I couldn't understand. The flutter of her hand made my head spin, and I closed my eyes again. Marina's hand squeezed mine. "I'm here, Tori. So is Grey. We've been here... waiting for you."

Holy shit, were they dead, too? Opening my eyes, I tried to shake my heavy head, not comprehending. "What, what happened?" My voice came out a soft croak, but they seemed to understand me.

Marina turned away briefly and then back at me. "We're not sure, really. You–"

"No, not me. You. Why are you here, too?"

Another voice chimed in, deeper and smoother. Grey. "Waiting for you," he said, echoing Marina's earlier statement.

"I don't... understand. Am I still in the kitchen?"

They laughed, though they sounded strained.

Another hand grasped the fingers of my free hand and squeezed lightly. "We're in the hospital," Grey said. He leaned over me, his head beside Marina's, giving me a better, but still fuzzy, look at him. His curly hair was a little longer than I remembered, with bits falling over the top of his glasses. His hazel eyes were watery, and he blinked a few times.

"I'm not dead?"

"You're not dead," Grey responded.

As soon as I asked, a third person was at my head, gently placing something cold, smooth, and wet in my mouth. Ice. Ice chips. I really was in a hospital.

My confusion probably should have subsided some at that

point, but it increased. I felt in my gut that I wasn't just injured; I was dead. Or had been dead. Or something. I frowned back at them. "Then why do I feel like I am?" The words made my throat burn, which was at odds with the dull ache overtaking the rest of my body. I let my head sink further into my pillow, the pain washing over me.

I took slow, deliberate breaths and focused on my surroundings for the first time to distract myself. Behind Marina and Grey, the walls were a sunny yellow, not the standard beige I'd seen in other hospital rooms. A string of crystals, in reverse-rainbow order, hung in the center of the wall. Blinds covered the windows, letting slits of bright sunlight in, but I couldn't see outside.

A TV mounted in the corner played a news station on mute. I squinted at it, but all I could make out were the words 'Governor Johnson,' because they were larger than the rest. I had never seen him before and paid him no mind. The ache was subsiding, so I turned my attention back to my sister, who was watching me with concern.

"It's a little better now. That must have been magical ice or something," I joked.

The person at my head cleared her throat, and Grey and Marina shared a look. "The doctor needs to see you now," Marina said. She let go of my hand but gave it a pat. "We'll be right back when he's done."

Within moments, a man with a stethoscope came into the room and began asking me questions about how I felt. The nurse returned and together, they prodded and poked, then sat me up and made me try to squeeze a stress ball—though I could barely close my fingers around it, much less squeeze it.

"I still don't understand what's going on," I said, focusing on the red ball in my grip. I glanced up in time to notice a concerned glance pass between them.

"Let's just get you into this wheelchair, honey," the nurse said with an empty smile.

"Where are we going? Why do I need a wheelchair?"

"Let's get some test results, then we can give you more answers," the doctor answered. He nodded to the nurse, who wheeled me through a maze of hallways until we reached our destination.

The nurse and a young man wearing teal scrubs assisted me onto a cold table, laying me on my back. Within minutes, my upper body was inside a huge contraption that whirred over and around me, which intensified the headache growing behind my eyes. Against the backdrop of the banging noises from the machine, I closed my eyes, held still, and tried to picture the last thing I remembered.

And came up blank. Nada. I remembered nothing. No fragments or flashes or feelings came to mind.

No one had told me anything about why I was in the hospital or how long I had been here, but from their reactions, it seemed like a long time. Had I been out for days, or even weeks? The thought made me shudder.

A voice interrupted me through the speaker by my head. "Try to be still, please."

Tears formed in my eyes—not from the lights this time, but from the confusion and frustration swirling inside me. I had spent an hour with the doctor and nurse, and still had no answers.

Finally, several banging noises later, the nurse pulled me out of the machine. She whispered some words I didn't recognize as she lifted the cage off my face. "For strength and healing," she said. She touched something smooth and cold to my forehead.

I had no idea what she was talking about, but I smiled and let her lead me back to the wheelchair. My feet didn't want to cooperate, and my legs threatened to buckle during the one step I had to take to sit back down.

Atrophy? I had been here long enough for my muscles to atrophy? Someone needed to give me answers. As soon as I saw Marina and Grey, I was going to demand them.

TWO

"WHAT DO YOU REMEMBER?" Marina asked a few minutes later, her voice hopeful. She sat on one side of my hospital bed, Grey standing beside her. He held a small basket of blueberries in one hand and ate them one at a time while we spoke.

Blueberries.

My last memory came back in pieces, broken and scattered. I cleared my throat, which felt perpetually hoarse. "Grey and I were... well, we were at home and–"

Her brows furrowed. "Home? You and Grey?"

I glanced from her to him, noticing the confusion on his face.

I took a sip of the water beside my bed. "Yeah, we were at our apartment. He was making pancakes, and I was getting ready for work. We started ... kissing ... and then there was this weird pain. I couldn't breathe, and everything sounded strange." A sensation creeped up my spine, and I shivered. "And then—poof! I was here. The lights were bright, and everything felt strange. I was sure I was dead, and this was some kind of afterlife. I don't remember being here at all. Isn't that weird?"

Grey made a noise akin to a squeak. "We, uh, we never–"

Marina smacked his arm. "Tori ... when did you and Grey move in together?"

I stared at her. What kind of question was that? She helped us move, for Pete's sake. "A few years ago," I reminded her. "You were there. You loved the kitchen but hated the color of the living room, and I said I wouldn't repaint because gray was the perfect color." I smiled up at the man with the same name.

They both shook their heads. Marina peered up at Grey, and from what I could see of her profile, she was worried.

He cleared his throat again. "Tori. We never moved in together. We had the place picked out, and we were going to move in November, so we could have our first Thanksgiving in that kitchen you and Marina loved so much. But then ..." He trailed off and looked at Marina, shrugging.

"And then you fell into a coma for four-and-a-half years," she blurted.

I chuckled. "Nice, guys. Mess with the half-dead girl. Seriously, though." Their faces stopped me from continuing. "Seriously?"

They nodded in unison. Marina squeezed my hand tighter than before. Grey leaned forward, his arm outstretched like he was going to touch my shoulder. It lingered in the air a moment, and instead he patted my hair a few times before shoving his hands into his pockets, averting his gaze.

"But I remember."

Grey shook his head, staring at the wall behind me. "You're remembering wrong. Maybe your mind was playing out some version of how you should have lived, filling in details so everything made sense."

My whole body prickled. I shook my head, blinking my eyes. My chest tightened and my breath hitched when I inhaled.

Marina reached up with her free hand and rubbed my forehead along my brow line, like our Grandma Lillie used to do.

When I spoke, my voice was shaky. "So, all these memories up here," I asked, pointing to my temple, "they're not real?"

"Maybe, maybe not," Grey said. "Some of them are, I'm sure." He finally looked at me, and his expression was sad and distant.

"The last memory I have, in the kitchen—our kitchen that you say we never moved into—that didn't happen?"

They shook their heads again.

The realization was bittersweet. They were telling me that Grey and I never moved into the apartment I loved so much, but also that I didn't really experience that mind-numbing pain, which was the only thing I remembered. Could it have been the pain of being awakened from my coma?

I sighed. "It felt like I was living a life. You say I've been gone four years, but for me, I've been living out those years. Grey and I were getting married. The wedding was coming up. Really soon," I added, trying to remember how soon. But I couldn't pinpoint a date in my mind, or even what time of year I died... or whatever we were calling it.

Grey's eyes were wide. He didn't look upset, just a little thrown off. This was all definitely news to him. Apparently, we were not engaged.

He must have read something in my face, because his expression softened. "We had just celebrated our second anniversary when the Unveiling... well, when you fell into a coma."

"The Unveiling?" I asked. "What's that?"

Marina grimaced. "Worry about that later." She began stroking my brow line again.

When she did, I noticed a flash on her finger. A ring. I grabbed her hand and inspected it, despite her trying to pull away. "An engagement ring?"

A small smile flicked across her face, and she averted her gaze.

"You've been gone almost five years," Grey reminded me softly.

I nodded. "My baby sister is getting married." It was strange, seeing as how I genuinely thought I was getting married soon a couple hours ago. "So, tell me about this guy. Also, I need to meet him pronto, since I didn't get to inspect him earlier and pass my approval."

Her eyes flitted to the wall. "Let's talk about this later."

I tried to shrug, but the movement made my shoulders and neck ache. "Why? It's not like I'm going anywhere. Seriously, Sis, tell me about him. What's his name? What does he do? Does he treat you right? And most importantly," I added, lowering my voice to a conspiratorial level, "does he know about your addiction to the TLC channel?" All the talking hurt my throat, so I reached for another sip of water, which caused Grey to take a step back out of my way.

Marina chewed on her lower lip, and her face scrunched up into an apology. She visibly gulped, then she removed her hand from my forehead and swept it out to the side. "You were sleeping, and we didn't know if you'd wake up."

It took several seconds for my eyes to follow her hand and notice where it ended up. Inside Grey's. My sister was holding my boyfriend's hand.

"Well, I'm awake now," I said cautiously.

Her face crumpled, her lower lip quivering. "It was four-and-a-half years, Tori. We were both by your side every day, and we were both grieving."

Grey coughed a little, then added, "We fought it for a long time, Tor. We didn't want to hurt you, and even if you never ... well, it just felt weird."

I stared at him, dumbstruck. Did I just hear what I thought I had heard?

"Tori?" Marina asked softly.

I turned my glare onto her without moving my head, which was pounding. "It just felt weird," I repeated. "Damn right it's weird! Were you going to hold hands over my grave? Give a sad toast at your wedding about how you thought you'd be marrying the other James girl, and isn't it funny how life turns out, hardy har har?" I could feel heat rising in my throat and face. The monitor beside me started beeping a little more loudly than before.

"Calm down, Tori," Marina begged. "Please. The important thing here is that we both love you."

I folded my arms and turned my head to the side, scowling. "I can't believe you'd do this to me."

"Victoria Margaret James," Marina said, standing abruptly, causing the bed to shake from her movements. "You were practically dead. Do you understand that? Dead! We were together every day, and in our grief, we fell in love. We just got engaged last month."

I clumsily wiped tears from my cheeks. My shaking hands didn't want to obey my commands, so I gave up. I breathed out hard and glared at them. "Okay. We are not done discussing this, but I'll table it before I say something I'll regret. Is there anything else I need to know while I'm already blowing a gasket?"

Grey and Marina shared a glance again, their expressions unreadable.

I sighed. "Fine. Save the surprise for another day."

Their faces showed immediate relief.

"Just get me the hell out of this place," I said.

"Yeah," Grey said, "about that."

I glared at him. "What about it?"

The door to my room slid open and someone in a jacket came in; she must have been a doctor. "How are you feeling, Victoria?" she asked as she approached.

"Tori," I said. As she neared, I noticed her jacket was tan rather than white. At a second glance, I saw it wasn't a jacket at all; it was more like a robe, the kind a wizard might wear in a movie. I frowned.

Marina and Grey showed no indication that anything was out of the ordinary. They must have seen this robed lady before, because they didn't seem concerned about her presence. Well, Grey didn't. Marina glanced away, and I thought I saw something akin to disgust flicker across her face.

"I'm Celeste," the lady told me. "We're going to do some bodywork. Your guests are welcome to stay, or they can leave if you'd rather be alone."

"I have no idea what you're talking about. What's bodywork?"

Celeste smiled warmly at me and pushed some stray blonde hair behind her ears. "Energy medicine, basically. I've been coming in for a while now."

I stopped her with a shake of my head. "Energy medicine? No thanks. I prefer my medicine traditional and scientific."

I noticed Marina wince. Maybe I was being too harsh on Celeste; she was only doing her job. I began to apologize at the same time she spoke, so I shut my mouth and motioned her onward with a clumsy wave of my hand.

With a little laugh, Celeste said, "Honey, traditional medicine flew out the window years ago."

"Excuse me?"

She frowned. "I mean, we still use it, of course. But we've found that magic and energy can speed up the healing process significantly. How else do you think you're moving around and talking as well as you are?"

I turned to Marina and Grey, who were both ashen and quiet.

Understanding dawned on Celeste's face. "Oh, no," she whispered. She turned to my visitors. "I'm so sorry. I'm going to let you guys talk."

Marina was obviously not happy that Celeste had opened a can of worms for her to clean up. She glared at Celeste's back as she walked out. Then she turned back to me and reached for my hand again. "Tori."

I tried to sit upright and winced. My whole body ached, but also felt incredibly difficult to maneuver. "Am I paralyzed?" I cried, the strange news momentarily forgotten in favor of a strong sense of fear.

They shook their heads. "The doctor said that if—when—you woke up, you'd have to go through intensive physical therapy to use your muscles again," Grey told me. "You won't be able to walk on your own for some time," he said in a quieter voice.

I shook my head slowly in disbelief. So, I wasn't dead, but my body had basically been. The news kept getting better.

Marina offered a small smile. "Tori, we need to talk about what happened the night you ... went to sleep."

"I didn't go to sleep, Marina. I was in a coma. Big difference. And yes, please, tell me what happened to me."

She nodded. "I know that. It's just difficult for me." Her eyes watered. "I've been without my big sister for almost five years, Tori. And a lot has changed since you've been gone. A lot. The Indianapolis you know is not the same one you're going to be living in. The entire world is different now. It's been a rough adjustment for all of us."

"So, fill me in. What could possibly be so different from four-and-a-half years ago?"

"You'll never believe who is President," Grey offered from the foot of the bed.

"Don't start with that," Marina chided him. "Just rip the Band Aid, guys. What the hell was Celeste talking about?"

Marina peered over her shoulder at Grey, who took a few steps to stand by her side. Not my side anymore, but my sister's. I tried not to show my emotions on my face.

She took a deep breath and let it out in a rush of words. "Magic is real. It happened the night you fell ... went into your coma. You were on your way to my Halloween party, but never showed up. Someone found you on the street, passed out. We don't know if it had to do with the magic surge or not."

I stared at her, unblinking. Finally, I let out the breath I hadn't realized I was holding. "Okay, go back a minute. What do you mean, magic is real?"

"Just what she said," Grey replied. "They call it The Unveiling. The night the veil between our world and another one fell, and their magic poured in."

I shook my head and pulled my hand out of Marina's grip. "Wait. I need ... this doesn't ... So, everyone is magical now?"

They both shook their heads. They spoke at the same time, and I shushed them with a glare. Laughing nervously, Marina tried again. "Not everyone. Some people have an innate talent for magic that's been hidden their whole lives, because magic didn't exist on this plane. Like a dormant genetic marker. When the veil dropped, their magic activated." She looked away.

Grey continued for her. "But not everyone has this magic innately. I don't. Marina doesn't."

"I'm so glad, too," Marina said, her tone darker. "Magicians are scary. They have no training, no control over their powers. They just use them willy-nilly, regardless of who they might hurt." She was bitter and upset. I wanted to press, but her tone made me think twice.

I inhaled slowly, trying to ward off the coming panic attack. This was too much to take on all at once. First, I was in a coma for almost five years. Second, my ex was marrying my sister. Third, magic was real. I shook my head, but it still didn't make sense.

They let me sit in silence while I processed. Finally, I found the words I needed. "You guys are bullshitting me. I can believe I was in a coma. Hell, I can even believe you two are engaged—which I'm still pissed about—but magic? That's too far."

Marina took my hand in hers. "It's a lot to get used to, believe me. When the veil dropped, it was hectic for quite some time. I don't expect you to understand it all right now."

"Good," I said, "because that's not going to happen anytime soon, maybe ever. This is all too much." The statement caught in my throat and my voice broke.

Marina glanced at Grey, who nodded almost imperceptibly. If it hadn't been for the wayward curl that flopped when his head moved, I wouldn't have seen it.

"No," I stated. "You don't get to say all that crap and then leave. Sit down and tell me everything." When neither of them moved, I added, "Now," pointing to the chairs against the wall.

They sat stiffly, neither looking at me.

"Start with Celeste. What was she talking about?"

Grey leaned forward and rested his folded arms across his knees. "Celeste is an energy healer. She has been coming in regularly and doing some basic stuff, like massaging your muscles but also channeling your aura and trying to talk to you on the astral plane."

I folded my arms across my chest. "Nope, didn't hear her on any plane."

Marina offered a sad smile. "The doctors said you may hear us, so I talked to you every day. Read to you, sang to you ... you didn't hear any of it?"

"Like I said, I thought I was living out my life. I didn't hear any voices talking to me while I did that."

She wiped her eyes. "I wish you had. I talked to you every day. Every day, Tori. I'm just glad you're awake now, and I can talk to you and know you're hearing me."

I was too, of course, but with all these revelations, I kind of wished I could go back to sleep. At that thought, I faked a yawn and watched as my guests jumped to their feet, all too ready to leave.

Marina hugged me and kissed my cheek, her tears spilling onto my face as she did so.

Grey leaned in for a hug, and I turned my face toward him expectantly. He jumped back, releasing me.

Realization hit me like a brick in my gut. "Oh." I couldn't even bring myself to apologize for wanting to kiss the man I still thought of as mine. So, I didn't.

Grey showed me a tight-lipped smile and hurried around the bed to join Marina in the doorway. They said their final goodbyes and walked out.

At least they had the decency to wait until they thought I couldn't see them before they held hands.

THREE

A WEEK PASSED. A week of painful physical therapy, strange energy healing, and awkward conversations with my sister and Grey. The hospital moved me to the rehab wing, where I had less supervision and a homier atmosphere. But despite the warmer paint on the walls and a couch in my room, I still felt like a lab rat in a hospital.

Today, though, was special. It was my birthday. And no amount of therapies and tests would take away my celebration.

I closed my eyes, the bright candlelight in front of me dimming, and wished with everything in my power that I wasn't in the hospital anymore, and that this was the dream instead of my life with Grey. But when I opened them, nothing was different.

The cake in front of me had two candles—a 3 and a 0—and vanilla icing, my favorite. A nurse had helped me onto the couch before company arrived, and she had placed the cake on a tray table in front of me. It was much better than celebrating stuck in bed.

Grey stood on one side of me and Marina on the other, big smiles on their faces. They had sung the birthday song, and I had smiled back meekly. This was not how I wanted to turn thirty.

But at least I *was* turning thirty. And awake to see it. I wondered how they celebrated my other birthdays, twenty-six through twenty-nine.

Marina leaned over and kissed my cheek. "I'm so happy," she

said through tears.

I smiled up at her and gave her an awkward one-armed hug, which made my IV line pull at my arm. I winced, and she cringed at my expression. "I'm okay," I assured her. "Thanks for all this. I'm glad you guys are here to celebrate with me."

"Where else would we be?"

I offered a sad laugh. "Oh, I don't know. Work, maybe. Wherever the rest of my so-called friends went when I didn't wake up. Or," I added as an afterthought, "on a yacht with the newest Mr. James."

It was Marina's turn to wince. "I don't think Mom has her boyfriends take her last name," she said, trying to lighten the mood. Anytime the subject of my mom—who had not yet visited me since I woke up—came up, Marina seemed to feel like she had to make jokes. It was something I always loved about her.

"All the same," I said with a shrug. "She's really just married to her job, anyhow." I swiped at the icing with my finger and stuck it in my mouth. It was so good; it almost tasted like old times. But not quite.

"Or one of the partners, at least," Marina quipped.

I smiled at her. Good ole Marina and her jokes. I had fulfilled my big sister duties when our dad died, but she was the one comforting me when it came to our absent mother. That's how it had always been. I brushed away the familiar ache that spread through me at the thought of my father.

"Are you ready to go outside?" Grey asked, swaying from side to side gently as he stood beside my bed. It was his nervous tell.

"Just a minute," I said. I took another swipe of icing and smiled.

"You know, the cake is good too," Marina said with a chuckle.

"But the icing's the best part. Okay, now I'm good to go." I pushed the tray away and glanced around the room. "Do I get to wear real clothes, though, or do I have to go outside in this gown?"

Marina motioned to an oversized bag on a chair by the door. "I brought some clothes for you."

I squealed. I had been in this hospital gown for a week—well, for a lot longer than that. Who knows how often they changed me while I was comatose? Grey grabbed the bag and handed it to me. "I'll, uh, wait outside." His smile was tense.

I realized just how weird this all must be for him. Coming to his ex-girlfriend's bedside every day because his current fiancée wanted him there? That had to be difficult. For a brief second, I thought I should be a little easier on them, but the idea passed quickly. However, before anger at their relationship could ruin my moment, I made myself move on. I would wallow when they left. For now, I was getting to feel the sun for the first time in, well, years.

Lifting the blanket that covered my lap, I eased myself onto the ground. It seemed I was healing faster than expected; just yesterday, the attending doctor told me she hadn't seen anyone walk so quickly after a coma, ever. I still had a way to go, but I could take care of myself now. Kind of.

When my feet touched the floor, a familiar ache crept up them, followed by an also-familiar tingling feeling. Supposedly, that was the magic helping dull the pain when it reached a certain threshold. I still wasn't sure how much I believed all the mumbo-jumbo, but I had to admit, when Celeste performed her energy healing, my spirits lifted and my pain dissipated somewhat.

Marina helped me stand, and I grinned at my reflection in the full-length mirror on my wall. I still looked haggardly, with dark circles under my eyes and skin so pale everyone was tiring of my vampire jokes. My hair, which had been cut to just below my shoulders and highlighted with cherry streaks last time I remembered it, was now long enough to sit on. The highlights had long since faded, leaving my natural dark auburn hair in its place. It was thick and wavy, and I had never loved it more. Marina kept trying to get me to cut it, to start fresh with this new life I'd been given, but I turned down her offers. My hair was the only thing that didn't look half-dead. It was too voluminous for my new lightweight body, but I liked it still.

She handed me a tank top, which I struggled to get over my head. My muscles were stronger than they should be, but everyday movements still required some work. The doctor said I'd be in physical therapy for a year, probably, although I was healing more quickly than they'd expected, even when using magic and medicine combined. The tank top Marina had picked up at Goodwill was loose and unflattering. I held onto Marina's shoulder while I stepped into a pair of sweatpants that were a size too big, then rolled the top twice so they wouldn't fall. At least my underwear fit; small victories.

Marina leaned in for a careful hug. "You ready for your big day? It's beautiful out, too. You're going to love it."

I nodded and stood on shaky legs. When Marina offered a wheelchair, I sat quickly, worried my legs would give out, and settled my feet in place while she slipped them into hospital sliders. "I've never been more ready to see the sun."

Marina showed a tight smile. "Things may look a little different." She pushed me through the doorway and toward Grey, who had been leaning against the wall waiting for us.

What could be so different about the hospital courtyard? "Let's just go, and I'll see for myself."

She was right.

When the double doors opened, I shielded my eyes from the bright light of the sun.... "The hell?" The buildings making up the downtown Indianapolis skyline were the same, but above them shone one spectacularly bright yellow sun and thousands of tiny twinkling orbs. I blinked a few times, then gazed upward again. Against the brilliant blue background of the daytime sky glittered millions of violet and white stars.

"I warned you."

"But, but why?" I shook my head in disbelief.

Marina handed me a pair of sunglasses. She was prepared. As I put them on, dampening the brightness, she shrugged. "Another product of the Unveiling."

We still hadn't talked much about the Unveiling or magic, despite my constant desire to learn more. My relentless demanding to discuss it was met with just as much resistance. Marina was afraid of something.

She pushed me to a bench and sat down next to me. "It's beautiful though, isn't it?" She donned a pair of oversized black sunglasses that matched her hair.

I nodded, glancing around the courtyard. Everyone was wearing sunglasses, which wasn't that unusual this time of year. The autumn sun was not only hot and bright, but lasted most of the day in Indiana. But this... "I've never seen anything like it." This must have been why all the blinds were closed throughout the hospital; I wondered how bright it would be inside if they were opened during the day.

"A lot has changed, Tori. A lot." She looked away, toward a small garden nearby. It wasn't anything special; I thought she was just trying to avoid my gaze.

"Tell me about it," I said.

When she was silent, I added, "No, seriously. Tell me about it. You keep alluding to the changes, but I don't know what they are. Every time I bring it up, you get distant, or worse — angry. Why do you hate magic so much? What does this magic look like in the real world? What ...?" I let my voice trail off and sighed.

My sister remained quiet, so I tried a different approach.

"Grey," I started.

He held up both hands, palms out—a sign of surrender. "Not my circus, Tori." It was part of a proverb he used to say all the time when he couldn't control something. He sat on the bench beside Marina, inches from her.

"It is both your circus and your monkeys," I told him, ignoring the raw emotion running through me at the sight of his leg so close to hers. "I deserve answers, and you are the only people who have been halfway honest with me. Even the hospital staff is keeping me on a need-to-know basis, and they've apparently decided I don't need to know that much."

Marina sighed. "Imagine all the magic you've seen on TV and those fantasy movies you like so much. People have basically unlimited power, I think. I'm not sure exactly how it works."

I raised my eyebrows. Unlimited power — was that true? Even in the fantasy stories I read and watched, magic was more controlled than that. But then again, those were fiction. This was reality. Who was I to enumerate the differences? I'd been half-dead for almost five years.

There was still a question she hadn't answered, though. It even seemed she was avoiding it. "But Marina... what happened? I know you said people have uncontrolled powers, but I feel like there's more to the story than that."

She sighed. "Tori, like I said, there have been a lot of changes." She passed a look to Grey, who nodded slowly.

I folded my arms across my chest. I gave Marina a stare I hoped said I meant business.

"For one, you know that bookstore I wanted to open up after college? I did it, but it's a bookstore-slash-magic shop. We call it Pages and Potions. We own it together," she said, reaching for my boyfriend's hand.

I had to stop thinking of Grey as my boyfriend. It was proving to be damn difficult, though.

Grey jumped into the conversation. "That happened even before we started dating. I just wanted to help somehow and saw a way I could."

"Wow," I said. "That's... different. And now I'm even more confused. I mean, you seem to have a disdain for magic, but you own a magic shop?"

She traced the lines on the bench's wood beside her, not answering. "It's complicated."

"Everything is complicated," I retorted. I waved my hands around, the stars driving my point home.

"I don't hate magic," she began calmly. She frowned for a moment, as if trying to come up with her next phrase.

"And I don't have a strong feeling about it either way," Grey added, filling the silence.

Finally, Marina continued. "I hate magicians. They are people who went to bed on Halloween night five years ago, woke up with magic, and don't know how to control it. It just exists inside them and comes out when it wants to—usually when emotions are high. Imagine having a three-hundred-pound linebacker angry at you for something stupid you did, like cutting him off in traffic. Except this linebacker shoots magical arrows from his eyes when he's angry. Or maybe he gains the strength of a hundred men and kills you with one punch, because his magic activates in anger. Or he can make his thoughts a reality—so when you cut him off in traffic and he wishes, in his rage, that the pipe truck in front of you would crash and impale you with a lead pipe, it happens."

My eyes widened. "Does that stuff happen?"

She nodded. "It can. Those were examples, of course, but

imagine someone who can do that stuff but doesn't take the time to hone their powers. That's what a magician is—someone with innate, uncontrolled magic. And they're dangerous." She rubbed the back of her head with her free hand as she said the last word.

"Is that what happened to you?" I asked gently. "To your head?"

She frowned at me, then sighed. "An encounter with a scared old lady who could move objects with her mind. She didn't know she could do it; this was just days after the Unveiling. We were at the market and the cashier was giving her a hard time. She was getting more and more upset, and when she boiled over, stuff started flying around. A cart hit me in the head and knocked me unconscious. The doctor said I was lucky I didn't have brain damage from the blow. I couldn't remember my address for a week! And do you know what a literature major does when she can't remember the last sentence she read, no matter how many times she reads it?" She paused for effect and continued when I didn't respond. "She flunks senior mid-terms. I had a four-point-oh my entire college career until those exams." She gazed into the distance.

"But you're better now, right?" I asked.

She squeezed my hand. "Yep. My memory came back, thank the stars. I was lucky, like the doctor said. But not everyone is."

I could imagine. That kind of unharnessed energy could be dangerous, even in little old ladies. What could a gang member or a politician do with that kind of power? I could see why she feared magic. Though it still didn't answer why she now owned a magic store. Or the absence of visible magic. I gestured around me. "I don't see chaos and mayhem. Why is everything so calm if what you said is true?"

Her crystal blue eyes flashed with anger, as if I had just called her a liar. "It's not a disaster movie twenty-four seven, Tori." Her words had bite.

I stared at the sky, silent. None of this made any sense, and I just wanted answers. But it didn't seem I was getting any more today.

Grey cleared his throat. "Magicians have had time to hone their magic by now, so it's better than when the Unveiling first occurred. But it's still far from perfect. You live in a bubble right now, where magic is regulated and harnessed for healing. If you're out in the real world long enough, you'll see that mayhem you mentioned."

I wanted to thank him for responding, but his answer wasn't exactly satisfactory, either.

"I'm done talking about the past, Tori," Marina said with a sigh, patting my hand. "Let's talk about the future."

I groaned. The doctors said I'd have a few more weeks of living in residential treatment until I could get out on my own. I had to walk around, feed myself a whole meal without my arms getting too tired, and stop having gaps in my memories before they would allow me to leave. I didn't really feel like I had a future with all that in my way. "Let's walk more instead," I said.

Grey stood and took hold of my wheelchair.

As we walked down the sidewalk, I admired the flowers while Grey and Marina discussed something about a new shipment coming in at the store. After a few minutes, I tuned them out. Would I ever understand this magic stuff? I hoped I never had to.

AFTER ABOUT HALF AN hour, they wheeled me back to my room and prepared to leave. As Grey held the door for Marina, he planted a quick kiss on the top of her head. I don't know if he didn't think I was looking or if he simply didn't care anymore. I wasn't sure which would hurt worse.

"Love you," I called after them just before the door closed. I didn't specify who I was talking to; surely, they would know I meant Marina, not Grey. Then again, I did love Grey. I closed my eyes and remembered the feeling of being wrapped in strong arms, kisses planted atop my head instead of my sister's. I didn't have many memories, especially around the time I went into my coma, but I didn't think I could ever forget that feeling.

Tears welled in my eyes, and I didn't wipe them away. No one was here to see them. I was, in more ways than one, alone.

FOUR

I SPENT THE NEXT month attempting to pry answers about magic from the hospital staff, who insisted on treating me with kid gloves. I had learned that the rainbow-colored crystals in my original room represented the seven chakras and which of mine were blocked. Celeste taught me some basics of energy healing, and I caught the janitor using cleaning spells in my room one night. Apparently, no one used an actual mop anymore.

The doctors were floored by how quickly I could meet their milestones. Before anyone knew it, I could walk a lap around the hallways without assistance and hold my arms up to feed myself and even brush out most of my long hair. Marina continued to bother me to cut it, and I refused. Since I was small and pale, my hair made me feel pretty. I annoyed her with my resistance as much as she annoyed me about it.

I sat on the edge of my bed, Marina helping me pull it into a thick ponytail, playfully complaining all the while. "Why do you insist on keeping it so long? It's already super thick."

I sighed. "I don't have control over anything in my life right now, Marina. I have no autonomy, no agency over my body. My hair is about the only thing I have a say in, and I like it. I'm done discussing it."

"Hey," Grey said from behind me. "Let's not argue over hair, of all things. Today is a great day, and I want it to be special. That means no cat fights."

I had turned to watch him as he spoke. "You have a point, Mr. Mackenzie. Today is not just a great day, it's an amazing day. The first day of the rest of my life." I grinned at him, the promise of living outside the hospital overwhelming my desire to punch him in the face that I still felt often. At that thought, I turned to my sister.

Looking smug, Marina responded, "So, you'll have autonomy and agency and all that stuff again. Which means you don't have to hold on to all that hair." I didn't have the urge to hurt her, but my resentment was probably another driving force behind my fight about the hair.

Grey groaned and I forced a laugh. I didn't want a silly half-playful argument to impede my release day. I was finally going home.

Well, not to *my* home, because of course that got let go of years ago. Grey had reneged on our apartment the day we were supposed to move in, apparently getting out without fines due to the circumstances, and he and Marina had brought all my boxes to a storage unit. At least I had already packed everything for them.

No, my makeshift home was in the most uncomfortable place imaginable—Marina and Grey's apartment. It made sense for me financially, and it eased Marina's ruminations about my health and safety. But damn.

I had always been the type to have a few close friends rather than a lot of not-so-close ones, and thinking of sleeping on my sister's couch reminded me of the fact that most of mine had been fair weather friends. They'd visited for a while after Halloween, but by the new year, it was mostly just Marina and Grey who came by regularly. A couple of my so-called friends had called or stopped by in the last five weeks, but none were close enough to offer me an alternate sleeping situation. I was stuck.

I changed the subject. "So, have you thought any more about me helping in the shop?"

Grey walked around me so he was standing next to Marina, his fingers brushing her arm as he did so.

I pretended not to notice, but my stomach knotted.

"Do you really want to spend all day with me?" Marina asked. "I mean, you'll be with me at home, then with me at work. We'll get sick of each other." She chuckled a little, but she sounded serious.

I shrugged. "Well, it's not like I can go back to my old job. I'm not sure how well I can teach classical languages if I can't remember that this is a spoon." I picked up the eating implement on the tray beside me.

"It's still that bad, huh?" Grey asked, sympathy creasing the corners of his mouth.

"Most days it's okay. The memory only crashes when I'm trying to think of something from the distant past, particularly around the time of the Unveiling." It still felt weird to use that word, even though it's what everyone called that Halloween when magic melted into our world. Since I wasn't conscious for it, it felt like I was speaking a foreign language and the borrowed word didn't sit well on my tongue. Foreign languages may be my passion, and pre-coma profession, but everything having to do with magic and veils was still strange.

He winced. "Can you remember much about it?"

I shook my head. "I remember you and I getting ready for Marina's party, but even that's spotty. I remember teaching class before that. We had a toga party in Latin four-hundred." I rubbed my temples. Just trying made my head hurt. "Aside from a few crude jokes and one particularly enthusiastic toga dance, I don't remember much from then either, though."

I sighed. I was a do-er, a go-getter, a learner. Sitting on my ass every day in sweats watching soap operas was not my idea of a good time.

"Hey, don't sweat it," Grey said, gesturing with his hands as he spoke. "It'll come back, eventually."

"Enough with the somber talk," Marina said. "It's a special day, remember?"

The thought perked me up from the rabbit hole of emotions I was about to go down. "Just one problem, guys."

They both stared at me, concerned.

"I don't have any real shoes. All this time here, I've just worn hospital slippers."

Marina let out a deep breath. "Don't worry. I brought all your clothes over from the storage unit. You have plenty of shoes at home."

Home. I turned the word around on my tongue, tasting it silently. I doubted Marina and Grey's apartment would ever be *home*, but it was a nice sentiment. "Thanks," I said finally, adding extra cheer to my voice.

"And so you don't have to leave here in slippers...." She headed for the duffel bag she had brought to help gather my meager belongings in and reached inside.

When she pulled out my favorite pair of black and white Converse sneakers, I let out a squeal. My feet had been neglected without my beloved sneakers—the only brand of shoes I have worn for years, even on some dressy occasions. Though they were mine, the T-shirt and capris she handed me were too big. I had lost so much weight that I wasn't sure if I'd ever get back into my old stuff. But seeing the shoes made me forget about the clothes. "Thanks so much, Marina."

She grinned. "I'm just sorry I didn't get into your stuff sooner."

"It's here now," I assured her. I scooted to the edge of the bed and bent to put on my beloved shoes. They were a little loose but would do. My toes felt happy, and I allowed the feeling to overcome me. I jumped up, excited, and clapped my hands. "Let's get me home!"

Robin, my favorite nurse—and a real medical one, not a hocusy-pocusy one—pushed my door open with a wheelchair. "I heard someone's ready to go!"

I glared at the chair. "You know, I can make it outside on my own now." It was the same argument I made every time I went outside.

Expectedly, she replied, "And it's still hospital policy for you to sit in this thing until you're discharged."

"Blah blah blah," I grumbled. But I put my feet up and let her wheel me out.

Grey ran ahead, his keys jingling, to bring the car around. He'd been in the background the whole morning and jumped at the chance to take a moment to himself.

Marina followed the wheelchair, carrying my duffel bag, a vase of flowers, and a festival of balloons. Somewhere in her arms was the singular bit of communication I had received from my mom during the whole time I had been awake—a "get well soon" card with a quick signature.

After a minute of waiting on the curb, saying my goodbyes to Robin, a dark blue SUV pulled up in front of us. The driver's door opened, and Grey stepped out.

I whistled at the vehicle. "A far cry from what you used to drive, huh, Grey?"

He nodded with a smile. "Hard work pays." He helped me out of the wheelchair, treating me as more fragile than necessary, and into the back seat of the SUV. Marina climbed in front and spun around to watch me.

"Hey, Marina." I tried to sound casual. "Have you heard from

Mom?" Though I hadn't seen her since a year before the coma, my heart still hurt that she hadn't been more involved in my recovery.

She scrunched up her face. "Mom is ... Mom. I called her last week, and she said to tell you it was nice to hear that you're well."

Grey chuckled. "That's Cora for you. Cold as ice."

I chewed on my lip, lost in thought. It seemed there were some major changes in the last four-and-a-half years, but Cora James' attitude didn't appear to be one of them. Fine then. I wouldn't go see her, either.

While I was pondering Cora's non-maternal instincts, Marina turned to glance at Grey with a wide-eyed, love-struck expression. She held out her hand, and he intertwined his fingers with hers and rested their hands in his lap.

I pretended not to notice them or the heat in my chest. I cleared my throat and Marina turned back to me, releasing her hold on Grey's hand quickly.

"So, Celeste was in today before you guys got here," I said, just for the heck of having a conversation. "She said my chakras are in better alignment. Also, that my aura is clean but strange. Do you know what a strange aura means?" I laughed a bit.

"No idea," Marina said.

"Strange, how?" Grey asked.

I shrugged. "How should I know? You guys have been in this world a lot longer than I have."

Grey turned down a road I didn't recognize, taking us to the heart of downtown Indianapolis. Some of the older buildings were familiar, but much wasn't.

Apprehension settled over me. With a sigh, I resigned to look outside at the buildings, both familiar and new. To the right, on the sidewalk, were big white letters spelling NDY. NDY? What was that supposed to mean?

Marina must have caught the puzzlement on my face. "You stand next to the N, and you make the I, spelling Indy. Get it?"

"Cute."

Grey added from the front seat, "You want to stop and take a picture?"

I cringed. "Isn't it a tourist thing?"

He shrugged. "I guess, but locals do it too. Pride in your city and all that." He said something else but was drowned out by the squealing of brakes and Marina's high-pitched scream.

Bright white filled my view as a truck, facing the wrong way, hurled toward us. Screams ricocheted through the car, creating background music for my terror.

I instinctively held my hands out in front of me to catch myself as the force of Grey's braking flung me into the space between the front seats.

When I did, an electric sensation brewed in my elbows and coursed down my arms and into tingling fingers. A burst of pale blue light emitted from my fingertips and in an instant, time stood still.

It literally stood still. I gasped—shocked, confused, and disoriented—and looked from Grey to Marina.

They sat frozen in the front seat, Marina's hands in front of her in a similar position to mine but minus the electric lights. Grey's hands clenched the steering wheel, his knuckles white.

I breathed out heavily and then made myself take a few deep breaths. What the hell was going on?

I glanced down at my hands, which were still glowing light blue. Outside, everything had stopped. Not even the leaves on the trees seemed to move with the wind. I hadn't been buckled, which was how I had ended up practically in the front seat, so I scooted backwards and sat against the back of my seat, breathing hard. I was glad time had frozen—however that had happened—or I probably would have been outside the wind-shield right now, ending up right back in the hospital.

Slowly, I inched toward the door and manually unlocked it. In shock, I stumbled out of the SUV. We were in the right-hand lane, so I was two steps from grass and sidewalk. I walked onto the pavement and peered around, unsure of what to do.

From the corner of my eye, I saw movement down the road. Movement when everything else was frozen still. I cocked my head to one side and frowned. I was moving, and I had blue hands. So maybe the person walking toward us also had … whatever that was. Electricity in their fingertips. It hadn't felt like what I expected "magic" to feel like, so it was difficult to call it that.

Magic was for movies and the fantasy books I liked to read, which Marina mocked since they weren't *literature*. At least, she used to mock them. She might even read them now, given everything that had changed. I didn't really know much any-more.

"Hello?" I called.

The man turned to me. He didn't say anything, but he began jogging toward me.

"I … I need help," I told him as he neared.

When he was close enough to talk to normally, I breathed a sigh of relief, taking a moment to let the breath flow out. As it did, I took in the stranger's appearance.

He sported a two-day beard, and his long, blond hair was pulled into a messy bun. He was a little taller than me and might have been handsome had I not been panicked.

"Hi," I said after inhaling again. I waved my arms, gesturing around us. "Can you explain this to me?" I was aware of the slightly frantic tone in my voice, but I didn't care. "Also, can you tell me how this happened?" I gestured again, this time toward

Grey's SUV and the white truck about to collide with it.

"I would imagine a drunk driver, from the looks of it," the man said. "I don't know why he's going the wrong way in that lane."

I rolled my eyes. "Not what I mean."

He frowned again. "Did you not do this?"

I shrugged, tears welling in my eyes. "I don't know. I put my hands like this," I started, showing him, "and then they got all electric and started glowing and then this happened." I swiped at my cheeks with my palms. This was not the time to cry. I had to fix this, somehow.

"How do you not know?" he asked, raising blond eyebrows.

"It's a long story."

He inclined his head, an invitation to continue.

"I was in a coma." I guess it was a short story, after all.

His eyes widened, but he didn't address it. "Look, I don't know how long everything will stay like this, since I didn't cast the spell. Honestly, I don't even know why I'm not frozen like everyone else. But I'll worry about that later. We'd better fix these cars before your friends unfreeze in the middle of a collision. I'm Bennett, by the way." He stooped to set a messenger bag on the sidewalk.

"Tori," I said absentmindedly, trying to figure out my next words. "I still don't understand what we're supposed to do."

He stood and smiled, showing nice white teeth. "You watch. I'll do." He moved his hands as if forming a ball from clay, slowly at first and then more quickly. After a moment, a ball of white light appeared between them.

I gasped, putting a hand to my mouth.

He winked at me and continued by muttering some words I didn't quite hear, but I thought I caught the Latin words for *movement* and *slow*.

My attention turned toward Grey's SUV. It slowly, so slowly, slid to the right several feet.

I stole a glance at Bennett while the SUV moved beside us. His eyes were squinted in concentration, and he continued to swirl his hands around the glowing orb between them. Beads of sweat formed on his forehead.

When it was over, the truck had moved several more feet to the side and straightened to fit in the lane properly instead of being skewed, like it had been. Bennett wiped the sweat off his forehead, and when he stopped repeating his Latin whispers, the orb blinked away.

He turned to me. "It's your turn."

I blinked back at him. I had no idea how I had done anything to begin with, and he wanted me to undo it?

Bennett caught my look and offered a small smile. "We'll start from the beginning." He took my wrists in his. "Think hard about what you want to do. Unfreeze time. Feel the energy inside you, coming from all over your body and into your arms, hands, and then out your fingertips."

I closed my eyes, sensed the warmth of his fingers around my wrists, and tried to conjure energy inside my gut. When I was warm all over, I grimaced and imagined the energy as air blowing through my body and out my fingertips, until ... nothing.

I shook my head. "I don't know how."

Bennett squeezed my wrists gently, like a reassuring friend. "You do. You have to."

"Can't you do it? Make a little ball of light thingy and unfreeze everything?"

He chuckled. "I could, but magic doesn't come naturally to me. I had to learn it, and it takes a lot out of me to do it. Besides, you need to learn to use your power."

I groaned, trying again to feel the energy inside me. "Why, though? Can't I just never use it again?"

He released my wrists and laughed. "On purpose, sure. But what happens next time you do something accidentally, and no one is there to undo it for you?"

He had a point. I closed my eyes again and breathed deeply, calling back to all those yoga classes I took pre-coma, feeling the breath in the back of my throat as I breathed in my nose. It was cool entering my nose and warm leaving. It was soothing, inviting, and calming. Warmth bubbled up inside me, and I imagined it this time as a light, spreading out all over my body instead of just my fingertips. I inhaled, and on the exhale willed all the light out of my body.

And time unfroze.

"WHAT THE HELL WAS that?" I turned wide-eyed to Bennett. My face was feverish, and my chest pumped with anxiety.

"Magic," he replied, as if that answered everything.

Grey's SUV came to a quick halt beside us, and the front doors flew open. Grey and my sister leaped out, both exclaiming in panic. "What happened?" Grey asked.

Marina grabbed my shoulders. "God, Tori. When I turned around and you weren't there, I thought you'd gone through a window or something. I'm so glad you're safe. But why are you not in the car anymore?"

I looked at Bennett and then back to them, holding my hands in front of me, palms up. Thankfully, they were no longer blue. "Well..."

Marina cut me off. "Who is this?"

"I'm Bennett. Bennett Weston." He held his hand out casually, as if I didn't just stop time and start it again in front of him.

Marina's own hand shook slightly as she took his and gave it a cursory pump. She jumped back, startled, as if there was an electric shock.

"That doesn't explain anything," Grey said, his eyes angry slits.

"I'm a mage," Bennett answered, as if that explained every-thing.

Grey urged him on with his facial expression.

"I was walking nearby and saw the commotion. I helped

Tori–"

"He used magic to move your car out of the way of the other car, so there wasn't an accident." I glanced at Bennett, hoping my look told him to shut the hell up. Marina wasn't exactly enthusiastic about magic, and I didn't want to freak her out any more than she already was.

He said nothing, nodding along with my story without adding anything to it.

Grey watched us both, seemingly unsure what was going on, but decided against questioning it.

"I hopped out, but you two seemed pretty stunned. I was worried about you," I added, hoping to appease his curiosity.

"Us? I'm just glad you're alright," Marina said, engulfing me in a hug.

"Whoa, whoa." I took a step back. "Too tight. Still sore."

She grabbed my arm and pulled me to the side a few steps. "Are you okay? Really okay?"

I nodded. "Just shaken up."

From behind us, a car horn honked, followed by a man yelling obscenities toward us. We were standing on the sidewalk, but Grey's SUV was still blocking traffic—which was attempting to move now that time had unfrozen.

I turned to Bennett to thank him for his help, and he reached for my hand. I expected a quick shake, but he placed something in my palm and held my hand a beat longer than I'd expected. He stared at me knowingly, like we shared a secret—which I guess we did—and flashed a quick smile. "We should scatter before the Department wonders why we're hanging around. I should get back anyhow."

I scowled. "The Department?"

Marina watched her feet, and Grey watched her. Finally, he answered. "The Department of Wayward Magic. The Department, some call them. Or D-Dub, if you're young or blasé about them. Either way, their job is to make sure magicians aren't flying off the handle, doing magic they're not supposed to."

I shook my head. "Wait. Magicians—those are people with innate magic, right?" When the group nodded, I continued. "So, magicians aren't supposed to do magic?"

Grey grimaced and Bennett rocked his head side to side, which told me the answer was "it depends."

I looked at Marina, who was still silent, her expression unreadable. "The old lady, did the Department come for her?"

She nodded. "We don't really know what happens after they take someone. They come, assess, and if the person is a danger, they get taken. If it's not a big deal, they may not even come. Like now, I doubt anyone will be alerted that wc avoided a catastrophe with magic." She watched at the ground.

I whistled. "It's a lot to take in."

Grey touched my shoulder quickly, then pulled his hand away. "It is. You'll be okay, though."

I flashed a quick smile. "Thanks."

The man in traffic laid on his horn, blaring it for several seconds. Others behind him followed suit.

I turned to Bennett. "We'd better go. Thanks so much for your help."

His smile was lasting and made his gray eyes shine. "I'll see you around, Tori."

"Yeah." I didn't know if I'd see him again or not, but I kind of wanted to.

When he let go of my hand, I scrutinized it. It felt electric, like he had residual magic or something, and it tingled. Inside my palm was a plain white business card, and as the sun hit it, blue letters appeared and swirled into words: *Bennett Weston, Intermediate Mage*. A phone number appeared beneath the words, and that was it. I flipped the card over. Nothing on the back, even after waiting for more words to appear.

This magic stuff was weird.

"Let's get going," Grey said tightly. I recognized that voice, anxious and frustrated. Grey was a stickler for being on time and, to be honest, a bit of a perfectionist. I had heard that voice a lot in the years we were together.

Except... had I really? Almost five of those years were not real; they were made up in my mind while my body was in a coma in the real world. But we were together for two years prior to my coma, so of course I knew when Grey sounded frustrated. But maybe I imagined the anxiety. It had been a while.

Marina tugged on my arm, and we re-entered the SUV. This time, I sat behind Marina instead of in the middle, buckling myself in tightly. We drove in silence.

After a few minutes, Grey cleared his throat. "Look, Tor. I know it's hard for you to hear about us, and I'm sorry. I really am." He paused for a moment, and I felt his apology in the air. "And I know it's weird to stay at our place. But you need somewhere to recover. Your mom's not going to help you, and we all know you're broke."

I did a double-take. "I'm what?"I could see him cringe in profile. "Your savings... well, you were in a coma after all."

Marina turned around, trying to look at me. "We used whatever we could to get you the best treatment, Tor. You understand."

I nodded, tears brimming in the corners of my eyes. I blinked them back furiously. I would not let this get me down and make me cry. I was stronger than that.

"How long until we're there?" I asked, trying not to sound like a whiny child.

"Almost there," Grey answered.

"So, you live downtown? Like, right downtown?" I hated

downtown. The traffic, the one-way streets, the lack of parking... it was all too much for me. I preferred suburbia, flora, and
houses with yards.

They both chuckled. They both knew how I felt about living
downtown.

"I work at the hospital," Grey said after a moment. "Living here
is convenient."

Marina chimed in, "And we are close to the store. I mean, we
could have opened it anywhere, but business is good here."

"Where is it?"

"Mass Ave," she answered. Massachusetts Avenue was, or at
least had been, the trendy area downtown. It was full of brew-
eries and boutiques and apartments for hipsters. And now, apparently, a magic store.

"We're here," Marina said suddenly.

We pulled up to an apartment community, big black gates
giving way for the SUV to roll into the parking lot. Grey parked
at the second building, and I craned my neck to see it stretched
several stories high. I really hoped we weren't too high up; my
legs were still iffy, and I'd only seen apartment elevators on TV.

"Don't worry. We're on the first floor," Marina said.

I breathed a sigh of relief and surveyed my surroundings.
The neighbors' cars appeared to be nice, like Grey's—mostly
shiny sedans and new SUVs, though a sleek black sports car was
parked down the street, too. The building itself appeared to be
newer, as the red brick and gray vinyl hadn't worn yet. Each
apartment had a large balcony or patio, some heavily decorated
with plants. I guess this was where I'd get my flora fix.

Grey parked and grabbed my belongings from the back seat
while Marina opened my car door for me. This whole situation
was bad enough without them treating me like a child, but I had
a feeling arguing wouldn't do any good.

Marina and I followed Grey through the door into a large living room with an open concept floor plan. The kitchen was spectacular—maybe even better than the one I had picked out previously. And the walls were gray. It was becoming more and more like Marina was living my life, or at least the one I was supposed to have.

After we settled, Marina headed to the amazing kitchen and whipped up my favorite comfort food, grilled cheese sandwiches and soup.

Marina and Grey chattered about business, occasionally explaining something to me or asking for my input, but I was lost in my own thoughts.

I knew why I hadn't told them about my magic on the road, but shouldn't I tell them now? What would it hurt if they knew?

She reached for Grey's hand, and anxiety burned in my chest. Watching them together, living their lives as if today was a normal day ... it hurt. Not just their relationship, though I had a feeling that pain wasn't going away anytime soon. But everything they represented—the nice car, the new apartment, their own business. They had the life I wanted, the one that had been taken away from me.

I may not have any money, or a job; hell, I didn't even have all my memories. But magic was mine, and it wasn't theirs. It was something I had that they couldn't take away. Kind of like they had taken a piece of each other from my life. Like the last four-and-a-half years had been taken from me.

Plus, Marina hated magic—at least, uncontrolled magic, which mine certainly was. She was even disdainful of Bennett, who wasn't a magician. He was just a mage, and she still didn't trust him.

We chatted for a while until I was yawning so much, I was annoying myself and probably them too. "Guys," I started.

Marina's eyes widened. "I told you we were pushing her," she said, smacking Grey on the arm. She turned to me. "You're exhausted, and all we did was come home and eat."

"And almost die," Grey reminded her, glancing at me for a second.

And use magic I didn't know I had, I added in my head. I decided to keep that to myself for a little while longer, though. There was no reason to worry Marina about my untamed magical abilities when she was still concerned about my memory and muscle tone. Those were more important.

"I'm just tired, guys. It's been an exciting day. Not quite what you had in mind, I'm sure."

Marina cringed. She started to apologize, but I cut her off.

"There's nothing to be sorry for. You didn't almost get in a car accident just to prove to me magic is real. Wait, did you?" I asked, looking at Grey.

They were both aghast, like they didn't realize I was joking.

I chuckled and shook my head. It was a long day, and I had a lot to think about.

"Take a nap," Marina urged after a long pause. "You can even use the bed. We've got a shipment coming in at the store, so we'll leave you alone for a bit. But if you need anything…"

"Yeah, yeah, I know," I said. "Wait. I don't have a phone."

Grey smiled and handed me a black device. "This is my personal cell. I have one for work, so you can use this until you get your own."

The phone was huge, much bigger than I remembered my old one being. Where was my old phone anyhow? I wondered how much technology had changed in the last four-and-a-half-years. "Uh, thanks, Grey." I turned it over in my hands. Just another thing that wasn't really mine, like the bed I was about to go nap on.

I wanted to fight it, but sleep sounded nice. They left a few minutes later, and I ambled into the big bedroom to curl up on top of the covers. The bed was soft, the comforter thick and smooth beneath me. A familiar scent lingered all around me and my eyes watered; Grey had worn the same cologne since before he and I had met, and its scent, strong and sweet, was both welcome and unwelcome at the same time.

My thoughts whirled with images of me and him interspersed with ones of him and my sister. Grey's arms around me as we watched TV. Nuzzling into the shoulder of his favorite sweater during a hug. Watching him kiss the top of Marina's head as they left the hospital room, him reaching for her hand in the car. Memories that weren't really memories flooded my mind, and I saw him proposing at our favorite restaurant, carrying boxes into our new apartment, and mixing fresh blueberries into our pancakes in the kitchen I loved so much.

I hugged a pillow to my chest and let the tears flow silently as emotions overwhelmed me. When my imagination took over, flooding my mind with movies of Grey and Marina intertwined on the bed I was lying in, I decided I had enough. I jumped up and trudged to the couch, falling into a restless sleep, dreaming about magic and past lovers.

I AWOKE TWO HOURS later and lay on the couch with my eyes open, staring at the textured ceiling. Whispers drifted in from the kitchen and I tried not to listen; it was difficult since my name kept popping up.

"... are we sure she's going to be okay on her own?" Marina asked.

The refrigerator opened and closed. "She'll be fine. Tori's strong," Grey responded.

"But she's not, Grey, that's the point. She just woke up from a fucking coma. A coma! Did you see her walking into the apartment? Her legs are still weak. Her speech is a little slow. Have you noticed?"

Grey sighed. "Of course, I've noticed, honey. But that's all normal. It doesn't mean she's a weakling. Tori can handle herself; I promise."

"But what about...?"

Silence.

"What about what?"

Marina sighed this time, loudly. "How do you think she's going to be when we start planning our wedding right under her nose? I can't exactly hide it from her. She's my sister. I've always wanted her to be involved when I got married, but I can't ask her to plan this with me."

Grey was silent. I imagined him shrugging, non-committal.

"That's what I thought," Marina said. The conversation ended, and dishes clinked a few moments later.

I yawned and rolled onto my side. This was going to be difficult. She was right about my physical and mental challenges. She was right about how fucking strange it was that she was marrying Grey. And no amount of wanting to help my little sister plan her wedding was going to change that.

I decided to lie down for a while longer, because it was too tense for me to announce I was awake just yet. Instead, I pulled Bennett's business card out of my pocket and checked it again. This time, under his phone number, the words *I can help you* appeared. After the initial shock of the magic words wore off, peace filled my body, and I could relax. I'd call him tomorrow; maybe he could be helpful somehow.

I had been home for only a couple of hours and there were already issues. I could use all the help I could get.

SIX

THE NEXT MORNING, I lay on the couch—which was fine but not as comfortable as the bed—and stirred to the sounds of Marina's footsteps thumping as she walked behind me. I sat up and stretched.

"Oh, shoot," she said. "I was trying not to wake you."

"Eh, it's fine." I yawned.

"Well, since you're up, do you want to come with me to work? I wanted to take a few days off, but–"

"I'll be fine. I promise. I really don't need a babysitter." Inwardly, I was excited about the idea of having the day to myself. After months of little to no privacy, with a steady stream of nurses in and out of my room, spending a little time alone wouldn't hurt anything. Plus, there was something I wanted to do.

AFTER MARINA LEFT FOR work, I ate Cocoa Puffs while standing in her kitchen and stared at Bennett's card. It didn't say anything new this time, which was slightly disappointing. I grabbed the cell phone Grey had left for me and dialed the number on the card.

A recorded message told me the number couldn't go through.

I tried again, and a third time, and received the same message each time. Confused, I dialed again, this time using the 317-area code before the seven-digit number. The call went through. Well, that was new.

"Hey, Tori," Bennett said after the second ring.

I was silent. How did he know who I was?

"I'm magic, remember?"

I took a deep breath, trying to recall something Marina had told me. "But you're a mage... which means your magic isn't innate. You have to study hard to learn it, and you have to perform spells to cast it. I'm pretty sure clairvoyance isn't a mage trait."

He chuckled. "You're catching on fast. No, I just had a feeling. Intuition, I guess. What's up?" he asked after a pause.

"I'm not really sure. Oh, now I feel stupid. I just felt like I should call you. Like maybe you could help me." I twirled my long hair with one hand, feeling embarrassed that I didn't have an actual reason for calling Bennett.

"No problem," he said. "I have a few things to do now, but we could meet for lunch if you'd like, and see what I can help you with."

I nodded, thinking. The Cocoa Puffs probably wouldn't last me very long, so lunch was a good idea. "I can't drive though," I remembered.

"Text me your address and I'll pick you up."

"Are you going to actually drive the car this time instead of moving it with a spell?" I asked, smiling.

He chuckled, probably out of pity at my poor attempt at humor. "Yep, with both hands on the wheel and everything."

We made our plans for lunchtime and hung up. I stared at Grey's phone in my hand, studying it. My fingers stumbled over the screen, pushing buttons I didn't know how to use. What little things had changed that I hadn't noticed yet?

After I texted Marina's address to Bennett, I scowled at the large machine in my hand and set it on the counter. I needed to shower and was excited at the thought—showering with no one waiting for me in case I fell, taking time to wash this grown-out mop of hair, shaving my legs. I glanced down at them, pale and hairy. Oh, God, they'd probably use two razors to get through. And I needed a tanning bed, pronto. Four-plus years of nothing but fluorescent lights had left me pale as a corpse. But that would have to come later.

AN HOUR LATER, AFTER a long, hot shower, I stood in Marina's bedroom again, staring at myself in her full-length mirror. I barely recognized the person staring back at me. My face was gaunt, my eyes sunken, and my skin sallow. I had gained weight and muscle tone during my months in the rehabilitation, but I was still barely a shadow of my pre-coma self.

I rifled through a box of clothes Marina had grabbed from my storage unit until I found my favorite skirt, short and pink and pleated. Once I put it on, it hung from my hips and threatened to fall if I moved my legs. I frowned. My favorite skirt! Before I took it off, I fastened the smallest bra I could find and slipped on a black T-shirt. It, too, hung loosely and was not flattering.

I stepped out of the skirt, kicked it across the floor, and pulled the shirt back off, throwing it with force at the mirror. The bra fit alright, even though it did nothing for my deflated boobs. But Marina's wouldn't fit me; she was more petite than me all the way around.

Still, I was smaller than I used to be. I snapped through the hangers in her closet, searching for something that might fit halfway decently. I settled on a pair of denim capris with a belt and a red V-neck t-shirt. It was athletic fit, so it clung to me a little better than some of the other shirts I tried on. And I had the perfect shoes.

I opened the box marked 'shoes' and smiled. Pair after pair of Converse sneakers welcomed me, all colors and models. I grabbed a pair of red ones with white soles and slipped into them easily. If I tied them a little tighter, they'd fit fine.

I surveyed myself again in the mirror. "Not bad, Tori," I mumbled.

I studied my leather jacket hanging in the hall closet; there was no way it would fit me now. It had belonged to my dad before he died, and I could only wear it because I had inherited his broad shoulders and long arms. Even with those features now, I knew I would swim in it. I touched it with my fingertips and my eyes watered. "Oh, Daddy," I whispered. "I wish you were here to help me through this."

An image played in my mind, one I couldn't forget no matter how many years I spent in a coma. In it, I held nine-year-old Marina's hand as a good big sister would. She was in her best dress, a purple so deep it was almost black, with a satin ribbon around the waist and a matching one tying her long black hair into a French braid. Little sparkles decorated her black tights and matched her black shoes. But what I focused on, as always, were the tears in her crystal blue eyes, which looked like wet ice.

We stood together, hand in hand, on the ground cover the funeral home had laid down, as everyone walked away slowly. The somber chatter of their voices faded, and occasionally someone would put a soft hand on our shoulders before walking away. Even Mom left us to stand there, at nine and thirteen, taking in the scene before us—Dad's casket lowering slowly into the ground.

Two men wearing bright yellow vests walked up to us, their expressions soft and sad. "You girls need to leave now. We can't finish if you're here," one said, looking at me.

I frowned and glanced between the casket and the man's yellow cap, rubbing the edge of my silky black dress between my thumb and index finger. "Why?"

"We have to, uh, cover the casket now," he said, shifting his weight from one foot to the other. He wrung bright yellow work gloves in his hands.

"You're going to throw dirt on my daddy?" Marina asked, her voice cracking.

The second man took a step forward and kneeled on one knee in front of her. "Your daddy's not in there, sweetheart," he said, at which point Marina looked like she was about to wail in confusion. "What I mean is, he'll always be in here." He took his index finger and put it to her chest without quite touching it, where her heart was. "We're going to bury the casket, but you'll always have him with you."

Marina sniffled. "How?"

The man smiled sweetly. "Because my daddy's in here." He pointed to his own heart.

Marina's lip quivered. "Is it lonely without your daddy?"

"Every day," he answered. "But I know he still loves me, just like I know your daddy still loves you."

"How do you know?" Tears spilled onto her cheeks.

"It's a daddy secret. You know, my daughter's about your age. I will never ever stop loving her, no matter what happens to me." He stood back up and wiped his knee off, even though it hadn't gotten dirty.

I flashed him a small smile. I wanted to pretend to be grateful that he helped my sister, but they also meant a lot to me.

He glanced at his partner and then back at me. "Now look, girls, I hate to make you leave, but it's the rules. You understand rules, don't you?"

I nodded. "Thanks," I said. "Come on Marina. Mom is probably waiting for us."

She took a step with me but shook her head at my comment. "I wish it was her," she said, barely above a whisper.

I pretended I didn't hear her and kept walking. But I did too.

Back in Marina's bedroom, I wiped tears from my eyes with the back of my hand and walked away from my dad's jacket. It would be a while before I could wear it, the thought of which made my throat burn. With one last glance over my shoulder, I left the room.

My cell beeped. Bennett was in the parking lot.

I texted him back, stating I was on my way, and peered around the living room. It felt so foreign, and so cozy, so different from the sterile environment that had been my home for the past months—or, really, almost five years. Even though I didn't quite feel at ease here—how could I, knowing my ex was sleeping with my sister in the other room?—it was a much-needed improvement. I hoped Bennett could help me so I could get back on my feet quickly, which included getting my own place.

I wasn't sure what I wanted or expected from him, but I had a feeling he was going to be a big part of my future.

The feeling increased when I got to his little red car, parked just outside the apartment door. Seeing him didn't put shivers down my spine like I used to feel with Grey early in our time dating—it was more of a comfortable, homey sense. Like I knew I was safe. Which was really something I needed right now, so I welcomed it with a smile.

"Hey, Ben... does anyone call you Ben?" I asked, sliding into his passenger seat. I'd like to say it was a graceful slide, but I'd be lying. Still, it was what my legs could muster at this point. They were still wobbly from the years of non-use. I leaned back into the comfortable seat and put on my seatbelt.

"Some do. I don't really like it though," he answered, waving a dismissive hand. "How are you doing? The post-coma life all you hoped?" He put the car into gear and headed out of the parking lot.

I had no clue where he was going, since I wasn't familiar with this area much before the... what did they call that night? The Unveiling. I didn't venture to this part of the city much pre-Unveiling, and I sure as hell didn't know where anything was now. New construction popped up all around, and everything was brick and crisp, including these apartments. I couldn't get my bearings as we pulled onto the busy city street and turned quickly onto another I didn't recognize.

"I don't hope for anything right now, except for these headaches to go away," I answered finally.

"Side effect?"

I thought about it for a minute. "Of what? The coma? Maybe. The magic? Maybe. I don't understand much of anything right now. Where are we going, anyhow?"

"Moe Joe's, you know it?"

"Nope."

"Well, it's a coffee shop a few blocks over. I used to go to poetry readings there when I was in college. Good memories." He made another turn, and this street was slightly familiar, but I couldn't place a specific memory. I didn't know if it was because of my brain trauma or because I just didn't recognize the street very well.

"We had those in the student center where I went," I offered. "I didn't go often. Unless the poetry was in Latin, it didn't interest me very much."

Bennett shot a quick glance my way. "You speak Latin?"

I nodded. "And Classical Greek, Sanskrit ... and a smattering of other Classical languages too. I teach it at the University of Indianapolis. Classical languages, that is." I paused, momentarily saddened. "Well, I used to. I don't know if I'll ever teach again, really. My memory's not what it used to be."

Bennett pulled the car into a small parking lot in front of a building with lots of windows and a sign that read Moe Joe's on the front. We were both silent—me feeling sorry for myself, and Bennett probably unsure what to say to my remark.

Still in silence, we got out of the car and walked inside. The interior of the building was littered with funky art displays and a large stage stood against the far wall, where I assumed they held poetry readings and maybe open mic nights. In front of us, the traditional glass case of bakery items sat waiting.

I ordered a plain coffee and a croissant, and Bennett ordered a fancy cappuccino drink I couldn't even say and a brownie. He paid for both of us, despite Marina leaving me some cash, and we sat at a tall table against a window.

"I'm sure you'll teach again one day," he said as I sipped my coffee in silence. He slurped at his drink.

I shrugged. "Maybe. I don't really know what else I'll do if I don't, to be honest. It's all I ever wanted to do, since I was a little girl. Teach and study languages. I never thought I'd end up studying dead languages, of course; that was a surprise when college came around. But I love it. The languages, the students, even grading papers. But now... I don't even know how much I remember." I stared at my pastry. It didn't hold any answers for me, but it kept me from seeing the look of pity I was sure was on Bennett's face.

When I finally looked up, that expression wasn't there. I was shocked, and a little off-put.

"The world is different from what you remember, Tori," Bennett said, taking a bite of his brownie. "I bet you'll find other ways to use those languages, even if you don't teach a formal college course."

I remembered the Latin words he had used to perform his magic yesterday. Maybe knowing classical languages would come in handy, since it seemed my new life was going to involve magic whether I wanted it to or not.

"I thought you have to do spells to use magic, but mine is innate?"

"Yes, but more complicated stuff will require the use of spells, potions, herbs, crystals, all that kind of stuff. You can't just *will* everything your way all the time. It's not like magic in the movies." He laughed a little, obviously thinking that would be absurd.

I contemplated what he was saying. I really had a lot of learning to do. "Can you teach me?"

He did a double-take and set his brownie down. "What? I'm not sure what I was expecting, but that wasn't it."

"Your card said you could help me," I said, confused.

Bennett shrugged. "My cards show people what they need in the moment. I don't control what they say."

"That's pretty cool, but it doesn't help because I need so much right now. My memories, for my head to not hurt all the time, a place of my own so I'm not staying on my ex-boyfriend's couch ...." I let my voice trail off. It was overwhelming to think about everything I needed to learn and do.

"To learn how to manage your magic so it doesn't hurt someone, including yourself?"

I nodded. "I know you understand how it works and can use it. I've only used it once, when we met, and I have no clue how it happened or how to make it happen again—or not make it happen, actually."

"You have innate magic, Tori. I don't know it's going to be possible to never use it."

That wasn't what I wanted to hear. Marina didn't seem keen on magic, and I didn't particularly want to keep this big of a secret from her. This new life was confusing enough without having to keep track of lies. "I was afraid you'd say that."

He took another bite of his brownie and contemplated. "I mean, I guess I could teach you. I've never taught anyone before, though. I'm still studying myself."

"Please? Help a freshly de-comatose girl out?"

Bennett chewed on his dessert slowly and then took a deliberate sip of his drink. "I don't know if I'm even allowed to. Helping you stop the car accident was one thing. I don't know that the Circle would want me to *teach* someone. Or the Department, for that matter."

I didn't know much about the Department, and I'd never heard of the Circle. But helping me learn not to hurt someone had to be a good thing, right? "Think of it more like studying together, rather than teaching me."

He was silent for a moment. "Studying together," he repeated. "They can't really be upset about that, can they?"

I took that as a yes and jumped from my chair. "Yay!" I leaned over the table and hugged him.

His eyes were wide, but he didn't pull back. He smiled. "I'm glad you're excited. I'm nervous."

"Well, now you can be like a master mage or something, right? Wear a robe and say important sounding things?" I sat back down and took an enthusiastic sip of my coffee.

Bennett chuckled. "Something like that, I'm sure."

We laughed and talked over the rest of our food and drink,

mostly about the differences between life pre- and post-coma. I was getting restless about the number of changes and squirmed in my seat.

"You about ready to go?" Bennett asked, eyeing my movement.

I nodded. We walked to the car, my head spinning with everything I had learned. Bennett had filled me in on celebrities, politicians, local happenings, and world news, and I could barely keep it all straight. "Is that all?" I asked as I got into the car and buckled my seatbelt.

Bennett laughed loudly. "That's about the gist of it. Nothing else important happened... except, you know, all the magic stuff. Fairies and trolls and shape-shifter–"

"Wait, what? Shape-shifters? Fairies? Trolls! I thought it was just, well, magic. Wave some hands, say some words, maybe throw some eye of newt in a cauldron."

Bennett pulled onto the road, and we made the way toward my—well, Marina and Grey's—apartment. He laughed again, throaty and loud. "It's something like that, yes. But there are a lot of supernatural beings in the Other Realms."

"Realms, plural?"

He glanced at me, then back to the road. "Yeah. The Unveiling dropped the first layer of magic, so to speak, between our reality and theirs, so we are a step closer to all the creatures who live over there. But only the ones in the realms closest to us came over. So, we have the magic-makers—magicians, mages, wizards. But the vampires, shape-shifters, gods, fae, and the like—those guys didn't get to come over right away, but their worlds are one veil closer to ours now."

I frowned. This was deeper than I had realized. "Vampires are real?"

Bennett nodded, keeping his eyes on the road.

"And shape-shifters are, like, werewolves?"

He nodded again. "But there are others too, it seems, who can shift shape to mimic something they've seen, and who don't need the full moon to do it."

I shook my head. "Wow. And... gods? Are we talking about Zeus and Hera here?"

He chuckled again. "I'm not really sure. I've never met a god or goddess. But my understanding is the various pantheons are, in some manifestation, real. Maybe not Zeus as we know him, but something similar exists over there. And it's only a matter of time before these guys cross over here and co-exist with us."

"Or take over our world," I mused. "I don't imagine gods and goddesses would want to harmonize with mere peons." We passed a statue I didn't remember seeing, either on the way to Moe Joe's or before my coma. "Where are we?"

"Just taking a different route back," he answered. "I thought we'd stop by Pages and Potions on the way. Have you heard of it?"

I nodded. "It's my sister's shop."

His profile showed his surprise. "I got the impression she wasn't happy about magic before."

"She's not enthused by any of this. I think she kind of felt forced into adding magic to the bookshop in order to keep it relevant. I don't think she likes it very much, though."

He nodded. "That's interesting. I don't know if I could do something I didn't like, or at least agree with, full time. Anyhow, not all gods just sat on thrones doling out storms and vengeance. Some were said to aid in fertility, agriculture, safe passage of sailors..."

"Yeah, so the sirens didn't eat them," I interjected. "Wait, sirens, too?"

"Probably, somewhere. The universe is a lot bigger than we

realized, Tori."

It wasn't the universe I worried about. It was the multiple dimensions inside it that bothered me.

We pulled into another parking lot, and I looked around. The lot was tiny and housed two buildings, both brown and red brick. One had a sign for psychic readings and the other for Pages and Potions. It was a larger than the psychic's building, with a big window on either side of the glass door. The window covers were beads of various colors, creating a fun and mystical vibe that was compounded by the smell of burning incense when we walked in. The door dinged, and Marina gazed up from the counter directly across from us.

"Tori!" She walked toward us and hugged me when she arrived. "I like the outfit. It looks familiar." She flashed me a smile and turned to Bennett. "Ben, right?"

He offered her his hand to shake. "Bennett. You were close."

"Sorry. What are you guys doing here?" She turned her head to check on a customer who was rifling through little packets that lined a shelf on the far wall.

"Just thought we'd stop by and see the place," I said.

"I've been in a few times myself. It's more for Tori," Bennett said.

"Well, welcome back!" Marina flashed a bright smile toward him. "Anything I can help you with this time?"

Bennett shook his head. "Nothing's on my list. Have you gotten anything cool in lately?"

I walked away and started looking at a rack of crystals, but I heard Marina say, "I got some interesting stones in just this morning. Want to see them?"

Bennett must have answered in the affirmative because they headed to the counter, which Marina walked around to head through a door that I suspected led to a stockroom.

I took in my surroundings. To my left were book-filled shelves that lined the walls and a few tables cluttered with stacks of books. From the looks of the genre signs, the store carried a little of everything, though it wasn't nearly as large of a selection as Marina had always planned on selling. She hadn't wanted to rival the major bookstores by any means, but the bookstore of her dreams had rows upon rows of books and a cozy reading nook tucked in the back. This was nothing like that.

The magic portion of the merchandise filled about two-thirds of the store. I wondered what that must have been like for Marina, to feel pressure to conform to a world she hated just to keep her dream afloat in some capacity.

Her laughter filled the air, and I glanced up to see her setting a box on the counter between herself and Bennett, her blue eyes twinkling. She was excited about something.

I looked around the rest of the store, but the trinkets all blended together in my mind. I didn't know anything about any of this. Yet. I picked up a light pink crystal and turned it over in my hands. It felt powerful, but I couldn't explain why. It smelled faintly of roses and baby powder. I pulled it to my chest and closed my eyes, feeling content and happy.

After a moment, I replaced the crystal and picked up another, this one a deep red. It shone in the light, and I felt motivated and energized when holding it to my skin. I wondered if others felt like this or if it had to do with the abilities given to me during the Unveiling.

I walked around the shelf of crystals, reading description placards, and feeling the items. When I got closer to the counter, Bennett's voice came into focus.

"You think any are spirit stones?" he asked, his voice childlike and loud.

I took a few steps toward them.

"Spirit stones are hard to find," he added.

"I don't know enough about spirit stones to determine yet." Marina held up a scarlet one for inspection. "I have to call in someone who can tell me."

"May I?" Bennett asked, holding out his hand.

Marina placed the scarlet rock in his hand and waited.

Bennett closed his eyes and mumbled something I didn't hear, so I took a few steps closer. He opened his eyes. "I can't sense anything. Doesn't mean there's not a special one in here, though. I'm not inborn, so I can't sense things like others can." He watched me as I neared, raising an eyebrow.

I took a few more steps until I was close enough to peer over the side of the box on the counter. There were six stones, all smooth and dark, unlike the crystals I was just perusing, and in a variety of colors. They appeared to be plain old colored garden rocks.

But they felt like something else. What, I wasn't sure, but intuition told me they were more than ordinary.

I leaned over farther to study them, afraid to touch them because of how strong the pull toward the box was becoming.

Bennett watched me with wide eyes.

I didn't want Marina to notice my pull to the stones, so I looked away, but I could still feel them. My skin tingled; my whole body energized. These were more than just garden stones; at least one of them was special. I just wished I knew more about myself and my newfound powers to figure out which one it was and what was special about it, or me.

SEVEN

THREE DAYS PASSED SINCE Bennett agreed to work with me, and I had spent a lot of time with him since then, mostly because I had nothing else to do with myself. In that time, I had made progress toward feeling my magic intuitively and using it with purpose. Though occasionally I threw orbs of light at the walls or moved something I wasn't supposed to. Just this morning, I had thrown an electric bolt at Bennett, barely missing his bun atop his head, and called it quits for the day.

I walked into the apartment and threw my jacket on the couch. And it was really my jacket, as Marina had taken me shopping for some clothes that fit yesterday while Grey was at work. We had hit some thrift stores in town, and I was able to load up with jeans, skirts, tops, and jackets. I didn't need shoes since I had an entire box of my favorites.

"Tori, you home?" Marina's voice called from the bedroom. When I answered, the door opened, and she stepped out. "I still love that skirt," she said, indicating the one I wore.

I twirled slowly, so I didn't get dizzy or lose my balance. It was like I had just gotten off a boat and still had my sea legs... for the last several weeks. "It is a pretty color," I commented, lifting the edge of the burgundy fabric to inspect. "Anyhow, what's up?" I sat on the couch and let her come to me.

She sat on the other end of the couch. "Nothing really. Just checking on you. I haven't seen you much."

I shrugged. "I'm just exploring. After you went back to work, I walked to Monument Circle. Had lunch on the steps with a bunch of other people on their lunch breaks. It made me feel almost normal."

"You are normal, Tori." Marina's voice was insistent and tinged with pain.

If she only knew.

"It's just, you know, I feel like my head's on sideways most days. And my legs too." I looked away and out the window. I wasn't lying, not really, but I hated omitting important things from my sister. Marina's feelings about magic made it pretty much impossible for me to be completely open with her. At least not right now, while my abilities were still erratic. Her fear of uncontrolled power was the problem, after all.

Marina leaned toward me and put a hand on my arm. "It's going to take some time. Remember, the doctors were surprised you were up and about as well as you are. It must be the magic behind the coma speeding up your recovery so fast. I'm just grateful you're awake, walking and talking and thinking as well as you are."

I scrunched my face up. "You're getting mushy again, little sis."

She held both hands in front of her chest and made a heart with her fingers. "I just love you, big sis."

We both giggled. It felt good. Even though my mind thought I had been laughing with her this whole time, I logically knew that I had missed out on almost five years of time with her, my best friend. And Grey, but of course, that ended differently.

I made a heart with my hands back at her and we giggled some more.

Marina cleared her throat. She scanned the kitchen, the TV, the front door.

"Is something up?" I asked, frowning.

"No, no. It's just, well. I hadn't planned on saying anything, but I feel I need to say it now." She wrung her hands together and finally turned to me.

I leaned forward a little, urging her on.

Marina took a deep breath and then blurted, "I'm sorry about what happened with Grey. I didn't mean for it to happen, and he didn't either."

I smiled. This was what she was worried about? "Sure, I won't lie. It's weird. Really fucking weird. But I don't, like, hate you or anything."

She wrung her hands together. "We didn't know if you were ever going to wake up, Tor." Her voice cracked. "We were both there with you every day, holding your hand, talking to you. He noticed I was sleeping there, so he started bringing me coffee in the morning—real coffee, not the hospital stuff. So, I brought him lunch a few times, when I'd finally get around to going out for it. At first, we'd eat separately so that one of us could be with you. But eventually we went to dinner together, not as a date, just as two people grieving, you know."

I nodded. A pit formed in my gut as she spoke, but I could tell she needed to get it out.

"It took a while to fall in love, I mean. Grey was hopelessly in love with you." Her voice drifted off, and she turned her head again. She spoke softly. "I sometimes wonder if he still is. Especially with you back—I mean, awake."

I scooted closer, tugging gently at her chin until our eyes locked. "Marina. Marina, look at me. He chose you. He wants to marry you. We never even talked about it. You guys have a good life, and I know it's weird with me being here now and all, but nothing's going to change that. Not me, not magic, nothing."

She offered a weak smile. "I hope you're right. I felt so bad about liking him, and then about loving him, Tor. But I couldn't help it. And then when you woke up, I felt bad all over again. And I couldn't help but wonder ... with you awake, would he still want to marry me?" She wiped tears that threatened to spill onto her cheeks.

I nodded. "That makes perfect sense. But I promise you, there is no Tori and Grey anymore; there's no us. There is a *you*, Marina and Grey. And I couldn't be happier." Okay, so it was a tiny white lie.

She sniffled. "You know, that's why Grey works at the hospital now."

I tilted my head toward my shoulder.

"Well, you know he started working for that company he hated when he got his MBA. After everything happened, he spent all his free time at the hospital. Then he thought that if he worked there, he could work from your room and spend every second with you. He slept in the chair so many nights he went to a chiropractor."

My eyebrows shot up. Grey hated the idea of chiropractors; he said they weren't real doctors and were basically charlatans out for the money of people in pain.

"I know!" Marina exclaimed. "That's how much he was there. He really did love you." She appeared sad again.

"And I loved him. But that doesn't mean I won't love someone again, and that he doesn't love you now. Every relationship is different, right?"

Marina nodded. "You're right. So," she said before clearing her throat, "now that you're out of the hospital and single for the first time in forever, is there going to be any dating in your future?"

I laughed. "Well, I hope so. I'm only thirty!"

She swatted at my arm. "You know what I mean. Like, soon. The near future."

I thought about Bennett, his short blonde beard and pale gray eyes. The messy bun he always put his hair in was growing on me. I wondered what his hair looked like down.

Marina was watching me think. "Ben? Err, Bennett?"

My cheeks heated, but I shook my head. "No, no. I mean, I don't think so. I don't know, I'm a little rusty at dating. I haven't since grad school, which now seems so much farther away than before."

"It kind of was," Marina said.

It was my turn to swat her on the arm. "Throw my coma in my face, why don't you? It wasn't my fault." I paused for a moment, almost afraid to ask the next question. "Whose fault was it, actually?"

"Huh?"

"My coma. What did the doctors say happened?"

Marina shook her head. "They didn't know. You were physically fit as a fiddle, and even your symptoms now are minor compared to what they'd expect from a coma that long. Your muscles should be completely atrophied; you should have had to learn to walk like a baby again. And talk again, too. But you're fine."

I'd hardly call these splitting headaches, memory loss, and baby Bambi legs fine, but I knew what she meant. I frowned. "So, it was magical?"

Marina nodded slowly and then shrugged. "Bennett seemed pretty interested in it the other day, didn't he?"

I thought about it. I vaguely remembered him seeming a bit weird when I mentioned my unexplained coma. Maybe he knew something I didn't—yet another reason to keep meeting with him regularly.

"He said he's a mage, so his magic is learned," Marina said. "But I don't know if we can trust him. What if he's lying?"

"What does he have to lie about?"

"Plenty of people are wary of innate magic, not just me," she countered, a bit defensively. "It's just so much more powerful, and harder to control, than learned power. And potentially so much more destructive."

I shook my head. "I don't get it, then. Why do you own a magic shop when you distrust magic? And don't tell me it's complicated again."

Marina scooted to the edge of her seat silently. After almost a full minute, she finally spoke. "I can't say, really. Pages and Potions started as a bookstore, and it did alright. But after the Unveiling, I read everything I could on magic. Of course, most of what was available was fiction or pseudoscience. There still isn't much written about magic, in our world at least. Sometimes you find a book from the Other Realm, but they're hard to come by, and even harder to read." She paused, long enough that I wondered if she thought she'd answered the question I asked.

Finally, she continued with a sigh. "I was enveloped in this world of magic, even though I hated it. Or fear it, really. It felt like a way to keep my eye on it, adding magic to the bookstore. My little shop is one of the biggest sellers of magical items in the state, believe it or not. Sometimes we're able to get our hands on artifacts no one else has. I feel like it helps keep them out of the hands of people who don't know how to control their magic. And my record-keeping is so tight the Department–" She stopped herself mid-sentence.

"The Department? You give them information on magic-users?" That pit in my stomach deepened, and I felt a little nauseated.

Marina wrung her hands and gazed at the floor sheepishly. "I can't really talk about it."

So, she worked with the Department of Wayward Magic, at least in an informal capacity. Did she have a hand in people getting turned over to the Department for not understanding their magic—the magic they didn't ask for and may not even want? Heat rose in my cheeks, and I looked away so she wouldn't see my face redden.

"I don't want to talk about it anymore," she said, standing suddenly.

I reached for her. "Sit back down, Marina. We don't have to talk about it."

She frowned but sat. "You don't understand what it was like, Tori. You weren't there."

Thanks for reminding me.

She continued. "People went out for trick-or-treating and came home with magical powers. They didn't know what to do with them. Lots of people got hurt."

I could imagine how easily that would happen, given what I'd seen of my own magic. But I'd also seen Bennett save my sister and Grey with magic. I wasn't sure what to believe. "Is that how it happened, that suddenly?"

Marina shrugged, her long black hair swaying with the movement. "As far as we can tell, yeah. Sometime Halloween night, the Other Realm merged with ours. By morning, all hell was breaking loose. Plus, that's when you fell into your coma."

I nodded. It made sense. As much sense as magical realms could, at least. Something Marina said caught my attention, though. She had said Realm, singular, not Realms, plural. "So, do you think that's the only other realm there is? I mean, you all talk about a great Unveiling as if this is the one and only time the worlds could collide. Do you not think there are more realms out there?"

Marina shrugged, leaning back in her seat and crossing her legs. "Some think so. I read something once about a multiverse. Under certain circumstances, all the realms in the multiverse can cross over with each other. So, like, wraiths could walk with werewolves and wizards, all together, with no ritual being performed." She shrugged again. "But I don't know if I believe all that. I mean, it's been almost five years and we haven't seen anything other than magic-users. No ghouls or vampires or zombies or whatever else may go bump in the night."

I crossed my arms over my chest. "So, you don't believe in it?"

"Oh, I believe in everything I sell, and some of what I read. I just think some people take it too far, wanting to raise the dead or whatnot. I don't think any of that is real. Those people have been reading too much science fiction."

"Makes sense," I said, drifting into a world of my own thoughts. Telling Marina what Bennett knew would blow her mind. On the other hand, according to Marina, what Bennett claimed to know might very well be speculation, or straight crazy talk. I didn't know what to believe at this point.

"Hey Tor," Marina whispered.

I looked back at her expectantly.

"Be careful around Bennett, okay?"

I stared at her, unsure of how to react.

"It's just that he plays with these forces, and we don't really know him. He has some power too, or he knows how to use it, to save us the way he did. He's not just making pencils float or doing light housework spells."

"That's a thing?" I exclaimed.

She sighed. "Not the point."

"Okay, okay, I'll be careful."

"But hey," she said, wiggling her eyebrows, "you can still get to know him. He is kind of hot, in a very non-Grey way."

"Yes, he is."

"Just promise me you'll be careful, right?"

Exasperated, I sighed loudly. "Yes, mother."

Marina reached up. I thought she was going to touch my cheek, but she pulled a few strands of hair out of my head.

I smacked at her hand. "What the hell?"

She smiled. "I know a thing or two about magic. And I'm going to make you promise to take care of yourself." She took a foggy white crystal out of her pocket and laid my hair over it. After pulling out a few strands of her own hair and placing it with mine, she closed her eyes.

I recognized more Latin as she spoke in short, simple phrases. She was making the promise binding from my body to hers. How cool. And how creepy.

When she was done, I asked her what was special about the crystal she used.

"Nothing really," she answered. "I don't have any magic, so I need a conduit. If I were one of those who gained magical powers, I'd just need the hair and the words."

I nodded. Interesting. Just how binding was that promise? I wondered what constituted being careful with Bennett. Could I not aim bolts of electricity in his direction now? Or would my magic not work around him at all unless I could control it? I had so many questions to ask my sister, but I couldn't bring myself to do it. She was too fearful. I felt like we'd rekindled our bond tonight, and I didn't want to risk that.

The front door opened, and Grey entered, carrying a pizza box. "Dinner is served, my ladies." He bowed in front of the couch as if serving us the entire box.

We laughed and waved him toward the kitchen where he set the pizza on the island. "So, anything exciting happen in your days?"

I shook my head. If he only knew.

EIGHT

THE NEXT MORNING, I rolled over and pulled my blanket to my chin. I had heard Marina and Grey leaving for work earlier and the sun was shining through the blinds, but otherwise I had no concept of what time it was. It could have been two in the afternoon for all I knew. I hoped not. I was supposed to meet Bennett at noon.

After a few minutes and several yawns, I rolled off the couch and glanced at the clock in the kitchen. It hazily told me it was just after ten. I rubbed my eyes and tried again. Yep, ten-thirteen a.m.

Breakfast, shower, then stretching on the living room floor. I had to see my physical therapist tomorrow and he would yell at me if I wasn't doing my stretches and exercises. Plus, they made my legs feel better.

At eleven-thirty I threw on some new clothes—a denim ruffled skirt, light green long-sleeved t-shirt, and a white infinity scarf with green polka dots. White Converse completed the outfit.

I made my way out of the apartment complex on foot. We were meeting in the park today. Bennett said that I was learning to control and understand my magic so quickly that I should be safe outside in public. I was excited. Autumn was my favorite time of the year. Being stuck inside all summer was bad enough; being inside all October would be horrible.

It took twenty minutes to walk to the park, but I didn't mind. My legs even held up pretty well.

Bennett was leaning against a tree near a large expanse of grass, and he waved as I walked up. "I don't have as much time as I thought I did today," he said when I reached him. "The Circle just called me in for something; I'll have to leave in a little bit." The Circle of Magi, he had told me recently, was the official council on mage magic.

"I didn't think they called you in very often."

He shook his head. "Not really. We meet regularly, but they only send out a bulletin if there are rumblings that something's up."

I cocked my head to the side. "So, there are rumblings?"

He nodded. "I guess there are rumblings."

"Hmm." I looked around. "Are you sure this is the place to practice?"

Bennett laughed, which was a sound I was beginning to like. "You're not the only one here with magic, remember?" He nodded toward my right, and I turned.

At the far end of the park, a small child sat on a swing, swinging herself. However, at second glance, I noticed a woman on a bench feeding an infant with one hand and making a back-and-forth motion with the other, aiming her fingers toward the swing-set. Her hand moved in time with the girl's movements.

Bennett indicated to my left, and I turned my head that way.

A group of college-aged young adults were running around a flat area in the grass, tossing a Frisbee—a seemingly innocuous activity. But then I noticed they weren't catching the disc in the air; the Frisbee would stop just before a person and fling back to someone else without ever touching anyone.

I had no words to describe how I was feeling about what I saw.

"Wow." Eyes wide, I took a closer look at the other inhabitants of the park. Not all of them were using magic, at least visibly. A group of children chased each other on the grass, playing tag, while others squealed on their way down slides and through tubes. A cluster of women with strollers laughed at the edge of the playground. A single man sat on a bench, peering in our direction. His gaze met mine, and he glanced away quickly.

Bennett smacked me in the arm with a smile. "See? You're not special, Tori."

I frowned at him.

"I mean, you're special, of course, but you're not the only one with magic," he stammered. "Though yours is pretty powerful, so maybe you are special in some way. I don't know."

I chuckled. "It's okay, Bennett. I know what you mean. So, what are we working on today?"

He took a few steps toward an empty clearing, and I followed. "You seem to have pretty good control over what you can do when you think about it. Except for the lightning bolt you threw at me the other day." He shot me an annoyed glance.

"Nah, that was on purpose," I told him, laughing.

His expression deepened for a moment, then his face went back to normal. "Ha, ha. I can throw one at you too, you know."

"But not before reciting at least five sentences in Latin and concentrating really hard. You know what I could do to you in that time?" I swatted at his arm so he'd know I was joking.

He shrugged. "Hey, at least I can remember the Latin phrases." Ouch.

He held his hands up. "Sorry, that was a low blow."

I chewed on my lower lip for a moment, then shrugged. "It's true, though. I have a good memory of what I taught, but the more obscure stuff—the stuff that made me good at my job—still escapes me." It made my stomach hurt to think about it.

"Well, your internal magic will only go so far. You'll have to learn, or remember, more of the Classical languages, especially Latin, to do anything big. Or even medium. But you still have a leg up on pretty much everyone else in the world. I mean, how many people spoke any Latin before the Unveiling, anyhow?"

I shrugged. "How many Catholics are there in the world?"

"How many of them actually know what they're saying?"

"You got me." We stopped. We had walked far enough away from others that I could still see them, but I couldn't hurt anyone with a stray spell. "So, what are we doing today?"

He turned toward me. "We are going to ramp up your magic with some extras," he said, pulling a plastic baggie out of his pocket.

I leaned forward to inspect it. "You brought drugs?"

Bennett laughed, hard. "No, no," he said between bursts of laughter, "I brought herbs."

I studied his face. "From the look of that herb, it's the same thing."

He shook his head. "Nope. This is bay leaves and basil."

I took it from him and turned the bag over in my hands. "So... you brought me Italian seasoning."

He chuckled, and I swore I could get used to that sound all day. I was developing a crush on my teacher, and I scrunched up my face at the thought. That was not in the plans.

"Essentially, yes. But fresh, and more concentrated than what you're thinking of. Both have a variety of magical properties, so I thought they would be good to have, regardless of what we do today." He reached into his other pocket and pulled out another small baggie. Inside was a finely grounded green and brown mixture. "Rosemary and vanilla. Both are good for memory."

"Do I... eat them? Snort them? Got a baggie of cocaine in there somewhere, too?" I joked.

He rolled his eyes. "You can eat the rosemary and vanilla, just a little on the tongue." He handed me the bag. "Every day, like a vitamin. The others, you can eat too, but we're going to play with them in different ways."

I was definitely curious now.

"And no, I don't have any coke. I bet that sketchy guy over there can probably help you out though," he said, nodding toward the man on the bench.

When he caught us watching him, the man turned away quickly.

Bennett was right; the guy did seem shady. Even his attire was suspicious—dark jeans, a tight charcoal T-shirt, and black shoes. He had an exotic appeal with coppery skin and jet-black hair, but he was too far away to see his features. None of the children had his skin tone, but that didn't mean one of them wasn't his. Still, it all added up to one word in my mind—creepy.

I turned away and cringed at Bennett. "What's he doing?"

"Don't ask me," he answered. "I'm not in his head."

"Can we do that? Get in someone's head?" I asked, a little too excitedly.

"You can do anything you learn how to do."

I crossed my arms over my chest. "Raise the dead?"

"You'd be a necromancer."

"See the future?"

"You'd be clairvoyant."

I squinted, trying to think of a good one. "Make someone fall in love?"

He paused. "I don't know what you'd be called, but you could do it. The right herbs, the right words, a little woo-hoo here—" he moved his hands around in the air, "and a little woo-hoo there, and poof. Someone's in love."

"You don't know how to do it, do you?"

He shook his head. "I never get my woo-hoo right."

We both laughed, and I touched his arm lightly when I spoke next. "I'm sure you don't need magic for that, though."

"Uh, thanks." His cheeks flushed. "But seriously, though, just because you *can* do something, doesn't mean you *should*. The magic community doesn't take kindly to forcing people into stuff against their will."

"Gotcha. No love magic." I nodded once for emphasis. A shiver ran through me, and I took a step closer, so we were almost touching. "But falling in love the old-fashioned way is still okay, right?"

He blushed again but didn't move.

I didn't plan it ahead of time; I just did it. My fingers grazed his arm as I leaned in and planted a kiss on his mouth. It was a simple, quick kiss, partly because I was unsure of myself, but mostly because Bennett didn't reciprocate.

He didn't push me away, which was a point in his favor, but he absolutely did not kiss me back.

I took a huge step backward, my face heating.

"Tori, I'm sorry," Bennett said quickly, his hands in front of him. "It's just that, well, it's not like that. Not with you."

I crossed my arms over my chest and tried to bury my face in my scarf, which naturally didn't work. "What's wrong with me?" I asked quietly. Grey didn't wait for me, and now Bennett didn't want me. The common denominator was me.

"For starters, I have someone. Casey. I wouldn't want to damage that."

I nodded. That made sense, even if it still stung.

"And for seconds, you're not a guy."

I looked up to see a smirk on Bennett's face. "Wait, what?"

"I like men, Tori. I'm gay. I mean, I'm sure I'd be into you if I wasn't, but I am, so I'm not."

I stared at him for a second, trying to decide if he was messing with me.

His expression seemed so sincere, my only response was to burst into laughter. "Of all the guys to throw myself at!"

He laughed with me. I still loved his laugh, but I'd have to get over that little crush.

"So, Casey, huh? You know, you could have just left it at that. I wouldn't have questioned whether Casey was a guy or girl," I said after I finished laughing. I was able to look Bennett in the eyes again, even though I was still a little embarrassed by my actions.

"I'm not ashamed, Tori," he said, shrugging. "It's who I am. Plus, maybe you'll meet him one day, and wouldn't you be surprised if he showed up and you were expecting a woman?"

I raised an eyebrow. Fair points, both.

"Okay," I said, changing the subject to move past the rest of my embarrassment. "What are we doing with your herbs?"

He poured some of his remaining herbs, the basil and bay leaves, into his hand and held it out to me.

"Shouldn't we, like, put them in a cauldron or something?"

He rolled his eyes. "Double double toil and trouble, huh?"

I shrugged. "I don't know about this stuff. Coma, remember?"

"How could I forget? It's not every day you meet someone who woke up from a five-year coma. Anyhow," he said, pinching the mixture of crushed herbs with his left hand as he held them in his right, "you could mix them into a potion. You can also eat them or mix them into water and drink them. However, for someone with magic like yours, I think just touching them will suffice. If not, we can give something else a try."

"I'm game," I said. I let Bennett drop the pinch of herbs into my outstretched palm. "Now what?"

"Now, close your eyes."

I did as he asked, albeit impatiently.

"Breathe in and out slowly, like you're meditating."

I cringed, as meditation was not in my daily activities, but I did as I was told.

"Concentrate on the herbs, on their powers."

"I don't know what they do," I reminded him.

I could hear him shift on the grass and fallen leaves. "Stop being so ornery. I'm going to tell you."

I blew out the breath I was holding. "Fine. What does basil do, besides make my spaghetti tasty?"

"Basil is good for bringing love to you, exorcisms—don't worry, that's not what we're doing today—wealth, protection, and courage. Some say it can aid in flying as well, but I haven't tested that theory. Bay leaves are also good for protection, but they also can enhance psychic and healing powers and are used for purification, strength, and divination."

I took another deep breath and let it out. "Wow, that's a lot of stuff. How can I concentrate on all that?" I opened my eyes to look at Bennett.

"Eyes closed."

"Why, though?"

"I don't know. It's easier to drown out distractions." His voice sounded irritated.

I closed my eyes again, becoming happy to drown out the distraction of Bennett being annoying.

"What do you want to do with your herbs, Tori?" he asked, his tone calm and low.

"Umm. Well, I'm not going to try flying," I said, laughing a little. "And bringing love to me is out, apparently." I giggled at that, as did Bennett.

"How about you try to move something, like we did the other day, but you can focus on protection while moving it?"

I had no idea what he meant. "Like, throw something at myself and hope the small spice rack in my hand will save me?"

"Something like that," he said, his voice serious. "Nothing big. Like, how about this pinecone?"

"Are you sure protection works like that? I mean, you didn't say 'force fields.' You said 'protection.' I assume that means protection from another spell, or from evil forces controlling my mind, or something." I frowned. I didn't want to get pelted with pinecones because someone misinterpreted the instructions.

"I think it can mean a lot of things," Bennett explained. He sounded a little condescending, like he was talking to a child.

"Fine," I said, being that child. "Throw a pinecone at me. But give me a minute. I'm concentrating."

After a moment, I asked, "Don't I have words to say or something?"

I could almost hear the smile in his voice as he gave me a Latin word to repeat—the word for *protection*, which I could have remembered without his help. Probably. I repeated it, but not very loudly, several times. The familiar tingle of electricity rushed over me, and I relished in it with a bit of excitement. It felt great, but I knew I'd be exhausted if I kept it up.

"Aha!" Bennett shouted, just when I was about to stop chanting.

I opened my eyes and jumped, startled. "What's wrong?"

"Nothing's wrong at all. Look," he said, pointing to the ground by my feet. Three pinecones lay there. Pinecones I didn't know he had thrown at me at all.

"What happened?"

"After a few times of you saying the word, I felt a surge of energy, so I threw the first pinecone at you. It got inches from you and just dropped to the ground. Same with the other two."

"I didn't like, start glowing blue or anything?" I asked.

He shook his head.

"Damn. That would have been cool."

"Pretty sure that only happens in cartoons."

I held my hands out to him, still holding onto my herbs. "These turned blue in the car that day, remember? So, it's not just for cartoons."

He chewed on his lip. "You're right. Maybe you are more special than I realized." We were both silent for a moment, contemplating his comment. Finally, he spoke up again, bouncing a little on his toes as he spoke. "I have an idea."

I peered sideways at him. "Should I be scared?"

"Maybe." He paused. "See those squirrels over there?" He pointed toward the nearest tree where two squirrels were picking up acorns.

"Yeah..."

"I'm going to throw a pinecone at them. But I want you to protect them when I do."

I frowned. "Seriously? What if it doesn't work?"

"Then I'll scare some vermin. No big deal."

I huffed and puffed, but gave in. "Fine." I closed my eyes and concentrated, saying the Latin word aloud but adding the word for *squirrel*. For the last few iterations, I opened my eyes and focused on the squirrels.

Bennett threw the pinecone, and it was a straight trajectory for the squirrels. He must have played baseball or something.

The pinecone got within inches of one squirrel and dropped straight to the ground, just like Bennett said happened with me.

I jumped and squealed. "Oh, my god! Look what I can do."

Bennett smiled. "I thought it would work. I can do it, but it's much more complicated for me, and it drains my energy to do any spells. How are you? Are you feeling tired?"

I checked in with myself. "Nope. Right as rain." I smiled back at him. "What else can we do?" I hopped on both feet, careful not to spill my pinch of basil and bay leaves.

"Hey," he said, leaning in with his voice low, "look at the guy. Don't let him see you, though."

I glanced over Bennett's shoulder. Sure enough, the guy in dark clothes had moved to a closer bench and stared in our direction. Specifically, he was watching me. He noticed me watching, but instead of turning away, he stared back at me.

I closed my eyes and started a new chant, wondering if it would work. *Invisible, clear, protection,* I repeated in Latin. *Invisible, clear, protection.*

"Whoa! Where the fuck did you go?" Bennett asked, alarmed and excited.

"Still here. I'm invisible, huh?"

Bennett nodded, his eyes wide.

I gazed past him at the guy near the playground, who was still staring in my direction. I wondered if he could see through my spell or if he just knew I was still there because Bennett was talking to me.

"How long do you think you can keep that up?"

"I don't know," I said. "Let me see." I had stopped chanting to speak, and that didn't seem to negate the spell. I threw the herbs on the ground, to which Bennett cried, "Hey!" but I was still invisible. Finally, I stopped concentrating. It took a few seconds, but my hands blinked into view and then finally Bennett told me I was solid again.

"That's so cool, Tori," he exclaimed. "I can't do that. Well, I've never tried, mainly because I've been told it's impossible. For a mage, at least."

"I wonder if I can do it again and get home without the guy seeing me. He's really creeping me out." I grabbed my scarf and tried to wrap myself in it, but it was still around my neck, so I couldn't hide very well. Plus, I didn't need a cloak of invisibility. I just needed my herbs and my Latin.

"Think I can do it without the herbs?" I asked. Before Bennett could answer, I started chanting the Latin words again, a little louder than before. After several iterations, Bennett's face told me it had worked. "This is amazing, Bennett!" I cried. I rushed forward and flung myself on him in a hug. It was probably strange to see him hugging thin air, but I didn't care. I was controlling my magic, and it was pretty damn cool.

"I think that may be enough for today," he said. "Why don't you come back, and instead of being invisible the whole way home, I'll just drive you home. I have to leave for the Circle anyhow."

"Fine," I grumbled, breaking my concentration until I was visible again.

"Still feel okay?"

"Yep. Feeling great. Charged up, actually."

He nodded. "Let's get going then. I don't want you walking home with that guy watching you like that."

NINE

BENNETT DROPPED ME OFF in the parking lot at my insistence that he didn't have to walk me to the door. I was wrong.

As I fumbled for the door key, a movement caught my attention in my peripheral view. I turned as quickly as my tired legs would let me, just in time to see a car come to a stop at the nearby curb.

Behind the wheel was the man from the park, watching me with an intense stare.

Startled, I jumped back, knocking into the brick wall beside me. "Damnit."

The man opened his door and slowly emerged from the car. After a brief pause, during which I remained frozen in place, breathing hard, the man took a step forward.

Fear and anger vied for my attention. I tried to take a step backward, but my foot met the wall. "You followed me," I accused. "Who are you? What do you want?" Electricity danced on my fingertips, and I wondered if I had enough energy left to defend myself with magic.

He nodded, walking toward me. "I'm not here to hurt you. I'm simply... interested in your skills." Despite his olive skin tone, he had no accent. But he did have the most crystalline green eyes I had ever seen, and the perfect amount of stubble. He was several inches taller than me, which was both impressive and intimidating.

"My skills? And why didn't you just come talk to me in the park? It would have been way less creepy than following me to my house."

The man grinned. "I didn't want to get pinecones thrown at me."

So, he had been watching me practice my magic. What all had he seen? Or not seen, rather.

He held his hands up in surrender. "I promise I'm not going to hurt you. My boss though, he might not promise that."

I gulped. "Boss?"

"I work for... Bram. He needs someone of your caliber of magic to assist us."

"My caliber of magic? That's ridiculous. I've only been practicing for a few days."

"I know, but Bram thinks there's a reason your magic is so strong already. Something to do with the coma you just woke up from."

I held a hand out, motioning him to stop. "How did you know I was in a coma?"

He smiled, equal parts sexy and unnerving. "Bram's been doing a lot of research. Apparently, several people around the world went into comas the night of the Unveiling. You all woke up at different times; some are still unconscious."

I shook my head, but I wasn't sure why I had trouble believing this. I had already learned that magic existed, I could use it, and it was likely responsible for my coma. Why wouldn't it make sense that I wasn't the only one? I wondered if I could find these other people and... I wasn't sure what. Talk to them, learn from them, simply not feel so alone?

He had paused when I shook my head. He flashed another smile—this one kind — and continued. "I don't know how to contact the others, and none of them are local. Bram mentioned one in England, one in Asia somewhere, another in the Pacific Northwest... I'm not sure how many there are. With all the havoc the Unveiling created, mysterious comas weren't exactly front and center news." He shrugged.

"Why, though? What does my coma have to do with me helping your boss?"

"In the time you've been practicing, you've been able to accomplish things I haven't seen before." He started to step forward before reconsidering. "I know you've just discovered your magic, and it may be a bit ... unpredictable ... but Bram thinks it's more potent than normal because of whatever put you in the coma. You're the one he wants, Tori. If Bram doesn't get what he wants, he's going to get upset."

Fear dissipated, and anger won the attention battle, at least momentarily. I leaned back, crossing my arms. "Why the hell should I care what this Bram guy does when he's upset?"

He sighed. "I've been instructed to offer you an ultimatum, Tori. Please don't make me do it."

"How do you know my name? Have you been watching me for longer than just today?"

He nodded. "I'm sorry, I really am. Bram had me watching you for the last few days."

"Who are you?" I asked again.

"Killian Costa. I'm kind of a hired hand. I want to talk to you about helping us out."

"What do you need help with?" I furrowed my brows and stared at him.

Killian crossed his arms, showing muscular biceps through his charcoal shirt. He was close enough to stare down at me, his green eyes boring into mine. "Bram is trying to perform some powerful magic. The problem is he's not magical. He's been practicing for years and made no progress. So, he has others to help him get what he wants."

"Which is?"

"Have you heard of the goddess Ophelia?"

I shook my head. Gods and goddesses, here we go.

"She's a demi-god. She is dormant in another realm, the Realm of Lost Souls. Bram wants to wake her up and bring her here."

I cringed. "Why the hell would he want to do that? Don't we have enough to worry about already?"

Killian laughed. "He has his reasons, I'm sure." His eyes clouded over, and he glanced away before meeting my gaze again. "I'm not exactly privy to that information. I just do what I'm asked."

Something about his comment didn't sit well with me, but I didn't address it. Instead, I tried to wrap my mind around the bigger picture. "Okay. So, this Bram guy wants me to use magic, which I am still learning, to help him raise a freakin' demi-god. Is that all?"

Killian cast his eyes downward, his mouth in a tight line. "He says if you don't help him, he will hurt your sister."

"My sister?" I raised an eyebrow.

"Marina."

"Yes, I know who my sister is. How does he know who my sister is?"

Killian shrugged. "I don't know. All I know is that Marina is in danger if you don't help us. We have already gone through three magicians at this point. You are the fourth and he's impatient. All Hallows Eve is coming and—"

"Wait. Halloween, again? Doesn't anyone want to get creative around here?"

His chuckle sounded forced. "It's the night when the veil between worlds is the thinnest. It's the easiest time to travel between realms or drop a veil altogether. And with the Unveiling five years ago, it's even easier now to do than it was before."

I frowned. "I missed so much."

Killian also shook his head. "Maybe, but you woke up with some fire in you, some genuine talent. You may not see it yet–" he said when I protested, "but I can tell you, it's there. It radiates off you."

I was still in shock from his statement a minute earlier, that this stranger would hurt my sister if I didn't help him. "So, this Bram guy, he's serious? Marina may be in danger?"

He nodded.

I narrowed my eyes at Killian. "And what do you do for him?"

He looked away for several seconds. "Look," he said when his eyes met mine again, "I was instructed to scare you into helping him, but I don't want to do that. He has others whose job is to ensure he gets what he wants. And believe me, when Bram wants something, he gets it."

"That didn't answer what you do for him. If you don't want to scare me, why are you here?"

He flashed a quick, sad smile, and I knew there was something he wasn't telling me, and probably wouldn't. Was Killian being blackmailed, just like he was trying to blackmail me? If I didn't do what he asked, not only might Marina be hurt—if I believed what he was telling me—but he might lose something, too. He didn't seem to want to share what was at stake for him, and I didn't ask. "What will happen to Marina if I refuse?"

He frowned at me but didn't answer. Instead, he pulled a phone out of pocket and swiped up on the screen. A photo appeared. It showed a man, his short blonde hair matted with blood, eyes swollen and purple. "Our last magician."

Fear snaked down my spine. "What do I have to do?"

Killian swiped the photo off his screen and showed it to me again. An address. "Tomorrow, noon. Don't tell anyone. Not your sister, or her boyfriend, or that magical friend of yours."

I was too scared for the mention of Grey to bother me. If he and Marina were in danger, I'd do anything Killian wanted. And I didn't want to involve poor Bennett, who was barely more than a stranger. I closed my eyes and took a deep breath. This Bram guy was preying on my vulnerability, which meant he had to know I was just in the hospital. Clearly, he knew about my family and friends. What was he truly capable of?

Opening my eyes again, I decided I didn't want to find out. "I'll be there."

Killian nodded. "Good choice." He walked away and stopped at the door to the slick black sports car I'd seen parked outside since coming home from the hospital. The bastard had been watching me this whole time.

I'd show up tomorrow at noon, and I'd fix this before anyone got hurt. I had to.

TEN

THE TAXI DRIVER PULLED up to the address Killian had given me yesterday and turned to give me a once-over. "You sure this is it, miss?"

The house in front of us was in a swanky neighborhood on the northeast side of Indy, and it blended in with the rest of the sprawling yards and big stone houses. But unlike the others, which had manicured bushes and expensive cars parked in front of four-car garages, this one seemed lifeless. If anyone actually lived here, it wasn't evident. Despite its beauty, the house gave off a vibe that said not to enter. I figured it was the right place.

"Yep, this is me." I thanked the driver and stepped out of the car. Glancing at my outfit, I realized why the driver had questioned if I belonged, given my denim jacket and sneakers. To be fair, I hadn't known I was being driven to a freaking mansion.

The taxi drove away, leaving me standing on the sidewalk, debating if I wanted to walk up the neatly trimmed driveway or turn and run. I didn't figure my legs would carry me very far, and I didn't want to risk Marina being in danger. With a sigh, I stepped forward.

Footsteps sounded behind me, and then a deep voice said my name.

I turned to see Killian approaching. He wore a similar outfit to yesterday, and I wondered if that was his standard uniform.

At least I wasn't the only one who appeared out of place here.

"No one's going to bite," Killian said, grabbing my arm and leading me up the driveway. "Well, I can't promise that. Just be nice to Bram, and you'll be fine."

I nodded, fear clenching my stomach. The sun felt a little too bright, and I wondered if it was stress or the light of the stars overhead. I didn't have much time to think about it, though, because Killian opened the front door and ushered me in.

Stepping inside, I gasped. The interior of the house matched the ritz of the exterior. The entryway seemed larger than Marina's entire apartment, with a grand double staircase as the focal point. At the base of each set of steps was a man standing guard, somehow mastering the balance between being expressionless and appearing fierce. The men's attire didn't match, but they were dressed similarly to Killian. Maybe it *was* a uniform.

Killian chuckled as I gawked. "This way." He guided me under an archway and into the living room. It must have been what I'd heard referred to as a *great room*, because it wasn't like any living room I'd ever seen. The walls stretched upward two stories, and the sun and stars were visible through a set of ostentatious skylights. Pristine white furniture that didn't appear to be for sitting clustered together around an enormous stone fireplace.

"Where *are* we?" I asked.

Killian laughed, more fully this time, but didn't answer. He continued to lead me out of the great room through another archway, and we navigated a hallway with a series of turns and corners, passing several doors along the way.

I surmised we were behind the grand staircase, and the doors were perhaps closets or servants' quarters, or whatever rich people wanted to keep hidden. Voices came from somewhere down the long hall and grew louder as we approached. Finally, we reached our destination—the kitchen of my dreams. Dark wood and marble countertops gleamed in the sunlight that shone through large windows. I glanced at the double oven and oversized range, wishing they were mine. The apartment I'd picked out with Grey had an amazing kitchen, and it paled in comparison to this.

I winced at the thought of my former boyfriend. What was he doing right now? Texting Marina from a conference, calling her from his desk, daydreaming about holding her? I shook the thoughts away. This was an important matter, not to mention a potentially dangerous one. I had to stay on my guard, not engrossed in thoughts of Grey.

"Good thinking," Killian whispered from behind me. "He's not worth your time, anyhow."

I spun around, frowning. Had I said that aloud?

Killian smiled, but didn't respond. Instead, he nodded toward the other end of the room, where two men sat at a breakfast nook.

One had red hair, a matching goatee, and dark wire-rimmed glasses, and was clicking a pen absentmindedly while talking with the other man, who had light brown hair and brown eyes. I watched them discussing for a moment and thought about what a normal scene this would be, if I wasn't here because I was being blackmailed into helping someone raise a sleeping goddess.

"She's a demi-goddess," Killian whispered from beside me.

I turned to him again, this time positive I hadn't spoken my thoughts. Had he just read my mind?

"I can't really control it. I hear some things but not others, and I can't always tune in when I want to. It's an unreliable ability," he said.

I pondered why Bram would blackmail someone with an un-reliable ability, but then I remembered mine was unpredictable, yet there I was.

The brown-haired man broke my thoughts. "Ah, Killian, good to see you."

Killian winced, but didn't address the man's words. Instead, he put his hand on my back and ushered me forward a step. "This is Tori."

I maneuvered away from his touch and stammered a hello.

The man stood up. "Ah, Tori. So glad to finally meet you." His voice was gravelly and low, like he had been yelling for so long he lost some of it. "I'm Bram. Welcome to my home." He spread his arms wide, showcasing the room with pride.

I turned back to Killian and then to Bram. This was not what I expected. I had expected some man with slick hair and a gold chain. Bram just looked like, well, a regular Joe. I must have worn my shock, because Bram chuckled.

"Expecting Tony Soprano, eh?" he asked.

"I guess," I answered softly.

"I'm not sure what Killian told you, but don't believe any of it," he said, peering over my shoulder at Killian. "I'm sure we'll get along just fine."

I also glanced over my shoulder and frowned at Killian, whose face was expressionless. Was he lying about Bram hurting Marina?

Killian stared right into my eyes and shook his head.

Was he reading my mind again?

He gave me a barely perceptible nod.

Okay then. It made sense that I couldn't trust the man behind this stupid scheme, but I wondered if I could trust Killian. When he didn't respond, I wondered if he hadn't heard me or was ignoring me. Either way, I'd worry about that later. I turned back to Bram expectantly.

"Let me tell you what I need from you, Tori," he said.

I stared at him, silent.

"I need something. Two somethings, actually. I have no magical power, as you three do. Killian's skills are less helpful at this phase, however, so that leaves the heavy lifting, so to speak, to you two. Oh, my manners," he blurted. "My dear, this fair-skinned man to my right is Poe. His abilities are very... precise... in nature."

I raised an eyebrow.

"I'm a necromancer," Poe said in a New England accent. I had a feeling that was the only explanation I would get for now. I didn't know much about what necromancers did, except what I had seen in fiction before my coma, but it probably wasn't pretty. It involved the dead, after all.

"Poe's abilities are limited in this realm, but he can help us with the greater task of awakening Ophelia. Killian told you of Ophelia, no?"

I nodded. "Realm of Lost Souls, sleeping goddess—demi-goddess—yadda yadda."

"Close enough," Bram said. "Ophelia has been dormant for centuries. She is, essentially, sleeping, and I wish to revive her."

"Why?" I asked, fidgeting with the hem of my shirt.

After a silence, Bram finally answered. "That's not important. Just know that when she awakens in our realm, she will be able to put us in touch with our loved ones who have passed on. She is, after all, the Keeper of Lost Souls."

"But I thought Poe is a necromancer." I gestured toward him as I spoke.

Poe nodded. "I am, but as Bram said, my powers are limited here."

"What does that mean?"

"It means I can talk to the dead, and even raise them to a new state, but it's more of a zombie-like state than lifelike. So, it's virtually no use to anyone."

I looked between Poe and Bram, trying to form an opinion about the motives behind this whole project. "I can see how that's not useful."

"If I were in the other realm, I could raise them to life. But the magic here isn't as strong." He peered at Bram, his voice soft. "I tried, but it wasn't possible to do any better."

"Are you... are you the strongest necromancer around? I mean, maybe–"

Poe stopped me with a shake of his head. "It's not just me, Tori. It's everyone with my powers. I've spent almost five years honing my magic in this one particular area, and I think—for this realm, at least — I'm as strong as they come."

I nodded. "Okay. So, you're trying to raise Ophelia because you believe she can bring someone back, right?"

Bram and Poe nodded. Killian moved from behind me and pulled out the bench at the breakfast table, putting one foot on it and leaning his arm on his thigh. He watched me while I talked with his associates.

"And why do you need me for this?" I crossed my arms over my chest.

"You are strong," Bram said quickly. "Your magic is palpable. Killian says you can also do things he hasn't seen before."

I flashed a glance at Killian, feeling betrayed that he told my secrets.

He offered a soft, unapologetic shrug.

Bram slid deeper into the nook's booth and patted the seat where he had just been. "Come, Tori. Have a seat. Let's talk."

Reluctantly, I sat down, keeping one leg outside the table so I could jump if I needed to. "So, what are these two somethings you need?"

Bram smiled. "Ah, yes, back to the basics. We are searching

for a necklace, silver and magical, and a spirit stone. Not just any spirit stone, mind you, but *lapis*. Specifically, it is the third *lapis manalis*, unknown to most of the human world but highly significant to our needs."

I raised an eyebrow, staying silent.

He correctly took that as a question. "The stone once belonged to Ophelia before she went to sleep. It has appeared at various places throughout time and is thought to be associated with ancient Roman culture. But our studies tell us it is actually older than that. The stone recently resurfaced a few years ago. We believe it's here, in Indianapolis, right now."

Frowning, I asked why.

"I have devoted my life to searching for something to connect me with Ophelia. Finally, the spirit stone came up on our radar. Mind you, it's been traveling over the earth for probably thousands of years, if not longer. Who knows how it ended up here?"

Killian sat on the bench his foot had been resting on and leaned his elbows on the table.

With everyone sitting, all eyes on me, I felt claustrophobic.

Under the table, I wrung my hands, looking around the kitchen for something to lessen my increasing anxiety. The brightness of the whites in the room felt inescapable. Not a speck of dust was visible on any surface. I couldn't find a single thing to focus on that wasn't glaringly perfect and shiny.

"So, again?" I asked, barely choking out the words. "Why do you need me? You have a necromancer, whose power it seems will be stronger on Halloween. Why don't you just wait a week and have him try to talk to your loved one?"

Bram chuckled. "It's not that simple, my dear. See, I have been waiting five years for this moment, and I can't wait any longer. If Poe can't get me what I need, I will have to wait another year. I simply..." he choked on the words. "can't... wait... that long." He paused and then continued. "I need assurance that this plan will work."

"Why me?" I glared at him, hoping I was giving him a defiant stare.

"I have been waiting for you to wake up, and luckily you left the hospital just when I need you. Your magic is powerful, as I expected. You will wield the magic — combine the stone and necklace then recite the incantation to awaken Ophelia. Poe will lend his strength, but his expertise was in creating the spell which we hope will revive her."

I shook my head. "I'm far from strong. I'm weak as hell physically and mentally and just started learning my magic."

Bram's eyebrows furrowed, as if he were contemplating this. He was silent for several seconds. Finally, he responded. "I don't care how long you have been practicing. Your magic is strong, even if you are not. Will magic like this take physical strength? Yes. You will probably be very weak afterwards if you are starting from a point of weakness. But you are sharing the load with Poe, and that will help. As long as you can remember the spell and withstand the magic long enough to do the job, you are sufficient."

My temples throbbed. "Look, I can't promise I can do what you're asking. Yesterday, I couldn't remember my thirteenth birthday party."

Bram heaved an exasperated sigh. "I don't care about your thirteenth birthday party. I care about your ability to remember spells primarily in Greek and Latin, and I am confident of those skills. And your ability to become invisible is invaluable. The last person in your position tried to perform an invisibility spell, and it went... awry. You created a spell out of thin air, from what I hear, and were able to sustain it. This will come in very handy when acquiring the spirit stone and the necklace."

I opened my mouth to protest, but Bram slammed his hands on the table. "Damnit, Tori, you are not getting out of this. I don't care what you come up with. You will help me, or you will suffer."

My mouth snapped closed as my body tingled so much it burned. My hands trembled under the table, and I clasped them together to stop whatever was happening to me. It felt like magic, but I wasn't doing it on purpose.

Beside me, Killian's eyes widened. He was silent, but stared at me. He knew something was wrong.

Poe and Bram were staring, too. Even though Bram couldn't feel my magic like the others, he could certainly feel the floor shaking beneath us. Cabinet doors opened and closed, exposing shiny white dishes that clanked together.

Something fell from a cabinet, its shatter echoing across the large room.

I slapped my hands onto the table, my fear rising. Marina had said magicians were unpredictable. If I couldn't stop this, would I hurt someone?

Would I be upset if I did? These people were, after all, attempting to blackmail me.

Still, I closed my eyes and breathed deeply, trying to stop the magic coursing through me. I couldn't hurt them on purpose, even though Bram had just threatened me.

When the magic increased, the room around us shaking uncontrollably, I sprung from the seat, knocking into the bench Killian sat on. He cursed, but I ignored him. My body felt like it was on fire. I waved my hands, but the feeling remained. I twisted and writhed against the pain, but the more I did, the harder the room shook.

Pain and magic churned inside me and when I couldn't take it anymore, I screamed. The magic released in an amazing rush of energy, leaving my body in a *whoosh*.

The room quaked violently for a few more seconds and then stopped.

I collapsed into a heap on the floor, panting. The throbbing in my head was gone, but I was left with vertigo.

The men continued to stare wordlessly. Around them, cupboards hung open, one having come off two of its three hinges and swaying precariously. Ceramic littered the floor, remnants of dishes that probably cost more than my old rent payment.

I sat up and blinked a few times. Had I done this?

"That was all you," Killian said aloud.

Bram cleared his throat. "Formidable magic. I told you."

No one attempted to help me up, so I stood and dusted my clothes off. "Unpredictable and uncontrollable. I told you," I retorted.

His lips stretched into a maniac's grin. "You'll do just fine."

"What part of that little show makes you think I'm the one you want?"

"The part where you exhibited more power accidentally than the other magicians have managed on purpose, on All Hallows Eve. This proves to me you're the one I need. And I will do anything to get what I want, Tori." His grin faded, and he glared. "Anything."

He made a small motion with his fingers, and two men appeared through another arched doorway. They wore dark tight-fitting shirts that showed off bulging muscles, jeans, and scowls. They stood silently, glaring as angrily as Bram. So, he had at least four goons working for him, besides Poe and Killian... if I could count Killian as working for him. Either way, I was outnumbered, and exhausted from the magic expenditure.

I grasped the edge of the bench where Killian had been before jumping up during the upheaval. My legs were wobbly, and

Bram's threat wasn't helping my nausea.

"You're powerful, Tori, so I don't want to hurt you. But I'm not beyond using those you love to persuade you to see things my way." Bram turned to Killian, who was watching me.

"Do what he says, Tori." Killian wouldn't meet my gaze. His tone was almost pleading.

I gulped. I still didn't have much proof Marina was in danger. Killian had showed me that picture yesterday, but was it enough to make me help this obviously unstable person fulfill a task that was likely to be horrible for the rest of us if successful?

Bram's fingers closed around mine on the back of the chair. "I said I didn't want to hurt you. That doesn't mean I won't. I just need you alive. Otherwise, your condition doesn't mean much to me."

"Where exactly am I supposed to find these items? And will I be doing it alone?" My tone was low and harsh.

"Is anyone else invisible?" Bram snapped back.

I kept my mouth shut. So not only was I being blackmailed into performing dangerous magic with unknown consequences, but I had to do the dirty work alone.

"As for where, we have a few ideas, but we will have to see if they pan out. If not, it's back to the drawing board. And we have less than a week to find these items and prepare the ritual. So, chop chop," he added, clapping to punctuate the words.

I nodded, unable to speak through the lump in my throat.

Poe slipped a piece of paper into my sweaty palm. "This is where you start. They tend to sell magical artifacts for much less than they're worth." He turned to Bram. "It's almost as if they don't study magic at all."

I glanced at the paper in my hand. It had an address on it; it was for some place downtown, but I had never been that familiar with the center of town. Too many one-way streets and difficult intersections. "Wait, so you want me to buy the items?"

Bram and Poe both laughed while Killian remained silent.

I wondered what he thought about all this. He didn't seem to jibe with Bram and Poe, and his current expression confirmed my suspicion that he was in the same position as I was. Would he help me escape this madness, or was he in too deep?

"Of course not, silly girl." Bram said through his laughter. "You're going to become invisible and steal them."

Of course, I was.

ELEVEN

MY DRIVER DROPPED ME off, and I ambled into the apartment, my left leg dragging a little behind me. As soon as Marina saw me, I cringed.

"Tori! Where have you been? Your leg... are you okay?" She dropped the dish she was rinsing into the strainer and rounded the kitchen island into the living room.

I put my hands in front of me to keep her at bay. "I'm fine, I swear; I just had a hard time at physical therapy." Wincing, I sat on the couch, my muscles sore. I had done a lot of walking today after meeting Bram and Poe, with the burden of what they'd asked me to do weighing on me the whole time. For blocks and blocks I walked, trying to think my way out of this conundrum, to no avail, until I had finally used a rideshare app to get home.

There was no way I could say no, or Marina would be in trouble. I had no choice, and I couldn't tell her. Grey would probably try to fight Bram to get me out of it, and I had a feeling that wouldn't end well for him. Bram didn't have any magic, but he had Killian, who seemed like an alright guy until I considered his muscles and unspoken experience in hurting people. I needed to save everyone from that, and whatever else Bram was hiding.

Marina sat next to me, wiping her wet hands on her pants. "Are you sure? I thought physical therapy was over hours ago?"

"I walked around the park for a while." It wasn't exactly a lie;

I did walk around the park; I just didn't go to physical therapy first.

"Why would you do that?" Marina leaned in to examine my legs.

I pushed her away. "Because I'm not a child."

Her mouth formed a terse line. She nodded curtly. But instead of lecturing me, she leaned in for a hug. "I'm sorry, Tor. You know I worry about you. I want you to be one hundred percent again."

I hugged her back. "I will be. It's just going to take time." And probably actually going to all my physical therapy appointments.

She pulled away. "Please don't push too hard."

I shook my head. "Of course not. Now, I smell something delicious. What's for dinner?"

Marina laughed and stood. "Spaghetti and meatballs."

"I knew it! Let me shower really fast and I'll be ready."

She shrugged. "I just put the sauce on so you're good. Grey will be home any time, too."

I grabbed sweatpants and a tank top and headed to the bathroom. The shower helped to unwind my tight muscles, and I stood under it for several minutes, continuing to go over the day's events in my mind, until my stomach growled enough to make me get out. I dried off, got dressed, and wrapped my long hair in a towel. Opening the bathroom door, I could both smell and hear that dinner had begun.

Grey and Marina laughed about something as their forks clanked on the dishes, and the enchanting aroma of spaghetti sauce and garlic bread wafted through the air.

My stomach growled in anticipation. I hurried to the table and sat down, my place already set. As I spooned the spaghetti onto my plate, Grey watched me silently. I caught him exchange a glance with Marina, but neither said anything.

Too hungry to care, I dove into my spaghetti. My head pounded, but I paid it no attention. Halfway through the plate, while I laughed at a story Marina was telling, my ears started to ring.

"Hey guys, I think I need to lie down," I said as the room swayed. I shuffled to the couch against the concerned questioning of Marina and Grey. As I lay there, staring at the ceiling, I noticed a familiar energy creeping up my spine. Magic.

Was this odd feeling related to magic? After all this time awake, was my headache a product of my magical energy? If so, what did it mean? Did I need to release energy for it to subside, or did it mean someone else with magic was approaching?

I had so many questions and absolutely no answers. But I knew someone who might.

"Hey guys," I said, holding the back of the couch as I sat up, "I need to go back out."

"What?" Grey asked.

"Now?" Marina cried.

"Yep. I forgot I'm supposed to meet Bennett," I lied again.

Marina frowned. "A second ago, you looked like you were going to vomit."

I stood up more quickly than I felt ready to, and the room spun for a second. I plastered a fake smile on my face. "I feel better. The ol' headache just flared up for a minute, that's all. I'll take something for it before I go. I'll be safe, I swear."

Neither appeared especially happy about me going out with the sun already setting and a leg that trailed a second behind my body.

"Need I remind you I'm a grown ass woman of thirty, and I don't need your permission to see a friend." I put my hands on my hips, hoping I seemed authoritative.

Marina also put her hands on her hips. "Need I remind you that you barely just got out of the hospital? After a four-and-a-half-year coma?"

Grey put an arm around Marina's shoulders. "Babe, she's right. It's only seven-thirty, and she's an adult. Why don't I give her a ride to wherever she's going while you take your shower? That way you're not walking in the dark with your legs tired from PT."

I felt a little guilty that they both thought I was worn out from physical therapy when I hadn't gone today. But I'd go tomorrow. Maybe. If I wasn't out stealing some spirit stone from wherever the hell it was hiding.

"Fine," Marina said begrudgingly. "While you're out, you can pick up that paperwork I need from the shop, too," she said to Grey.

While they discussed the paperwork, I texted Bennett. He replied immediately and gave me his address.

"Ready?" Grey asked, heading for the door.

I nodded and followed him.

The car ride was mostly silent. This was the first time Grey and I had been alone together since I left the hospital. Sure, sometimes Marina was in the cafeteria or bathroom or at the shop, but that didn't happen often. I imagined it would feel weird for Grey to visit me without her now that I wasn't his girlfriend anymore.

I wracked my mind for something to break the uncomfortable silence. I couldn't say what I was thinking—I miss you, I want you, I love you—but no other thoughts were forming.

"Mind if we drop by the shop first, since it's on the way?" Grey asked.

"No problem." I stared out the window. "Wow." I had been too preoccupied as we walked to the car to realize what the night-time sky looked like, and I hadn't been out at night until now. It was almost dark, and the stars shone brightly, like streetlamps high above us. The violet starlight didn't permeate the air, but it created an amazing effect shining beside the bright white stars.

"I guess I forgot how amazing it is," Grey said. "The first few weeks, months maybe, I watched the sky every night. Those purple stars, and how bright they all are... it is really deserving of the word *awesome*. But after a while, it became normal."

I couldn't imagine ever getting used to this.

We pulled into the shop's parking lot, and I stepped out of the SUV with Grey and followed him in.

My skin prickled as we approached Pages and Potions, and when Grey opened the door, a burst of energy slammed into me. I took a step back and held onto the doorframe. Luckily, Grey had walked in before me and didn't notice.

This didn't happen before when I walked in, so I wasn't sure what it was. Maybe they had gotten a new artifact that was more powerful than they realized. Or maybe my magic was more tuned in since I had been practicing with it. Whatever it was, my entire body tingled, and I could feel magic in the surrounding air.

While Grey went into the back room, I strolled around the store, waiting for the jolt to hit and tell me what was giving off such a physical aura. It was strongest at the counter, so I walked around it, checking out all the small items on the countertop. Grey had gone through the door to the stockroom, so I had to be quick in case he came back out.

I crouched to examine the shelves below the countertop. Some gnomes with silly outfits—I touched them and felt nothing. A bag of crystals of assorted colors; they gave off a faint magical energy, but it wasn't what I was searching for. But I was getting closer. My heart beat faster when I touched the side of a brown box. I recognized that box as the one Bennett and Marina were pouring over the other day. I had felt something then, too, but it hadn't been this strong.

When I reached for the box, the stones sat there, glimmering in their magic. Sweat beaded across my face, and my body tingled. Squatting on the floor, I pulled the box onto my knees and peered into it. I tried to balance the box on my legs and reach into it, but I was too uncoordinated, so I stood up and placed it on the counter. I reached in to touch a random stone, wondering which was special.

The door beside me opened.

I pulled my arm back and took a step away from the box.

"Find anything interesting?" Grey asked as he stepped out, holding an armful of paperwork.

I shook my head. "Just wandering around. I don't really understand all this," I said, gesturing to the products in the storefront.

"I don't really, either. I just lend my business acumen to your sister." He laughed like he had said something hilarious.

I kind of missed that laugh, but I pushed the thought aside.

"Let's get you to your friend's then," he said, making his way toward the door.

I followed him, turning around once to look at the box on the counter. It beckoned me, but I couldn't go to it right now. I'd have to come back another time, when Marina and Grey wouldn't question me.

FIFTEEN MINUTES LATER, WE pulled into a neighborhood of small houses. They looked cozy, and I was momentarily jealous of the inhabitants. Grey pulled into a driveway. "Here you go."

I pretended I knew exactly where I was. "Thanks, Grey. I'm sure I can get a ride home."

"Well, if not, call us. One of us will be here." He flashed me his pearly white smile before pulling out of the driveway.

I sighed. My heart still ached around him, but it was getting better. Time had gone on for him and he had gotten over me and fallen in love again, but time hadn't moved for me. The pain was still fresh, and I had to cover it up most of the day. And, of course, the guy I wanted to rebound with turned out to be gay and betrothed. I couldn't win in the love game right now.

The front door opened, and Bennett stuck his head out. "Tori! Come on in. Hey, I love your outfit."

I cringed. In my haste to get out of the apartment, I had forgotten to put on real clothes. I was wearing gray sweatpants with the word LOVE in pink down the side, a pink racerback tank top, and black flip-flops. Not only wasn't I dressed for company, but I wasn't dressed for the cool October weather. And my hair was unbrushed. I blushed.

"Hey, I'm playing," he said as I approached. He gave me a playful punch in the shoulder. "No worries. Look, I'm in sweats too." His hands directed my gaze toward his black sweats. He wore a white t-shirt and white socks. His hair was pulled into a bun, and he was unshaven. He was the complete opposite of Grey, yet they were both so attractive. Why was I surrounded by hot guys I couldn't have? I decided Casey had better be ugly.

I stepped inside and glanced around. We were in a small foyer with a stone floor that led into hardwood floors out of two exits. Through the first, I could see a kitchen and dining area, and we walked through the second, which housed a couch and recliner facing a large flat screen TV. On the wall was a brick fireplace and a wooden built-in bookcase. It was so homey I wanted to stay forever.

A hallway connected to the other side of the living room, and a man walked toward us. He was probably my height, just shy of six feet tall, with short brown wavy hair and dark brown eyes.

He wore black, red basketball shorts, a black t-shirt, and was barefoot. And he was hot.

Damnit.

"Tori, come meet Casey," Bennett said excitedly, moving me forward with his hand on my back. "Casey, Tori."

Casey held out his hand, and I answered with the firmest shake I could muster. I was tired and weak, so it probably wasn't the best, but Casey didn't complain.

"Have a seat," Bennett said, gesturing to the couch.

I sat on one end, and he sat on the other.

"Coffee? Tea?" Casey asked, raising a mug in a sort of salute.

I shook my head, not wanting to be more of a bother than I already was. "Thanks though."

"You sure? I can make anything you want. Water ... wine? One's just as easy as the other."

Now I was curious. "If I say yes, are you going to magic my drink?"

He grinned, a dimple appearing in his right cheek. "Why do you think I became a mage?"

Bennett swatted at him, fingers grazing Casey's bare legs. "Since you're so hell-bent on showing off, I'll take some tea."

"Sure thing, babe." Casey held the mug up to his lips as if he were going to drink from it, but instead whispered a few words I couldn't hear. Then he smiled again and handed the mug to Bennett, who sniffed it and nodded. "I don't know why you do that. You know it's going to be perfect, every time."

Bennett shrugged and took a timid sip. "It's hot."

I chuckled, but stopped when my head pounded more.

"So, what's up?" Casey asked, settling into the recliner across from us.

"Two things," I said. I held up one finger. "First, I think my headaches are connected to magic, but I don't know how."

Bennett set his mug on the coffee table. "Why do you think that?"

I leaned forward. "I've had a strong one all night. But it got me thinking, my headaches are better when we're practicing. At first, I thought it was the fresh air, but I'm wondering if it has to do with using my magic. Or maybe being around someone who practices. I don't know." I leaned back again.

Bennett nodded and turned to Casey, who shrugged. "What's the second thing?"

I took in a calming breath. "Well, on the way over we stopped at Pages and Potions."

Bennett nodded, gesturing for me to continue.

"As soon as I stepped out of the car, I felt it."

"Felt what?" Casey asked, leaning forward and clasping his fingers together in prayer hands.

"Magic. That's all I can say. It was pure energy. I had felt it before, but not this strong. I searched the shop while Grey was busy and found the source. Those stones," I said, turning to Bennett, "they were putting off a strong magical energy. I almost puked getting so close to them."

He frowned. "But you weren't that affected the first time you saw them."

I shrugged. "I could feel it the first time, but not like this. This time.... it was so strong. It was almost scary."

Bennett and Casey looked at each other. Neither spoke for several moments.

Finally, Bennett asked, "Could it really be?"

"A spirit stone," Casey said, his voice full of awe.

"You think?" I asked. I didn't know what a spirit stone did, but I knew I was searching for one that was supposed to be in this area. I even had an address of a place to look, but I hadn't even paid much attention to it yet. What were the odds it was for Pages and Potions?

But I couldn't tell Bennett about Bram and Ophelia. It was one more secret I'd have to keep for now. For his safety.

Bennett cocked his head to the side. "Is it possible there was a new stone in the box that wasn't there before?"

I shrugged. "I didn't count them. It was dark too. It's totally possible."

"One of them could be a spirit stone."

"What exactly is a spirit stone?"

Bennett and Casey looked at each other again, as if playing a game to see who got to—or had to—answer my question.

Finally, Casey answered. "They're really rare, and each one is from a different being or realm, so they're not identical."

"It could hold the spirit of an Otherworlder, or be connected to one in some way," Bennett added. "They sometimes end up here even if we aren't connected to the realm they came from due to travel between realms, different people using them in spells, private auctions, what have you."

"Travel between realms?" I asked, my eyes wide.

"So we've heard," Casey said.

"Why would I feel them?"

Bennett shrugged. "Maybe your inborn magic makes you susceptible to potent magic."

"And spirit stones are very potent magic," Casey added.

Bennett nodded. "Or maybe you're connected somehow to it. Somewhere in your family someone used it, or you are connected to the original holder somehow... though I don't know how that would be."

I did. Ophelia. I wasn't connected to her, per se, but I was now searching for her spirit stone, which would make it possible the stone sensed a connection.

Wow. Here I was, thinking about a stone sensing something.

How my life had changed.

I rubbed my temples. "Okay. So, I may be connected to a powerful magic stone that made its way to my sister's shop. I might get magical headaches. And I still don't know why I went into a coma and woke up just as suddenly. I'm not really getting any answers here, guys; just more questions."

Bennett sighed. "Let's tackle these one at a time. Casey, can you grab the book?"

Casey nodded and left the room again.

"What book?"

Bennett took a sip of Casey's water and set it back down on an end table between the couch and recliner. "A magic book."

"Is it from the Other Realm? My sister says those are really hard to find."

He nodded. "The Circle scoops them up when they are discovered. That's how I ended up with this one. I'm only borrowing it, though. And it tends to have a lot of questions, and only a few answers." He smiled wryly at me. "Seriously, you may leave here more confused than you were when you came."

Awesome. Just what I needed.

"What do you think the book can help us with?"

Bennett rubbed his chin with his thumb and forefinger. "I'm wondering if there's anything about, well, anything, really. But I think we'll have the best luck finding information on spirit stones, though it may not be much. As for the coma, I–"

"I found it!" Casey interrupted, walking back into the living room. In his hands, he held a large book bound in brown leather. He laid it on the coffee table before us and sat back in the recliner.

I followed the guys' gazes and watched the book.

It didn't do anything.

"Uh, guys?"

Bennett nodded and reached his hand out, allowing Casey to put something in it. Bennett rubbed his hands together and closed his eyes.

I raised an eyebrow at Casey.

"We have to make the book show us what we're looking for. Otherwise, we'll be at it for days."

"You mean there's no index on that thing?"

Casey shook his head.

Bennett shushed us both. He held his hands above the book, palms down, and recited a chant in Latin. It sounded familiar, like I should know the words, but I couldn't place anything except the word for book. After a few recitations, it opened, and the pages flew. Bennett opened his eyes and mumbled something I didn't catch.

The pages continued to turn until we were looking at the back of the book.

I frowned. "What does that mean?"

"It means there's nothing in the book about headaches," Bennett said. "I'm going to try again with spirit stones."

We went through the ritual again and the book pages turned quickly in the opposite direction. It opened to a page with a black-and-white picture of several stones. There were only a few sentences on the page, and they were not in English or Latin.

Bennett glanced at me. "Greek?"

"It's a Brahmi script," I said, squinting at the squiggles that all seemed to jumble together. "Not quite Devanagari, but close. Maybe an early form of Classical Sanskrit?" I rummaged through my mind for more information. Vedic Sanskrit was an oral language, but maybe this was something between the two, or a language from around the same time that died long ago. Whatever it was, my head was pounding, and it was difficult to read. However, if I pushed hard enough, I could get an idea of the sentences, assuming I was close to the origin of the language.

"Um. I think it says that stones of the spirit are attached to their maker, with a piece of their... soul? Yeah. The stones contain a piece of the maker's soul." I stopped reading and peered up at Bennett. "They're not inherently good or evil; they just are. They take on the powers of their maker, and kind of act like a proxy for that god."

"So, they're only made by gods?"

I nodded. "Yeah. I'm not sure why they are made, though; it doesn't say." Silently, I wondered if Ophelia was enough of a god to make her own spirit stone, or if there was some kind of loophole that allowed half-humans to make the spirit stones, too.

Casey leaned forward in his chair. "If they are imbued with their maker's magic, it sounds like a god or goddess could place a spirit stone somewhere to watch over a community."

Bennett nodded. "For protection, maybe, or to keep their presence in the city, so the people continued their sacrifices and work."

I nodded too. There was another sentence on the page, but the words were blurring a little as my head hurt even more. "Um, it says that performing the spirit spell will bring the god's soul to the spell-caster. That's it."

This made perfect sense related to Bram using the stone to find Ophelia. But it didn't explain why the stones' power pulled me in like it did. And, of course, I couldn't tell the guys about Ophelia.

Casey whistled, which made me cringe. He flashed an apologetic look and said, "We never would have read that without you here. It looks like gibberish to me."

"Mages learn spells mostly in Latin," Bennett added. "I've heard some magicians who specialize their magic — necromancers, pyromancers, what have you — use Greek, but that's out of our league. Whatever you just read," he said, shaking his head, "is way beyond us."

I offered a small smile, rubbing my temples. "I think I understood it, but it seemed to be older than what I'm used to."

"Your head's really bothering you, huh? Do you want something—aspirin, maybe?" Casey asked, standing.

I shook my head. "It hasn't been helping. That's another reason I think it has to do with magic."

Bennett reached over and rubbed the back of my neck with one hand. "We'll look into it, see if we can figure anything out," he said.

I turned my head toward him as the pain grew louder. My ears felt full, and the room started to spin. Then I was slammed into darkness.

I AWOKE WITH MY face wet and cold. I felt my forehead with an arm that was heavier than it should have been. A cold rag laid across my skin. That would explain the slow dripping into my eyes.

"What happened?" I whined, trying to sit up. It was a slow movement, as my head pounded with every muscle twitch.

When he answered, Bennett's voice sounded like it was from far away. "Slow down, Tori. Don't overdo it." A warm hand stroked my upper arm.

I moved the washcloth and opened my eyes. Bennett was crouched beside me on my couch—well, Marina and Grey's couch. Casey stood behind him, a worried expression on his face.

"What's going on?" I asked. "When did I get home? Where are Marina and Grey?"

"One thing at a time," Bennett said, his voice calm. He put his hands on my back and helped me sit up. My head throbbed and I could barely keep my eyes open.

"You got home last night," Casey offered, starting the much-needed explanations.

I raised an eyebrow. "I don't remember."

"Do you remember anything?" Bennett asked.

"We were reading the book at your place, and my head hurt, and then I woke up with water in my eyes." I tossed the wash rag onto the coffee table nearby.

"Okay," Bennett said, sitting beside me. "Short version is—you got that headache and passed out at our place. You woke up and were groggy but asked to go home. We told your sister you had a headache–" He paused when I glared at him. "She thought you over-exerted yourself doing ... whatever it is she thinks you're doing."

I made a motion with my hands for him to continue.

Casey chimed in with, "Marina let us in this morning to check on you, since you were still sleeping beauty when she was leaving for work."

"Thanks for coming by." I pushed myself to sit up even straighter and blinked several times. There were literal spots in front of my eyes. What the fuck was going on?

"I have a theory," Bennett said.

I raised another eyebrow. It was easier than talking.

"Do some magic. I think you were right, and your headache will go away."

"Either that, or you'll have to stay away from mages," Casey added. His voice didn't betray whether he was joking.

I wasn't sure if I could conjure up the strength to do any magic right now. But I leaned forward and closed my eyes, imagining a ball of light in my hands, like the one Bennett had wielded the first time we met. I whispered the Latin words for ball and light, which was all the Latin I could remember through the pain.

After what seemed like several minutes, but probably wasn't, a small orb appeared between my opened hands. I kept my hands open, hoping the prolonged magic would ease the pain in my head.

It did.

It was a slow release, but it was working.

I smiled at Bennett, the only move I could muster. But as the moments passed, so did the throbbing.

Once my head became more normalized, I experimented with my hands, stretching the orb into a long blob, molding it into a heart, and finally expanding it until it was as large as I could make it. The more energy I put into it, the more it pulsed with light.

"Wow," I said finally. "I feel so much better. I can't believe that worked!"

Casey nodded, but continued to look worried. "Tori, I know plenty of people with innate magic. None of them have complained about headaches when they don't use it."

Bennett shook his head in response.

"Hmm," I mumbled. "Well, maybe they just don't mention it?"

Casey shook his head. "I don't think that's the case."

"What do you think it means?"

"Maybe it has to do with your coma?" Bennett suggested.

I stared at him, leaning forward in my seat a little more. "What do you mean? Also, Casey, sit down. You're freaking me out standing over us like that."

Casey moved to the armchair nearby and smiled at me.

Bennett laughed his rich laugh and then looked back at me. "Well, I was thinking–"

My phone rang. Well, Grey's phone rang. I recognized the number, and I didn't want to answer it. But I knew I had to, or else Killian would probably show up to drag me out of the house.

I held one finger up to Bennett and put the phone to my hear as I stood. "Hello? This had better be good."

Killian chuckled. His laugh wasn't as nice as Bennett's. It was less melodic and more rugged. "Oh, it is good. The necklace has been spotted at an underground auction, and it's going up for sale tonight. You need to be there; it will be much easier to get it once we're invisible."

I felt my eyes widen. "An..." I moved to the kitchen. In a lower voice, I asked, "An auction?"

"Yep. Poe wanted to go with you, but I thought you'd be a little more comfortable with me."

"Why would I be more comfortable with someone who can read my thoughts?" I peeked at the guys in my living room. They weren't watching me, so that was good. I turned my back to them.

"Because Poe is... well, Poe has a thing for women." He let his voice trail so I could imagine the implications.

"Oh."

"Yeah. So, be ready at eight, and wear something nice."

I gulped. "How nice?"

"Ever watch any spy shows where they have to go to a black-market auction, and everyone's dressed to the nines?" he asked.

"Yeah."

"It's based on real life."

"Shit," I muttered. "Goodwill doesn't exactly have a selection of ball gowns."

"I'm sure your sister has something."

"I'll figure it out. My house, eight o'clock," I repeated.

"See you then, sweetheart."

I growled just loud enough he could hear it and then hung up the phone. I returned to the living room after grabbing three bottles of water.

"Here you guys go. All that magic made me thirsty," I added.

Bennett looked me square in the eyes. "So, we're supposed to pretend we didn't hear that?"

My heart pounded. "Hear what?"

"You have a date tonight!"

"Oh, that," I exclaimed, waving a hand around. "It's nothing. Just some guy I met at the park one day." It wasn't a lie. Not totally.

Grey's phone rang again. This time it was Marina. "You were passed out when I got up for work. Are you feeling okay?" She is always worried about me. In her defense, if she were in a four-and-a-half-year coma, I'd worry about her too.

"Yeah, just tired. All the therapy's been taking a toll on me." I winced, feeling bad for lying again.

Bennett shook his head as if he couldn't believe I was lying to Marina, but he didn't comment.

"Well, hey, come have lunch with me," she said. "I can come pick you up so you don't have to taxi." She paused. "I feel like we aren't spending enough time together, Sis. I'm coming to get you for lunch."

"Don't worry about that. I bet my friends can bring me to you." I glanced at Bennett and Casey, who nodded.

"Cool," she said. "See you soon."

"We can top off some magic supplies while we're there," Bennett said when I hung up.

"Two birds with one stone," Casey added.

They waited while I dressed and brushed my teeth and hair, then we headed out—them to do some shopping, and me to spend an hour lying to my sister. What a fun way to spend the day.

At least my headache was gone.

THIRTEEN

THAT EVENING, AFTER LYING to everyone in my life about where I was going, I stood in the living room in Marina's only evening gown. It was black with a deep v-cut neckline and a slit in the hip up to the mid-thigh. It was sexy as hell on her, but I didn't think it did my skinny body any justice. I wondered if I'd ever get to wear any of my favorite clothes she had saved for me again.

"I can't believe you're going to a gala for a first date," Marina gushed. "But you look amazing."

I avoided her eyes, but caught Grey's gaze.

He tilted his head in a half-nod, then turned away.

At least I knew I wasn't the only one who still felt awkward.

"It's not our first date," I said. Oops.

Her eyes widened. "You have a secret boyfriend? That's where you keep running off to! It's Bennett, isn't it?" Her words rushed out too fast to answer.

When she stopped talking, I held my hands out in front of me, palms down. "Calm down, Marina. No, it's not Bennett. I thought maybe... well, but he has a... Casey."

"What's a Casey?" Grey asked.

"A boyfriend."

Grey nodded again, fully this time.

"So, who is it?" Marina asked loudly. "And where did you meet him? Physical therapy?"

As far as she knew, that was the only place I had been. Besides the park, that is. "The park," I answered honestly.

"Oh, that's sweet. Well, still. What kind of gala is this?"

I frowned. "Something for his work. I'm not really sure." Another half-truth.

"His name?" Grey asked, getting in on the game.

"Killian," I replied before I could stop myself. That one was true, after all.

Just then, there was a knock on the door. Damnit. I had told him to wait for me in the car. "I'm not sure how long we'll be gone, so don't wait up," I said, trying to be nonchalant as I walked to the door.

Marina winked. "Oh, we won't."

I opened the door to find Killian standing on the welcome mat with a long-stemmed white flower in his hand. He was exquisite in a black tuxedo with a black bow tie. His dark hair was combed neatly, rather than the tousled look he had been going with before. He looked absolutely ravishing. And just perfect for my excuse.

Marina nudged me. "Damn, girl."

Grey edged toward the door. He stuck his hand out for Killian to shake, in perfect fatherly fashion. "Killian."

Killian glanced at me, then back to Grey. He shook Grey's hand, his expression confused. "Random guy I don't know."

I giggled, mostly out of nervousness. "This is my sister," I said, feeling a rock in my gut. I wasn't sure if Killian had ever seen her or not, but he surely knew her name already.

He nodded, not giving anything away.

"So, you must be the ex who's marrying Tori's sister," Killian said, releasing the shake and sneaking a glance at Marina.

My eyes widened. I looked at Marina and Grey, ready to apologize.

Marina shook her head. "It's fine. Really."

Grey shifted his feet, a stance I recognized as anxious. "Yeah, it's fine."

An uneasy silence followed.

"Well, we're off," I said, stepping forward, hoping everyone would take the hint and let us leave without more awkwardness.

But Killian didn't move. Instead, his eyes moved from the tip of my open-toed shoes to the dress's thigh-high slit and lingered on the low point of the V-cut before finally meeting mine. "Wow, Tori. You look amazing. I can't believe that wasn't the first thing I said." He shook his head and handed me the flower. "And this is for you."

I turned to give it to Marina to put in water, but Killian stopped me.

"Bring it with you."

Curious. But I obliged. "You don't look so bad yourself, Mr. Costa."

He raised his eyebrows, showcasing his clear Caribbean green eyes. "You ready?" he asked finally, offering his arm.

I nodded but didn't take his elbow.

"You kids have fun now," Marina joked.

Grey stood back, his arms crossed, glowering.

A pang of guilt shot through me for a moment, until I remembered Grey wasn't mine anymore, and had no reason to be jealous or angry or whatever the hell that expression was about. "Don't wait up," I said again, winding my arm through Killian's and letting him lead me forward. I didn't turn around to see Grey's expression.

Killian pulled his car into the parking lot of an old warehouse on the edge of town. The sound of gravel crunching permeated the air despite the closed windows.

It was dark already, so I couldn't make out many features of the warehouse, but it was big. I wasn't sure what it used to be, either. I didn't frequent this side of town much if I could help it.

"Ready?" he asked. Before I could answer, he turned off the ignition and got out of the car. As I was fumbling for the door handle, he opened my door from the outside and held out his hand. "Allow me."

"You can cut the act now, Killian." I stepped out on my own but struggled to stand up from his low-riding car.

He raised an eyebrow and kept his hand out.

Finally, I took it and let him help me up.

"See? That wasn't so hard, was it?"

I shot him the dirtiest look I could muster and released his hand. "I can manage myself, but thanks for the help."

He rolled his eyes. "You're wearing high heels on gravel. Take my arm. Please."

After stumbling a few times, I finally obliged.

We walked in silence until curiosity got the best of me. "Why are we dressed like *this* to go *there*?" I asked, emphasizing my words with hand gestures.

Without breaking stride, Killian laughed. Finally, when we were almost to the door, he responded. "You can't exactly buy and sell rare magical items at the farmer's market." He glanced at me, and I motioned him to continue. "When people started discovering artifacts with powerful magic—not just jewelry and stones like we're looking for, but enchanted items, scarce spell ingredients, anything really, even weapons—they brought them to the big auction houses. But the public got scared. More than they already were, I mean. So, the Department was created, and one of its jobs was to round up these objects and keep them out of the general population."

I stopped, wanting to hear the rest before we were inside. "Meeting secretly makes sense, then. But it doesn't explain why I'm dressed like a movie star, in shoes that were not made for gravel." I kicked at a rock with my toe.

Killian grinned, his green eyes sparkling. Instead of answering, he shrugged and began walking again.

A small group of people, all dressed to like movie stars, clustered around a double door in front of us. Each woman carried a single white flower. I quickly figured out it was a signal to allow entry to the event. I watched them silently for a moment, marveling at the women's grace in heels and the idiocy of wearing formal attire to a warehouse.

Just when I was about to prod Killian further, we stepped past a black-clad doorman and into an enormous open space, and my jaw dropped. I wasn't sure what I had been expecting, but this wasn't it.

"There were no big auction houses in Indy," Killian said as I marveled at the view. "So, they made one."

I nodded, barely listening. Those magicians, or whatever they were, had wanted a lavish auction experience, inconspicuously. It was genius, really. To the rest of the population, this was an abandoned warehouse in a crummy part of town. But to those in the know, it was the Ritz of underground bidding. I wondered if other cities boasted this glamorous of auction spaces, or if this was the only one.

Killian tugged on my arm, and I let him move me toward a wall so I could gawk without being in the way. He released my arm and stood beside me with a chuckle. "I was awe-struck my first time, too. My search led me to a similar place in Kansas, where I had been looking for this thing for a long time. I don't know if this is what all magic auctions look like, but at least two of them do."

Something he said stood out to me, but I was still taking in the bright white paint, rows of glittery lights, and fancy chandeliers. His words were forgotten as I noticed the amount of expensive jewelry worn by other attendees. My stomach growled when I spotted the tables on the far side of the room, spread with finger foods and champagne glasses. I shook my head, trying to process the difference between the interior and exterior of this place. Maybe looks weren't the best judge of something, after all. I glanced sideways at Killian, wondering if that sentiment applied to him, too.

"Let's grab a table," he said, nudging me toward the center of the enormous space. Small circular tables with crisp white cloths littered the room, some with people sat at them while others remained unoccupied. Without offering his arm again, Killian led me to an empty table on the edge of the arrangement closest to the bathrooms. He pulled out a chair and motioned for me to sit.

Just before I moved to sit, a man with white hair came up to us with a smile. "Killian. So nice to see you." He patted Killian on the back with barely a quick glance at me.

"Johnny Boston. How's it going?"

The man's smile grew. He was handsome, but his grin was unnerving.

I glanced away, unsure how to respond to the creepiness in his eyes.

"Doing well, Mr. Costa, doing well. Just here on a little business." He emphasized the last word. "Here for anything specific tonight?" He finally noticed me, his gaze starting at my face and moving down my body before our eyes met again. The action felt stranger than it had when Killian did it earlier.

Killian saved me from the creepy glint in Johnny's eyes. He

put his arm around my waist and pulled me closer. "Why else would I be here?"

"Touché," Johnny responded.

Someone tapped on a microphone from the stage. "Three-minute warning everyone," a woman with a British accent said. "Please collect your auction placards and find your seats."

"Well, it's been nice. Until next time," Johnny said. He touched my arm before walking away.

"Ew," I said once he had left. "What's his deal?"

Killian leaned in and whispered, "We've worked together a few times. We're not friends."

It made sense, in Killian's line of work. I wasn't exactly sure what that was, but there had to be a reason Bram wanted him, other than his erratic mind-reading ability. What else was he hiding behind that handsome face and tailored tux? I cleared my throat and re-focused on our current situation. "Boston?"

"Maybe it's his real name, maybe not. Like I said, he's not my friend." He motioned toward the chair again. "Wait here. I'm going to collect a placard."

I obliged, happy to give my feet a break, even though we hadn't done much walking yet. "I thought we were stealing the item, not bidding on it."

He sighed. "You've never been covert, have you? We are undercover, Tori. That means we have to blend in with the surroundings. If everyone thinks we're here to bid, we should act like it."

I nodded. "What about Johnny?"

Killian scowled for a moment, then comprehension gleamed in his green eyes. "Ah, Johnny. He may be a scoundrel, but he's a noble scoundrel. As long as we aren't after the same item, we won't have any problems with him."

"Okay," I said, only slightly understanding the rules of the underworld. "So, I'll just wait here like a good piece of arm candy, and you go do manly things."

"Exactly." For show, he kissed me on the cheek before he stepped away.

While I waited, I took in my surroundings, trying to memorize the layout of the floor for later. I wasn't sure where the necklace was, but my guess was it was behind the stage which sat in the center of the floor. Two security men, dressed all in black, stood at the back corners of the stage, bulky arms crossed over their chests. I presumed they were guarding doorways to the storage area.

Hearing Killian's distinct laugh, I turned to see him slapping another man on the back. "Old buddy, it's good to see you. But I must get back to the lady."

He headed toward me, and for a second, I forgot we were here to be thieves. He was so handsome, his expression cocky, that I could almost imagine we were here as a couple.

Our eyes met as he approached, and I let the thought run wild for a few more seconds. When he was beside me, Killian leaned down, his lips to my ear. "I know where the necklace is."

My breath caught in my throat as the scent of his cologne wafted toward me. It was fruity, woodsy, and sexy as hell. I had picked up on it already, but we hadn't been this close before. All I could do was nod at his statement.

Killian pulled back enough I could see his face, but whispered. "Some of the auction items are on the stage already, but it's not. It's behind the stage." He gestured toward one of the security men I had just observed.

"How do we get back there and get it out of the case?"

He flashed me a fabulous smile. "You leave the last part to me. But you, my dear, need to get us back there."

I stared at him, momentarily forgetting the plan. Realization dawned as I stood, and I grasped the back of the chair with white-knuckled hands. "No, no no. I can't."

He continued to smile. "Sure, you can. I saw what you did on the fly. I could hear your thoughts, remember? You can make both of us invisible if you try hard enough, I bet."

"Why didn't we practice this before?"

He put an arm around me like we were cuddling and leaned in close to my ear again. "Because I just found out about this auction twelve hours ago and was a bit preoccupied securing us a spot in this highly selective, highly illegal activity."

His phrasing played again in my mind. Magic was out in the open, so why was purchasing magical items illegal? Further, why didn't Bram just use his enormous wealth to buy them in the first place? Confusion and anger clouded my mind. Why was I even necessary for this scheme, other than to perform the spell on Halloween?

"Whoa, slow down there," he said with a chuckle. "Those are all valid questions, but this isn't the time or place to answer them. We need to focus on what we're here for."

Nodding, I tried to clear my mind. Images of white sand and endless ocean replaced the swirling questions. I took a few deep breaths, eyes closed. Despite hearing waves lick the shore in my mind, anxiety threatened to take over. "I can't do this."

Killian pulled my body toward his until the fabric of his shirt met my bare collarbone. "Yes, you can."

My breath caught in my throat, and I gulped. Something in his voice almost made me believe him. "I'll try. But not here."

Killian backed up and held out his arm so I could take it again.

This time, I laced my arm through his without a fight. My skin was clammy, and my heart pounded in my ears. My headache was gone, thankfully, but I had spent so much energy earlier in getting rid of it I didn't know if I had much left to do an invisibility spell for me, much less for both of us.

We made our way through the crowd, pushing against the stream of people moving toward their seats.

The restrooms were tucked into the corner opposite where we needed to go. I would have to keep us both invisible as we made our way behind the stage and past the intimidating security guards. No pressure, Tori.

Killian ushered me into the women's bathroom. He looked around, giggling like he wanted someone to see us, and then followed me in.

"What was that about? I thought we were covert?" I asked when the door shut behind us.

He assessed the two stalls in the room, whose doors were open. We were alone. "If anyone wants to account for us, maybe someone will remember we snuck off to the women's bathroom after being close and cuddly at the table."

My stomach dropped. Was every instance of him being touchy and pulling me close just part of his plan to assure no one questioned our whereabouts? I discovered I was more disappointed than I liked at the thought. It wasn't a bad plan, though I would have preferred to stay under the radar entirely. But it was what we had, so I nodded.

"Okay. What do you need to do this?" Killian reached into the pocket on the inside of his jacket and produced two small baggies of crushed herbs. "Basil and bay leaves like before?"

I shrugged. "Might as well give it a try. I'm really worried about covering both of us, though."

He rested his free hand on my arm. "I'm not." Before I could respond, he handed me a pinch of each herb, his fingertips lingering in my palm.

I gulped as I closed my hand around herbs. "What's the actual plan?"

"Just get me back there, and I'll take care of it," he reminded me.

"Okay. Grab my arm; you probably shouldn't let go." I took a deep breath, trying to ignore the sensation of his skin against mine. Was it the magic we shared, or something else, that made it hard to focus? I let my breath out, reminding myself it might be neither of those. "Here goes nothing."

Then I closed my eyes and chanted the Latin words, which I could remember more easily now without the headache, for *invisible* and *both*. I squeezed the herbs in my hands.

"Hey," Killian whispered after a moment. "You did it."

I opened my eyes. "Whoa!"

"Shh," he said. It sounded like his finger was in front of his lips, but I couldn't see him to tell.

"I thought we were supposed to be making out in here. That's our cover, right?"

"Aw, you think we're just making out? How cute," he responded.

I was glad I was invisible, so he wouldn't see the blush I was sure had crept up my neck and cheeks. At the thought, my whole body heated. In an instant, my hands came back into focus. Shit.

Killian's husky laugh echoed off the walls. "Magic doesn't work when you're hot and bothered, huh?"

I gritted my teeth. "Shut up so we can do this." I concentrated, harder this time, until my hands disappeared again.

"Okay," he said, his tone still light. "I don't know how long you can hold this, so we need to go."

"Agreed."

We exited the bathroom, him holding onto my arm. The crowd had dissipated as most people took their seats, so crossing the floor was easy. As we neared the stage, workers clambered about, some holding items for bid. We walked carefully, so as not to bump into anyone.

The area behind the stage wasn't a room, but rather a large space cordoned off by temporary partitions. Three steps led up to an open doorway which was guarded by the eagle-eyed security man, hands now at his hips.

I stopped in front of him, holding my breath. My heart rate quickened as I thought of what might happen should we be seen entering a place we didn't belong.

Killian's thumb rubbed my skin, the rest of his hand still in place. He could probably hear my thoughts and was trying to comfort me. It worked, at least a little, and I stepped past the guard into the item storage zone.

As we stood just past the entryway, I took in my new surroundings. Tables outlined the area, with the space immediately to our right reserved for larger items on carts. Across the room was another doorway sandwiched between two short tables. The tables were filled with jewelry, paintings, knick-knacks, and other odds and ends. How would I know which necklace Bram wanted? And would my magic hold long enough to sort through it all?

I breathed deeply and let Killian pull me toward the right-most table. A golden chalice sat by itself nearest us. It looked old and worn, but was probably precious, if it was showing up here. Or maybe it wasn't, and some fool was going to spend a lot of money on a fake. The thought made me almost laugh aloud, but I caught myself before I gave us away.

Using slow, small steps, we walked along the edge of the table, perusing each item. I tugged him to a stop near the middle of the table, where a necklace with a thin yellow gold chain and a large sapphire pendant rested on a white cloth.

Killian whispered, "no." He led me around a man who inspected a jewelry box with a magnifying glass.

As we walked, so slowly it barely seemed we were moving, I glanced at our surroundings. At the end of each table stood large men, much like the ones in Bram's house. This was going to be more difficult than I had originally imagined—which had been bad enough. I felt my energy wane and stumbled a little. As Killian steadied me, I focused on the guard in the farthest corner.

He wasn't *like* one of the men from Bram's. He *was* one of the men from Bram's house.

Killian and I stood still for a moment, and I caught my breath, which was shallow and quick. I didn't know how much time we were going to have until I couldn't hold the spell anymore.

I had to keep the magic going long enough to get out of here. There were half a dozen other people in this room, so just appearing in the middle would not be good. Especially since all the security people I'd seen were visibly armed. They expected people to use magic to try to steal things, so I was surprised there were no wards against the magic I was doing. Then again, the others had made it seem like no one had successfully remained invisible, so maybe this magic was undetectable to their magical security system. I hoped.

I also hoped I could keep the magic up long enough to not find out just how good their security was.

After viewing a few more items, we came to a table beside the other door. It had a few small art pieces and a lot of jewelry. Killian strolled along the side of the table, stopping when someone came near. Finally, he pulled on my arm to get my attention.

Before us lay a large necklace of white gold or platinum, I couldn't tell which. My specialty was ancient languages, not precious metals. The chain was thick and shiny, reflecting the light from above us. It was beautiful and fit for a god. I wondered if it, too, came from Ophelia. I'd have to ask Killian about it later.

He edged us closer to the necklace, pulling me toward it until my legs were crammed up against the table's edge.

I was worried we would make a sound knocking into it, but somehow we didn't. I stared at the necklace, its power raising goosebumps on my skin. My eyes closed, I reveled in the magic, momentarily forgetting my mission. As I reached for the necklace, strong hands pulled me backward.

Killian's voice appeared inside my head in a whisper. *Someone senses us.*

My eyes widened, and I was so surprised I almost dropped my arm that he was holding onto. Since when could he talk to me in my mind?

It's new to me, too. I'm just as surprised as you are. But don't think about that now, his voice said. *We need to do this and get out of here.*

My chest tightened. I was already weakened from using so much magic. I was pretty sure the head of this black-market auction didn't take security—or thievery—lightly, which meant we could be in a lot of trouble if I couldn't hold myself together.

Outside, the auctioneer was talking faster than I could understand. The people inside the room buzzed around, barking orders to each other about which items were up next and conferring with security on little radios. I wasn't sure which one of them had sensed us, so I froze, along with Killian. Worried my anxious breathing would get us caught, I held my breath. But it was difficult; I was draining fast.

Get ready, his voice said in my head.

This method of communicating was definitely safer than whispering aloud, but it was still an odd sensation, and I jumped at his words. I wasn't sure what I was getting ready for, so I braced myself and took another breath. It wasn't deep, though, because suddenly, the table in front of us overturned. Priceless items crashed to the ground, the sound echoing in the small room.

Killian's voice was in my head again. *Run. But don't lose me.* He led me to the nearby door.

I stumbled, expecting stairs again but getting a ramp, and nearly fell to the floor. Running in heels was bad enough, and running down a ramp while clasping herbs in both hands, with Killian holding onto my arm, was almost impossible. But I managed to do it.

We ran through the crowd that had gathered around the door after hearing the commotion, pulling each other to keep from running into someone.

The auctioneer was looking toward the ruckus, but continued his counting. He was in the hundred-thousands, but I didn't know what people were bidding on. I didn't care. I was more concerned with making it out of this warehouse alive.

Killian took the lead, pulling me behind him toward the main doors.

I let him lead me and began running through the Latin words in my head again, hoping that would help keep the spell powered up. We were too close for my magic to fail.

A few more feet. Almost there.

I stumbled, grasping at the air to keep from falling.

My hand touched someone's arm, and it wasn't Killian's.

An angry man with a bald head and bigger biceps than I'd ever seen stood at the doorway, blocking our exit. And staring at the space where my invisible hand touched his skin.

FOURTEEN

I DODGED TO THE left, but the man clasped his other hand onto mine, holding me in place. He glared toward me, but not quite at me. "You think you were going to get away with that?"

Gulping, I didn't know how to answer. Or if I should. I couldn't run because his hand had grasped mine and held me still. I still had herbs in my free hand, but the painful tingle all over my skin indicated my magic wasn't going to hold.

Killian had the necklace. He could try to get away, but as soon as he left me, he would be visible again and would inevitably be caught by one of the security guards who closed in on us.

I apologized to him in my mind, hoping he could hear. Then I opened my hand and let the bay leaves and basil fall to the floor. My skin appeared instantly.

So did Killian's, and when he turned to me, his eyes were wide. "What did you do?"

Before I could answer, large hands grabbed my shoulders. "Come with me," a deep voice said.

Men pushed me and Killian toward a corner of the building, where we would have no chance of escape.

We walked silently, and I was acutely aware of the patrons' eyes on us.

The auctioneer had stopped speaking. Security guards from almost all points of the building were around us or moving toward us. It seemed the only ones who had stayed in their positions were the two guarding the storage area behind the stage.

I stared ahead again, focusing my attention on Killian. If he was speaking to me mentally, I didn't hear it. Then again, I wasn't giving him an opening to between the repeated apologies in my mind.

The guard shoved me into the corner and spun me around. With a hardened gaze, he began patting down my dress, rough hands quick but thorough.

When he was confident I didn't have the necklace, the guard turned to Killian. His search was fast and easy, and the necklace was in Killian's breast pocket. "You didn't put much thought into this, did you?" the guard asked.

Killian didn't speak, and something told me to follow suit.

The guard opened his mouth to speak, but another gruff voice cut him off. "I'll take it from here. You can get back to the door."

Was this the head of security? I gulped, not wanting to think about my next few minutes. Hoping they weren't my last.

The guard left and another man, also wearing all black, took his place. His familiar face gave me no comfort. Was he going to report back to Bram that we had failed?

Killian's fingers found mine, and they laced tightly together. He didn't speak, which was probably wise.

The guard, who stood several inches taller than both of us, glared down at us with disapproval. After what seemed like several minutes of silence, he spoke again. His voice was low, but still gravelly. "I thought you guys had done it. But no. This magician—" he spat the word, "couldn't keep her shit together."

"What's going to happen to us?" I asked in a shaky voice.

"I imagine you'll be tasked with finding the necklace again," he said, as if the answer were obvious.

I supposed it should have been, since Bram was hell-bent on

using this particular piece in his spell. But part of me had hoped we could put him off for another year. Maybe he'd forget the whole thing.

A quick chuckle burst out of Killian. "Don't think that's going to happen."

The guard glanced between us and shook his head. "It's still freaky when you do that." He straightened his back and motioned with his hand. "Come with me."

Our linked hands trembling, Killian and I walked beside the guard to a side door. On the way, I noticed the auctioneer had resumed speaking and the other guards were back in place around the building. It was as if nothing had happened. The whole situation was taken so nonchalantly by everyone else that I wondered how often something like this occurred. I also wondered what awaited us on the other side of the door.

Holding my breath, I followed Killian outside, the guard behind me. I expected someone with a gun, or a powerful magician—I had heard them called *wizards* by some—to be waiting for us. Instead, I was greeted by crisp autumn air and crunchy gravel beneath my feet.

I spun around, sure this was a trick.

The guard didn't smile, but his eyes twinkled for a brief second. Or maybe it was a trick of the light. The stars were spectacularly bright. Whatever it was, it was gone in an instant. "You can't come back here now. You're going to have to find a different way to get the necklace." He began to shut the door between us.

"Wait," I said, grabbing the door to stop it.

He looked offended and surprised, but he waited.

"Why do we need this necklace? Can't we find a different one?" I glanced between the guard and Killian.

The guard shrugged. "I just go where the boss says. Tonight, he said, *go to the auction and make sure they don't fuck up.* I'd better not get in hot water for this," he added with a glare.

"Sorry," I muttered.

The guard shut the door and left Killian and me standing beside the old warehouse, the white and violet stars casting more light than I was used to at night.

Killian dropped my hand and smoothed his jacket with both hands. "The necklace is powerful. Maybe the strongest of its kind. There's no way Bram's going to let us off the hook."

I stared at my feet. We had been almost home free, and I had failed. My stumble had put Marina in danger, as well as endangered whatever Bram had over Killian. Emotions and exhaustion overtook me, and I slumped against the wall, closing my eyes.

"Breathe," Killian said quietly. He rubbed his hands up and down the goosebumps on my arms. "It'll be okay. We'll figure it out and we'll get the necklace." His green eyes grew cloudy, haunted.

"I'm sorry," I said, my breath ragged. I was too drained to form many more words, and standing was becoming difficult as well.

"Let's talk about that later." He slipped my arm over his shoulder and slowly led me to the car. A wall of disappointment stood between us, but he opened my car door and helped me slip inside without saying anything else.

Killian drove us away from the warehouse, and I stared out the window. Little light trails appeared on the stars overhead as he whizzed down the road too quickly for my comfort. I couldn't bring myself to say anything, so I just watched them wordlessly. Violet mixed with white until I had to close my eyes to still my churning stomach. I leaned my head against the cool glass and waited to arrive at my makeshift home.

━━━━━━━━━━━━━━✦

FIFTEEN

LIGHT FILTERED THROUGH SHEER curtains, shining onto my face the next morning. I lay on the couch, my body weak and exhausted from last night's activities, mentally cursing the early morning sun.

A sound from the kitchen startled me, and I sat up quickly to peer over the back of the couch.

Grey making breakfast. He held the skillet in one hand and flipped a pancake in the air, a trick that always made me envious because I could barely turn one with a spatula.

I smiled a little at that thought, then laid back down with a sour taste in my mouth. Grey wasn't making pancakes for me. He was making them for Marina.

I felt a small pang in my chest. It wasn't that I wanted Grey back—was it even wanting him back if we never really broke up in the first place? It was unrealistic to think we could ever be together again, but it was difficult to be this close to him daily.

In that moment, I decided I would move out. I wasn't sure how or where I would go, but I couldn't stay in his apartment anymore. It would surely be better for Grey and my sister if I weren't crashing on their couch forever, too.

I smiled wider at the idea of independence, then closed my eyes, prepared to go back to sleep for a couple of hours. But my phone rang.

I'd have to get my own phone, too. Hmm. The expenses were

racking up already. I silenced the call and put my arm over my eyes, ready to go back to sleep.

"Hey baby," Marina said from across the room. She sounded sleepy and sultry, and I cringed.

I contemplated whether to pop up and say I was awake, but I decided against it. I figured if I stayed still and quiet, I might actually go back to sleep.

No such luck.

My phone went off by my head again, and I glared at it to see who was calling. Killian. He could wait. When it stopped ringing, Marina's singsong voice filled the room. "Tori. You got in late last night! I'm guessing things went well with..."

"Killian," Grey offered, his mouth full.

I sat up and twisted toward the kitchen. Grey popped a blueberry from the package to his mouth, the purplish berries giving his lips a dark tint.

The sight caused me to flash back. The memory was so vivid I dropped the phone as it engulfed me.

Blueberries spilled all over the countertop. I grabbed at them as they rolled, but most slipped through my fingers. Behind me, someone let out a deep, throaty laugh. Grey.

I turned to look at him. His curls were slicked back, except for one little one on his forehead. His tie was unfastened, hanging loosely from his shoulders, and his white shirt was unbuttoned half-way down to show the red and yellow S on his chest. His regular plastic-framed glasses completed his Clark Kent look.

A blueberry flew off the counter and hit my leg. I peered down to make sure my knee-high red boots didn't have fruit splatters on them. The blue skirt was one thing, but Wonder Woman didn't need to look like she had been kick-boxing a Smurf.

"Diana Prince," Grey said, his voice low. "You look amazing."

I wiggled my eyebrows at him. "And you, Mr. Kent, are super

handsome." I tugged at the ends of his tie with each hand and used it to pull myself closer to him until his face was within touching distance.

He kissed the tip of my nose, then side-stepped me to reach the counter. "You're going to be late for class. Leave the fruit and I'll pick them up later." He reached forward and plucked a blueberry off a pile. "Mm. Maybe after the party tonight, we'll get these back out with some whipped cream..."

"I like how you think," I interrupted. "Although the party doesn't even start until eleven, so it's going to be pretty late before we get done."

Marina's annual Halloween party typically went until the next morning, which would not leave much time for blueberries and whipped cream before I had to teach my eight-a.m. class on Sanskrit and ancient Indian culture.

"Halloween only comes once a year, babe. You know it's my favorite. Let me celebrate." He wiggled his eyebrows back at me.

"Yeah, yeah, we'll see." I shook my hips, making my short skirt flare, exposing my garter belts. "Just don't forget to clean up the blueberries at some point."

He popped another into his mouth. "Maybe I'll just leave them here and put them in our pancakes in the morning," he said through a mouthful of fruit.

Blueberries were his favorite, after all.

"Tori, are you okay?" Grey asked, his mouth full of blueberries.

I blinked and then nodded slowly. I turned toward the kitchen to see Grey and Marina both wearing worried expressions.

"You spaced out for a minute there," Marina added. "Did something happen?"

Before she could go into worried-sister overdrive, I held my hands up and said, in what I hoped was a reassuring tone, "I'm fine. I just, uh, had a flashback."

"What was it?" she asked.

I shook my head as I sat up on the couch and bent to pick up the phone from the floor. "I think I need my own phone," I said, changing the subject. "I feel bad keeping Grey's for so long."

"Tori, it's been a week," he said, his voice less mumbled than before. "Don't worry about it at all."

I stood up and pulled at the bottom of my t-shirt. "I know, but I feel like I'm taking advantage of you guys already. The place, the phone...."

"Nonsense," Marina exclaimed. "You're my sister. We love you. You're sticking around and we're helping you out. Get over it."

I frowned. Over Marina's shoulder, I could see Grey plopping blueberries into his forming pancakes. Fucking blueberries.

"I don't know, Marina."

"It's been a week, Tori. One week." Marina stepped into the living room. Grey's t-shirt hung to her mid-thighs and swayed as she walked. She made it look better than I ever did. "Tori, you were missing for fifty-eight months and two weeks. And a day—if you're counting. That's almost five years I went without my sister. Do you really think I'm going to be ready to kick you out after one freakin' week?"

I hung my head. It was selfish of me to think of leaving when she put it that way. "I just don't want to be a burden."

"You're not–" she began.

"No way–" Grey started at the same time.

I held my hands out to them, my eyes wide. "Okay. Fine."

"Who was on the phone?" Marina asked. "Your phone rang and now you're talking about leaving." She tilted her head, and something dawned in her eyes. "It was Killian, wasn't it?"

She was right, but not about him making me want to move.

"Ooh," she said. "Killian makes you want to move out, huh? Are you in love?"

I grimaced. "With Killian? No. Hardly." It took a second for me to realize I had told them I had actually been on a few dates with him, so I added, "It's too soon to be in love. I've only been home a week, as you so recently pointed out."

She wagged her finger like a parent scolding her child. "Maybe it's subconscious, but you brought all this up after he called. Don't deny it."

I rolled my eyes. "Fine. I don't deny it. Now, may I please go to the bathroom?"

In the bathroom, I sat down, figuring I might as well take advantage of being in here, and scrolled through the messages on my phone. Killian had been texting me the whole time I had that ridiculous discussion with Marina.

Call me.

Need to meet.

Bram wants to see you.

Call me.

I rolled my eyes and deleted the texts one at a time. This guy was high-maintenance for sure.

I texted him back, telling him I'd be with him in a few minutes. Apparently, that wasn't good enough.

It's important.

Now.

Still, I waited until I washed my hands before I called him. From the bathroom, I could hear Marina giggle at something Grey had said, and I knew they were too busy to listen in on my call.

"Finally," Killian answered after the first ring.

"What is so damn important you can't let me pee in peace?"

Killian sighed. "Sorry, Tori. Bram is freaking out. He wants to see you."

I groaned. We knew this was coming, but I had hoped to get a little more sleep first. "He's going to have to wait."

"I don't think he's going to like that," he said. Caution laced his voice, and I wondered briefly if I should take him at his word.

My stomach growled. Bram was seriously going to have to wait until I ate breakfast. And maybe took a shower. I glanced down at my tank top and pajama pants. I'd have to change, too. "I need a couple of hours."

"You have thirty minutes." The line clicked.

I glared at the phone and then set it back down. After splashing water on my face, I left the bathroom to find two sets of eyes staring at me.

"Everything okay?" Marina asked. "Before you worry, we couldn't hear what you were saying. But your tone sounded upset."

"Everything's fine. I just need to run some errands." I hated lying to my sister, even if it was for her own good. But was it, really? Wouldn't knowing about Bram's plan allow her to get to safety... whatever that looked like? I flashed her a tired smile and bent to rummage through a box for clothes. I needed to get ready.

As I stood beneath the warm shower water a few minutes later, my mind drifted to another time, one I didn't even realize I had remembered.

I was walking along the sidewalk, my red Wonder Woman boots clicking with each step. It was a particularly warm October, so I was able to wear my corset and tiny skirt with garter belts outside at almost eleven. It was so warm, in fact, I wondered if Grey would have stripped out of his second shirt by now. He was walking from his apartment while I walked across campus from my menial office to Marina's apartment, just off university grounds.

The sky around me was dark and starless. Even though trick-or-treating hours ended at nine, there were costumed teenagers about still, mostly walking around with friends. Down the street, a masked trio threw toilet paper rolls over tree branches, giggling. I watched them as I walked, a small smile on my face. Marina was four years younger than me, but in our teenage years we had toilet-papered a house or two on Halloween—usually belonging to whoever Mom was dating, when we could keep up with the rotation.

I turned to my left to watch the moon as I walked. It was full and white and cast an eerie glow on the trees. Something in the air changed, and I frowned. It felt heavy, thick. I looked around, but no one was watching me or following me. I considered calling someone to talk to me, but I was only blocks from Marina's apartment she shared with two other college seniors. Nothing was going to happen in the next five minutes before I got there.

Still, I picked up the pace a little.

And then—

A knock on the bathroom door stirred me from the flashback. "Better hurry, Tori," Marina shouted. "It's been twenty minutes, and you said you only had thirty."

That memory had captured me more than I'd realized. I thanked Marina and turned the water off. After a quick once-over with a towel, I dressed, the clothes clinging to my damp body. I was attempting to run a brush through my wet-but-unwashed hair when Marina popped her head into the bathroom.

"Finish up, Sis. He's here."

I groaned. I wasn't even really mad at him, except for his impatience with the texts earlier. But I was not looking forward to another meeting with Bram. Especially since we didn't have the necklace.

"I heard that." Killian's husky voice wafted through the open doorway. "I'm glad you're so happy to see me." He didn't sound angry, so that was good.

I set my hairbrush down and walked into the living room, very aware of Marina and Grey's eyes on us. Despite not wanting to see Bram, I couldn't act wary of leaving with Killian. He was supposed to be my boyfriend, after all. "Just tired," I said as I neared.

He nodded in understanding. "Ready?"

"As I'll ever be," I muttered. For my sister's sake, I added, "Errands aren't going to run themselves."

Killian's face didn't betray any confusion. He was probably used to lying to those he loved. Who knew how long he'd been involved in Bram's scheme? "Wouldn't that be nice," he said instead, holding out his hand for me to grasp. He was taking this boyfriend charade seriously.

I took his hand, lacing my fingers through his. "See you guys!" I called as I grabbed my purse and followed Killian out the door.

SIXTEEN

I STARED OUT THE window of Killian's sports car as we whooshed past other cars on the road. Soon, we pulled up to the home where I had first met Bram, and Killian parked in the driveway. "How bad is this going to be?" I asked him.

He sighed. "Pretty bad."

"Will he..." I couldn't even finish the sentence as the image Killian had showed me on his phone filled my mind.

"He'll probably just yell and make threats. He only got violent with the others when they refused to help." Killian opened his door and stepped out.

"So, I just can't stop until we see this through. Oh, that's good news." I wasn't sure what the result of this plan would be, but it felt like something I should try to sabotage. How could I do that without ending up like that man in the picture?

Killian sighed, harder this time. "You can't, Tori. Don't you get it?"

Man, that was still freaky. After taking a deep breath, I followed him up the walk and through the front door without knocking.

Before it shut behind us, Bram's voice boomed through the foyer. "What the hell happened last night?"

I winced and instinctively reached for Killian.

He jerked his arm away before I could touch it and turned toward the voice. "Bram, we had the necklace."

155

"It doesn't matter that you *had* it if you don't have it now." Bram's footsteps echoed through the entryway as he thundered toward us. He stopped before us with clenched fists. "The incompetence displayed last night is unacceptable." He turned his attention toward me.

My pulse thrummed in my ears. I didn't even try to speak, furtively praying to whatever gods were out there that Killian was right, and my lashing today would only be verbal.

"Tori," Bram repeated through gritted teeth, "what the hell happened?"

"I tripped," I said in a small voice.

"You *tripped*? That's what might cost me the chance to—never mind." He turned to Killian. "You will remedy this. Remember what's at stake if you don't."

Killian's eyes clouded over, but he remained otherwise emotionless. "How could I forget?"

I wondered what Killian had been blackmailed with—harm to a loved one like me, or something else entirely? It dawned on me that, though he had been nice so far, I didn't know anything about him. He could be hiding a horrible secret in exchange for helping Bram. Was I partnered with a criminal?

That's not important right now, his voice said in my head.

Well, that wasn't reassuring.

Though still intimidated, my fear was less paralyzing than it had been a moment ago. I lifted my chin and glared at Bram. "We have options, you know."

Both men snapped their heads in my direction. *Whatever you're doing, stop*, Killian told me silently.

Despite the gurgling in my stomach, I ignored Killian's pleas. "We don't have to stand here and be threatened. I could call the police."

Bram's head threw back, and he cackled. "Naïve girl."

The term left a sour taste in my mouth. I began to protest, but he cut me off.

"Would you like to call Sheriff Anderson? I have his number saved in my phone. Or perhaps we can call David—you know, Mayor Stone?"

I stared at my shoes, unsure how to proceed. That he was chummy with the local authorities wasn't a good sign. What could he get away with?

"That's what I thought." He paused and crossed his arms over his chest. "I had higher hopes for you two. Tori's ability to become invisible should have gotten you out free and clear. As it was, you're lucky I had the forethought to put a man on the security team. Do you understand what would have happened if he hadn't been there?"

I squared my shoulders and glared at him. "If this is so important, why did you send us in, anyhow? Amateurs who don't even want to be here. You could have sent someone who believes in your mission. Or, hell, why didn't you just go yourself? I'm sure you have the money to win the auction." I gestured to our extravagant surroundings for emphasis.

Killian sucked in a breath.

Bram laughed, softly this time, which was more disconcerting than his cackle. "Abraham Johnson cannot be seen at such a place."

Hearing his name created a flashback to the television in my hospital room when I woke up. Not realizing years had passed, I'd assumed the governor being interviewed was for another state.

It took a few seconds for the implication to set in. When it did, my eyes widened. We were being blackmailed by the fucking governor. There was no telling what he could do with that much power.

Silence filled the air as we all took in the gravity of the situation. During that time, two of Bram's thugs approached, flanking him.

I got the picture. This time, when I resigned, I meant it. "Fine. Do we really need that specific necklace? Maybe there's another item we can find that will work."

Bram and Killian shook their heads. Killian spoke up first. "I've been searching for years for something this powerful and haven't found anything else. There's no way we could come up with something in a few days."

So, Killian had been working with Bram for years? Or working *for* him, rather.

Bram waved his hands, shooing away Killian's words. "Don't worry about Killian's search, dear. He may be a magician, but he didn't have my reach until we stumbled upon one another."

Killian averted his gaze. There was more to that story, but he wasn't going to tell me right now.

I didn't know if it was important enough to try to pry out of him or not. But first things first.

"However," Bram continued, his tone much more level than before, "Killian's right. Even with that reach, we haven't heard of any artifact that has the same amount of power as that necklace. Of course, we haven't been able to try very many, because the other magicians haven't been as... cooperative... as you." He flashed me a wicked grin.

I grunted in response.

My lack of enthusiasm didn't appear to affect him. "Now, where are we with the spirit stone? We have less than two days left to use it, which means we need to find it, preferably yesterday."

Before I could admit that I hadn't investigated the stone at all, Killian spoke up. "I'll go with Tori to Marina's shop and see if she knows about the stone."

Did Killian know the stone might be there? Or at least *a* spirit stone, if not *the* spirit stone?

He turned to me. He did now.

"What do you know?" he asked me.

"I don't want to mess with these things," I said honestly. "I did some reading on them, and they're pretty badass."

Killian frowned. "Where did you read up on a spirit stone? They're so rare, I haven't been able to find anything on them."

I clamped my mouth shut. I didn't want anyone to know about Bennett and Casey. Enough people were potential targets of this stupid scheme already.

"Who's Bennett?" Killian looked up at me.

"Damn you, Killian. Stay out of my head."

He shrugged. "I told you I can't help it. I think I can hear more of your thoughts than anyone else's because your magic is so strong. Is Bennett that guy I saw you with in the park? Man bun?"

I scowled at him but didn't answer. That was probably all the answer he needed, however, because he appeared satisfied.

"Tori. Forgive me for my anger moments ago. Let's sit and discuss what you know and the future of this endeavor," Bram said, motioning toward the great room beside us.

I crossed my arms and planted my feet firmly in place. "Look, Bram. I don't know what your deal is or why you want this so badly. But I won't put my friends and family into harm's way just so you can get a stupid rock and bring Ophelia's soul to our plane."

"Her soul?" Bram asked.

I nodded. "I read that the god's soul will come to the spell caster. I don't know much else. But why would you want Ophelia's soul?"

Bram made a fist and clenched his jaw. "I don't want her soul.

I want her."

I shook my head. "I don't know if you'll get her or not. All I know is the spirit stone is imbued with a piece of her soul and when you cast the spell—"

"When *you* cast the spell," Killian repeated.

"When I cast the spell, it will bring a piece of her soul... Oh my god."

Bram and Killian both watched me curiously.

"My memory is faulty after the coma. It's worse when I have the headaches. And the script was so..." I gulped. "I translated wrong. Oh God, I was wrong." I leaned against the nearest wall and closed my eyes as dread churned my stomach. I was so wrong.

"Damnit, Tori, what's going on?" Killian asked, his voice loud.

I opened my eyes and peered into his. "It didn't say her soul would come to the spell caster. It said realm. Her realm would come to the spell caster." I looked at Bram, fixing him with a hard gaze. "We'd bring the Realm of Lost Souls to earth," I told him as anxiety rose in my chest. "We can't do this."

Bram met my stare without averting his gaze. "Are you sure? You said you were wrong before."

"I'm clear-headed now; I'm as sure as I'm going to be."

"What does that mean?" he asked, raising an eyebrow.

I exhaled sharply. "The text is similar to classical Sanskrit, which I can read, but it's a little different. Older, I think. But even with the differences, I'm pretty sure I'm right this time. My head isn't foggy."

He nodded while processing the information. "We'd better prepare then."

"For what?" Killian asked.

"For Ophelia's realm to merge with ours."

"What?" I cried. "You can't be serious!"

Bram stomped his foot, the sound echoing off the bare walls. "I will do whatever I must to bring Ophelia here. If her lost souls come with her, so be it." He looked at Killian. "We have survived the Unveiling. I'm sure we can survive the undead, too."

Shocked, I continued to stare at him. "You've seen Romero movies, right? Do you really want the undead here in our realm, with your wife and children or other loved ones, Bram? I sure as hell don't." Not to mention we didn't know exactly what types of undead we were talking about. They could be Poe's zombie-like raised dead, or vampire-like creatures, or poltergeists instead of Caspers. I hoped Killian could hear my thoughts now, though I was sure they were frantic and largely incoherent.

Bram took a step toward me until his face was inches from mine. "I am thinking about my wife and daughter," he said. His voice was soft and pained. "That's why we will continue with the original plan. This information is not a setback."

So, Bram's lost souls were his wife and daughter. As sad as that was, it wasn't sad enough to make me willing to risk bringing that realm here.

"I won't help you," I told him.

"You have no choice," he answered coolly.

"We all have choices, and this is one I'm making for myself and all the innocent lives in our world. I'm not helping you bring those monsters here. Ophelia would be bad enough, but everything she brings with her is even worse."

Bram looked at Killian. "Killian has a soft heart. He's been trying to protect you from the gravity of this situation. But I don't. Not anymore," he said, looking back at me. "I have plenty of others who will do what it takes to get you to comply."

I frowned. Was he threatening me?

A small smile played on Bram's lips. "Your magic will open the gate and bring Ophelia and her little lost souls here. And if it doesn't, your magic will not be enough to save your sister and her lover. You're right, Tori. We do have choices. Those are yours."

I turned to Killian, who averted his gaze, and then back at Bram, whose expression told me what I need to know. I didn't doubt him for a second. Still, I couldn't do what he asked. I couldn't live with myself if I did.

"That's the point," Killian said softly. "You won't live."

I watched the turmoil on his face for a moment and then turned and stomped out the front door.

SEVENTEEN

Sitting on the front stoop, I contemplated my next move. I was angry enough to take Killian's car, but I couldn't drive a stick-shift. Walking home was out of the question because I didn't know where we were. And as much as I wished it to, my magic didn't let me fly or teleport or anything cool enough to get home. So, I was stuck waiting on a guy I barely knew, who had coerced me into a scheme I wanted nothing to do with.

"Don't shoot the messenger," he said, the door clicking closed as he stepped outside. "I'm not as bad as you think I am."

I didn't really know how bad I thought he was, since I was pretty sure he was also being blackmailed into helping Bram. But why? What did Killian have that Bram needed so badly—a sporadic mind-reading ability? Surely, Bram didn't want him for his chiseled chin and sparkling green eyes.

Which stared at me in amusement. "They sparkle, huh?"

I groaned. Why couldn't his magic have fritzed out just before I thought that?

He chuckled and held his hand to help me up. "Ready? Or do you want to sit here and think about my chiseled chin some more?"

"Let's go," I said, ignoring his hand and his question. "Want to check out Pages and Potions while we're out? Then you can bring me home."

He nodded and headed for the driveway. When we reached

his car, he didn't try to open my door for me, and I couldn't decide if I liked that or not.

As he pulled out of Bram's neighborhood, his phone rang. He hit a button on his dash to keep the call private and held the phone to his ear. "Hey." His jaw clenched as the other person spoke. "Uh huh. No, no, don't do that. Yeah. I'll be right there." He set the phone back in the cup holder and turned to me. "Change of plans."

I ignored him and glared out the window in silence. I wasn't really mad at Killian, but I couldn't take my anger out on Bram without consequences, and Killian *was* doing his dirty work, after all. The drive took several minutes, but finally we pulled up to a house in a neighborhood of small old homes. It was probably a cute bungalow in its day, but now was just an old brick house with small front windows and weeds overgrowing the lattice on the front porch.

We parked on the street in front of the house, since there was no driveway. "Stay here," Killian said, killing the engine. With no other words, he got out of the car and walked through the grass. He let himself in the front door without knocking or announcing himself.

I watched him go in and then turned to look at the other houses on the street. Occasionally, fresh paint or trimmed bushes made a house stand out, but they were all pretty similar—older styles, in various states of disarray.

A loud ring pierced the silence, and the menu screen on the dashboard displayed Bram's name.

I reached forward to hit the answer button, but thought better of it. After a few more rings, the sound stopped.

Then it started again. Bram was calling back. He must really need something to not even leave a voicemail or text message.

I watched the screen continue to light up with his name as he called again and again. Finally, I had had enough. I grabbed the phone and put it in my pocket, getting out of the car.

The grass was tall, cool, and a little itchy on my sockless ankles. It was probably going to stain my white Converse, and then I'd be really pissed. I got to the front door and paused. Should I knock? Call for Killian? I pondered the options as the phone vibrated in my pocket, its ring muffled by fabric.

I opened the door slowly without announcing my arrival and took a step inside.

The interior of the house was incongruous with the exterior. A brick fireplace was the focal point of the living room I stepped into. Pictures adorned the cream-colored walls, and a burgundy and cream rug accented the hardwood floor. The furniture coordinated with the rug, soft and inviting. To the right was a hallway which I assumed led to bedrooms, since the small eat-in kitchen was through a doorway to my left. Peeking in it, I could see it was painted in the same cream color, with a floral border and pink accents adorning the small amount of wall space. It was quaint and pretty. Did a woman live here?

I tiptoed through the living room, looking around. What the hell was Killian doing here? Did he bring me to visit his girl-friend?

As I neared the hallway, voices floated toward me. One was Killian's, though I couldn't make out what he was saying, as it was soft and calm. The other was more frantic, higher pitched and scared. Not a girlfriend.

Was Killian pressuring someone else to join this crazy scheme? And just how much coercion did he use before letting Bram's henchmen take over?

I crept forward, now determined to remain silent. When the phone vibrated again, I yanked it from my pocket and turned the ringer off, inwardly groaning. I should have just left it and waited in the car like I was told to, or even found someone else to bring me home, but I couldn't. Not when the woman sounded scared.

I pressed against the wall and tried to peer around the corner, but there was no way I could see without being seen. Even though I had made myself invisible before, I didn't think I could do it without preparation. Plus, my heart was pounding in my ears, which made it difficult to concentrate. I settled for listening without being heard.

"I don't understand," the woman was saying through tears.

"You don't need to," Killian said. He almost sounded reassuring.

"Help me, Killian. Please help me."

She knew his name?

Well, of course she did. I knew his name, and he was still acting on behalf of a blackmailer.

"Mama, I'm trying to help you. You know that."

Mama? This was Killian's mother?

Killian sighed. "I just have to do this one more time. This is going to be it, I know it."

There was silence, except for the sound of the woman sobbing.

"Mama, I found the necklace. The one that can help us. Once I have it, I can use it before giving it to Bram. I can probably get this new one to help me use it, too, if her smart mouth doesn't get her killed."

I felt my eyes widen. Was he talking about me?

"My boy, my brave boy," Killian's mother said tenderly. She didn't sound especially old, but her voice was muffled with tears.

Something creaked, and I imagined Killian kneeling in front of a rocking chair to talk to his crying mother, though I could have been way off base.

"I don't want to be brave," Killian said softly. "I don't want to do this, Mama. But I will, for you."

"Don't hurt anyone, Killy," she said.

"I'm trying not to, Mama. So far, I haven't been put in that position. If Tori can follow directions, I shouldn't have to."

I sucked in a deep breath. He was talking about me. What did I have to do with anything? What the hell was he talking about?

There was a pause. Did he hear me? Or my thoughts?

Finally, he continued. "I'm going to fix this, Mama. I promise. We'll get you back to normal. This curse won't take you."

I frowned. His mom was cursed—that's what Bram was using against him. And he needed the necklace to cure her... the same one he was using me to steal. If he was just pretending to work with Bram, would I get caught in the middle of their power struggle?

The phone vibrated in my pocket, and I instinctively put my hand over it to further muffle the sound. I needed to get back to the car before Killian heard me. What would he do if he knew I had come in here, to his mother's home?

I tiptoed back to the car and buckled my seat belt just as the front door opened and Killian stepped out, shielding his eyes against the light of the sun and stars.

"Let's go," he said, putting the car into gear. "We need to find that spirit stone."

EIGHTEEN

I RECOGNIZED THE LANDSCAPE as we drove toward Pages and Potions, which was downtown not far from Marina's apartment. Some of the buildings were familiar from before my coma, while others I was getting used to from the last week of being driven around.

After a few minutes of silence, I cleared my throat. "So, are you going to tell me what that was about?"

Killian shrugged.

"Did you bring me along while you blackmailed someone else?"

"I told you, I'm just the messenger." His lips turned into a small smile. "And I'm a monogamous messenger, no worries."

I laughed a little. "Oh, you know how to get to a girl's heart," I joked.

Killian turned to glance at me, then back at the road. After a long pause, he asked, "Why is it so important to know what I was doing?"

That was a good question. I really didn't know why, but I made up an answer that sounded good. "If I'm supposed to trust you, I don't want to think that you have me waiting in the car while you're, I don't know, tying someone up in a chair or whatever it is you do."

Killian laughed. "You watch too many movies. I don't tie anyone up in chairs."

169

I shrugged. "How am I supposed to know? You won't tell me what you were doing."

He scowled. "Because it doesn't concern you, Tori. Not everything concerns you."

"Fine. How long until we're there?"

"A few minutes."

I grunted and leaned my head back. Why was this man so difficult?

If he heard that thought, he didn't respond. Instead, he glanced at his phone and cursed. "Bram called a dozen times. Why didn't you tell me?"

I remained silent as he redialed, purposely repeating lyrics to an old song so he couldn't read my thoughts and find out that I'd been in the house with him.

After a moment, Bram's voice filled the car. "Finally, Killian. Where have you been?"

Killian sighed. "You don't own me, Bram. I stopped... somewhere. We're headed to the magic store now."

I was proud of him for his show of defiance, however small it was. But it would take more than that to get out of Bram's ridiculous plan.

"Never mind that," Bram said, his voice laced with irritation. "Do you know Dax Jaxon?"

"Who?" I asked.

"Only one of the biggest rock stars alive," Bram answered.

I shrugged.

"What about him, Bram?" Killian asked, even more annoyed than Bram.

"I'm sending you a tweet he just sent out." A quick chime filled the air, followed by Bram's sigh. "Look at it, will you?"

Killian passed me the phone.

I clicked on the link that popped up and gasped. "He's wearing the necklace!"

"Where is he?" Killian asked, reaching for the phone.

I slapped his hand away. "Eyes on the road." I scanned the tweet. "He's playing downtown tonight at White River. Tickets are still available."

Killian turned to me with a grin. "Looks like we're going to a concert."

"This isn't for fun," Bram snapped. "Don't fuck up this time." The line clicked.

"He's so pleasant," I said as I set Killian's phone back in the cup holder.

An overwhelming sense of magic filled the air, and I realized we were pulling into Pages and Potions' parking lot. I put a clenched fist to my chest, my eyes widening. Why was the magic stronger each time I came here? And how was I going to hide this reaction from Marina?

"You okay there?" Killian asked.

I shook my head and choked out, "I don't know."

Killian turned to me, concern written across his face. "It's strong, huh?"

I nodded. "Do you sense it?"

He unbuckled and reached over to unbuckle me, too. "Yes, but not like you. My magic is more intermittent than yours, and not as strong."

"So, I feel this way," I emphasized by pointing to my chest, "because my magic is stronger than yours?"

"I think that's how it works. Anyhow, you ready to go in?"

I shrugged. It was now or never. Really, it was now or five minutes from now, since I didn't have many options in this situation. I opened my car door. "Let's get it over with."

Outside the car, Killian grinned at me. "I love when a woman is so willing to spend time with me."

I rolled my eyes. "Well, if I wasn't being blackmailed to do it, I might feel differently."

His sarcastic grin faded. He didn't respond.

A bell over the door dinged when we entered. I took another deep breath and let it out slowly as we walked past a row of dream catchers and other ornaments.

"Tori! What are you—oh." Marina scowled at Killian before facing me. "It sounded like there was trouble in paradise earlier." She had a box of crystals in her hand and was squatting in an aisle, pulling some off the shelves and putting new ones on.

I shrugged. "I don't know what's going on," I said honestly.

She eyed me suspiciously and didn't greet Killian. "Well, can I help you with anything?"

"I was wondering if you have any, uh," Killian began, looking around, "amethyst powder?"

The powders were across the store, which was probably why he was looking around. "I should," Marina said. She stood, leaving her box on the floor. "Let's take a look over there." She gestured toward the far wall.

Killian flashed me a quick look that I took to mean I was supposed to snoop around while he pretended to be in the market for amethyst powder.

They walked away, a sour expression on Marina's face. I watched her disappear behind a shelf and then I made my way behind the main counter where the stones last were. The magic in the store was so thick I couldn't differentiate between items. Not that I had much experience in doing that anyhow. But as I searched for the box of stones behind the counter, nothing jumped out at me. Everything was a sea of similar magic.

Plus, the box wasn't there. Damnit.

"Looking for something?" Marina asked.

I jumped, guilty. "Um..."

"I told her the good stuff's behind the counter," Killian said with a grin. "She was curious to see what people buy in a place like this."

Marina shrugged. "It's a little of everything, really. And I keep the *good stuff*, as you call it, in a case under a lock." She pointed toward the nearby wall, unwittingly showing me where to look next.

"Thanks," Killian said. He glanced at me, and I gave him a small shake of my head. "I'm going to look for that crystal you told me about," he said to Marina.

"I'll show it to you." She walked away, and Killian followed.

He looked at me over his shoulder, telling me with his eyes to search for the stones.

I nodded but was confused. All the magic was overwhelming my senses. I couldn't distinguish one feeling from another, let alone one magical item from another. I did know, however, that the box of stones wasn't behind the counter anymore.

Pretending to meander aimlessly, I headed straight for the locked case at the back of the store.

"Oh, that's cool," I heard Killian say.

"What do you want these for? I can recommend other items that could help you out if I know more," I heard Marina ask.

There was a pause, and I cringed as I imagined what Killian could possibly say.

"I'm hoping to increase my meditation skills," he said finally. "I heard amethyst was a good potentiator."

I crouched to look at the shelf next to the case. It held books, which normally would be of big interest to me, but today that's not what I was interested in. Standing, I peeked into the case. There were crystals, some vials of liquid, and some stones. Was it my imagination, or did the magic in the air just get thicker when I saw them? I moved to lift the lid, but it was locked, like

Marina said it would be.

I had contemplated asking Marina if I could just have some stones because I thought they were pretty, but that had been before, when they were in a simple box behind the counter. She obviously knew they were special, or at least could be, to have locked them up.

Sighing, I tuned back into Marina and Killian's conversation.

Marina's tone was less friendly than it was a moment ago. "... you got magic during the Unveiling, then."

"Sure did."

Shit, Killian, you didn't just tell her you're a wizard. The only thing she hates more than wizards is—

"... more of a magician, actually," he said.

We were fucked.

I took a few steps closer and hid behind a row of bottles filled with colored liquids, listening.

"I see," Marina said. "So, you have innate magic, but haven't studied enough to harness it properly."

"Well," Killian stammered. He was sweating, his crystal green eyes darting around the room until they locked on me. His face screamed for help, but he continued to stammer through a response to my sister.

Her demeanor was still friendly, since he was a paying customer, but she already didn't like him, and finding out he had inborn magic but didn't study enough to control it like a wizard... well, that just made her move from disliking him to hating him.

"Hey, guys," I said, coming up behind Marina. "Did you find what you're looking for?"

Marina gave a curt nod. "Your friend here is a magician. He's looking to increase his meditation skills, and he heard somewhere that amethyst is good for that. How about that?" She gave Killian a fake smile, then turned to me. The emphasis on her words told me all I needed to know — she had no interest in magicians, even those I brought around. Which confirmed my reasons for not telling her my secret.

"I did," Killian answered. "Did you?"

Marina's eyebrows raised.

"Oh, I didn't find anything interesting." I gave my sister a quick smile. "I mostly looked around while you guys chatted."

"Can I ring anything up for you?" Marina asked, looking back at Killian.

He smiled brightly. "Not right now. But thank you so much for the help. I'm sure I'll be back once I do some more research."

Marina flinched, barely noticeable to outsiders. But I was her sister, after all, and I saw it. "Great. Do some more research. That's always a good idea."

"I guess we'll be out of here then," I told her. I leaned in to hug her. "I'll see you at home later."

She nodded. After I pulled away from the hug, she exclaimed, "Oh! Do you still need a ride to physical therapy?"

I shook my head. "I'm good."

"Okay. Love you. Nice to see you again," she added to Killian, though there was no warmth in her voice.

"And you as well." He reached for my hand, and I reluctantly let him grasp it.

He dropped my hand as we walked to his car. "Do you think it's there?" he asked, opening his door.

"I don't know. I mean, there were stones there, and they were powerful. One of those stones might be the *lapis manalis*." I whispered the last words as I slid into my seat.

"Any idea what that thing is, anyhow? I mean, Bram said there were three of them, right? How do we know we'll get the right one?"

I shrugged as I buckled my seatbelt. "We don't. At least, I don't.

But if you think about it, of the three known stones called the *lapis manalis*, only one of them was likely made by Ophelia... maybe two, if we stretch."

He started the car but turned back to me.

I counted off on my fingers as I explained my thought process. "One is said to make rain—that has nothing to do with what we're looking for. One was said to be part of the doorway to the underworld in Roman culture. That could be Ophelia's stone, but she's not the Roman god of the underworld that we know of, so I think that's the stretch."

"Do we know that for sure, though?"

"We don't know anything for sure at this point." I sighed. "I wouldn't be surprised if there was one set of gods and goddesses, but different cultures made their own versions of them. So, Ophelia might be the real-life equivalent of Hades and Osiris and the like, the underworld gods. I think. That's the best equivalent of lost souls I can think of."

Killian nodded. "I guess that makes sense. Assuming you're right, though, that doesn't tell us anything about the third *lapis manalis*. Which we know nothing about," he said in frustration as he pulled out of the parking lot. "And I can't be of much help; I don't know anything about mythology. My family is Egyptian, and I can barely name any of the gods from that part of the world."

"It was a big part of my education. But I'd never heard of the third *lapis manalis* until Bram mentioned it." I paused, glancing out the window at the passing cars. "Do you think it's real? The third one?"

Killian shrugged. "You know more about this than me. All I know is we need to find this stone, pronto." He was quiet as he drove. After a minute, he said, "That didn't go well."

I shook my head. "Marina hates untethered magic."

He looked at me, confused. "Yet she owns a magic shop?"

"She studied business and literature in college. Her plan was to open a bookstore. I guess it didn't go as well as planned until she added the magic side to it. In her mind, I think it's more a bookstore that sells magical items than a magic shop that sells books."

"Something must have happened to her while you were in your coma."

"I don't know. I've gotten that impression, though." She had shared about the old lady's uncontrolled magic, but I wasn't convinced that was the whole story.

Killian nodded silently. Finally, he asked, "So, how does that work with you? I mean, you guys are obviously still close despite your magic, which is pretty powerful. And you're basically a novice."

I cringed.

Noticing my lack of verbal response, he glanced at me. "She doesn't know, does she?"

"I'm afraid of what will happen if I tell her. You heard her disdain for you in there, and you were potentially a paying customer."

"It's a wonder she stays in business," he added.

"They say she has the best inventory in town," I said, shrugging.

"Well, we need a new plan." He took a corner more slowly than necessary and appeared to be lost in thought.

I waited for him to continue and sighed when he didn't. "I don't know. Maybe we... don't?"

The car stopped at a red light and Killian turned toward me, his brows furrowed. "What do you mean, *don't*? You think we can just walk away at this point?" When I didn't respond, he continued. "What interaction with Bram so far leads you to believe that's an option?"

I picked my nails, focusing on them rather than his intense gaze. When the car started moving again, I spoke up softly. "I know about your mom."

"What about her?" he asked, his tone icy.

"I know she's cursed, and you're planning to keep the necklace to cure her."

Killian whipped the car into a parking lot, and it lurched to a stop. "Did Bram tell you that?"

"No."

He slammed his hand against the steering wheel. "Damnit, Tori! Talk to me. How do you know about my mom?"

I lifted my chin and found him staring at me. "I overheard you talking to her. In her house."

His handsome face contorted in confusion. "Can you... did I somehow...?"

Shaking my head, I waved my hands to stop him. "I heard the good old-fashioned way, not magically. I snuck in when you were with her."

He continued to stare in silence.

I continued, my words rushed. "Bram kept calling, and I got annoyed, so I went in to find you, and I heard you being so sweet, and I realized it was a private moment and I didn't want to intrude so I left before you could find out." I took a deep breath.

His head bobbed slowly. "Okay."

That was it? Or was he about to explode on me, messing up this whole plan and putting everyone's lives in danger?

"I wouldn't do that," he whispered. He ran a hand over the stubble on his chin. "And I did plan on keeping the necklace for myself, but I don't know anymore."

"Why not?" He had told his mom something about being able to complete the plan if I followed directions. I hadn't done anything to throw Bram's plan off course, so I hadn't messed anything up for Killian. At least, I thought so.

He placed a hand on my arm. "It's nothing you've done. Also, you worry too much."

I chuckled and glanced at his hand. My skin felt warm under his. I blushed and looked away.

"No, Tori, to be honest, I'm not sure what to do," he continued. "See, that necklace is the whole reason I'm in this mess with Bram in the first place. When he realized I was after the same artifact as him... well, he expects me to use my research to find the necklace and give it to him, and if I don't..."

"He'll hurt your mom," I finished solemnly. I pondered what he'd said. "So, he recruited you for your research, not your magic?"

"Not quite. I was in the wrong place at the wrong time and tried to outsmart the wrong person. I wasn't recruited in the same sense you were. He didn't know a thing about me until I sweet-talked a woman in Chicago into helping me steal the necklace—yes, I know, I shouldn't have done it," he said when he caught my raised eyebrow. "But it's important. And I wasn't going to hurt her; I just wanted to use her connections to get to the necklace before it moved again." He ran a hand through his hair and stared out the windshield.

"So, Bram realized you knew a lot about the necklace and wanted that knowledge."

He nodded. "And here we are. I told him I wouldn't hurt anyone, so he doesn't ask me to. But I still feel dirty when I follow his orders." He rubbed his arms with both hands.

I completely understood that sentiment.

We sat in silence for a few minutes, me twisting strands of long hair around my fingers, and Killian facing the side window, brooding.

"I kind of hate my sister," I whispered. I stopped twirling my hair and waited for his response.

He turned to me with a frown. "What?"

"Wouldn't you, if she fucked your partner while you were in a coma, and they plan their wedding while you're sleeping on their couch? Not to mention that I don't think she would take it well if she found out I'm a magician. Like, at all."

He laughed. "Yeah, I can see that. But hate? That's such a strong word."

I wobbled my head in indecision. "I said kind of."

"Why are you telling me this?"

Shrugging, I sighed. "Even though I feel that way, Marina's the only family I have. Dad's dead and my mom hasn't even cared enough to check on me since I woke up. Marina said she only visited me once in almost five years. I'll bet she doesn't come to the wedding, either. She's just—well, Cora James is a bitch."

Killian chuckled, but still appeared confused.

"I need Marina in my life. You need your mom in your life." I grasped his hand in mine. "As much as I hate this with every fiber of my being, we have to see this through. For them." Tears burned my eyes but didn't spill. "Maybe once Bram uses the necklace, you can use it for your mom. Then we'll all be happy and safe and free of Abraham Johnson."

He squeezed my hand. "I love your optimism, and I agree that we need to see this through for my mom and your sister. But I don't know if I can be responsible for the realms merging. Plus, I'm not sure we'll even be completely free of *Governor* Johnson."

The tears began to flow. "I don't know how to fix this, Killian. I feel so helpless."

With a sad smile, he used the thumb of his free hand to wipe the tears from my cheek. His green eyes bore into mine, but I couldn't look away. He didn't speak; he didn't need to. We were in the same boat with no oars. The only way to get to shore was to follow Bram's lead. Killian was the first to break our stare after a moment, and he dropped his hand from my face and cleared his throat. "So, what's the plan now?"

I sighed, my skin feeling cool and naked without his comforting touch. "I guess we need to come back when they're closed."

"Why, Ms. James, are you suggesting we break into your sister's store?" he acted aghast.

"If it saves her life, then yes. I think I know where the stones are, but they're locked up."

"Alright then. We can hit it after we get the necklace back. In the meantime, you need to get to physical therapy, no?"

I groaned. I hated physical therapy. Not only was it painful and tiring, but it kept me from doing what was truly important right now.

"Staying healthy is important, too," Killian said softly. "Now, where is therapy?"

NINETEEN

AFTER AN HOUR-LONG PHYSICAL therapy session, a walk home, lunch, and a long nap, I once again stood in front of Marina's full-length mirror, hands on my hips and a scowl on my face. I had listened to a couple of Dax Jaxon songs to get the feel for what to wear to the concert and had raided Marina's closet for clothes suitable for a rock show. Dressed all in black with my long hair in a braid, I figured I'd fit in alright with the crowd. Dax was around my age, so hopefully his fans were, too.

With a groan, I remembered I was thirty, not twenty-five, so I was probably a couple of years older than the singer. Still, I didn't expect to stand out too much. I couldn't afford to. This was too important.

I waited in the kitchen for my ride, who was, of course, Killian—I'd been spending pretty much every waking minute with him lately. Which wouldn't have been bad under normal circumstances. But these definitely were not normal circumstances. I was getting a free concert and extra time with an attractive man out of the deal, but it still didn't seem like I'd come out ahead. The Realm of Lost Souls sounded like a place I did not want unleashed on Earth. But Killian and I had agreed earlier that there wasn't a way around this.

Taking a sip of coffee, I decided I'd try to get through this phase of the plan and figure out how to avoid the realms merging later. If I could. I leaned against the counter and played various scenarios in my mind, but they all ended up with either the realms merging or someone I cared about dead.

A ding from my phone brought me back to the present moment. Killian had texted to say he was outside. Apparently, we'd moved past the phase of the relationship where he'd show up at my doorstep. I sighed and put my empty coffee cup in the sink. Show time.

It didn't take long to get there, and Killian knew just where to park. He knew how to dress, too. I took in his dark jeans and the black t-shirt that hugged his frame, realizing his "rock concert" outfit was strikingly similar to his "spy on Tori" one.

"Is your closet full of those shirts?" I asked him with a nudge of my elbow. We waited in line for the V.I.P. experience he'd bought, which ensured us a chance to get up close and personal with Dax—and the necklace.

Killian grinned. "Would you rather I went shirtless?"

"It's a little cold." I turned so he couldn't see me blush.

He held up his arm, emphasizing the jacket draped over it. "I'll be fine. Plus, I happen to have a style," he said with a faux haughtiness.

I couldn't help but smile. "Yeah, yeah. You just like the looks you get in public."

"Doesn't hurt," he said with a shrug. After a moment of silence, he nodded. "They're about to let us back."

"Is it hard, sorting out the thoughts in a big place like this?" I asked, leaning in to whisper.

The teenagers in front of us squealed in delight. The line was moving. I guessed I'd have to wait for an answer to my question. I fought the urge to tap my foot as we waited impatiently for the groups before us to meet and greet with their favorite artist. I watched the sea of fans huddle toward the front of the stage as the opening band began to play, for a moment forgetting why we were there.

Then it was our turn.

The security guard ushered us to a small make-shift room backstage. Band and crew members scurried about, making it difficult to focus.

Killian's hand on the small of my back gently urged me forward. It was now or never. Maybe literally. He plastered an ecstatic grin on his face and stepped toward the figure sitting on a barstool across the room. "Dax! I'm so happy to meet you." Killian crossed the room in long strides and held out his hand for a shake.

Without missing a beat, Dax grabbed Killian's hand, but instead of pumping it, he pulled Killian in for a hug. "The pleasure's mine, man." After releasing Killian from the surprise embrace, Dax ran his hand through his shaggy neon green hair. He turned his attention toward me. "Much pleasure." He spread his arms for a hug.

I leaned into a quick embrace and stood back. Hugging a stranger was awkward, but I had to pretend I was a huge fan. After all, we paid for the now-sold-out V.I.P. experience. I leaned into Killian with a smile as fake as his. "We are just so excited to be here."

"I love meeting fans. It's why I do what I do, you know?" Dax sat on his barstool and motioned toward a nearby set of stools. "Have a seat, guys. Unless you want the picture first?"

Killian nodded eagerly. "Yeah, let's do that." He handed the assistant his phone and motioned for me to stand beside Dax, opposite him. "Can you take a couple?"

The assistant, a petite woman probably a little older than me, smiled. "Of course. Say cheese!" She snapped a few pictures, then handed the phone back and stepped to the side.

Killian remained beside Dax and kept his voice low. "We need a favor, Dax."

The singer looked at him, surprised.

Killian's fingertips grazed the necklace. "We need this."

Dax jumped up, his barstool falling over. Several people glanced at us but went back to their work when Dax appeared to be unharmed. "No can do, man."

"It's really important," I added, moving to stand beside Killian. "Life or death important."

Dax frowned. Before he could speak, Killian cut him off. "We can pay."

Dax raised an eyebrow but shook his head. "I paid good money for this just last night. No way am I letting it go."

I shot Killian a look that meant "I told you so." I didn't think this would be that easy, but he wanted to appeal to Dax as a human rather than use magic or steal the necklace from him. "We only have a few minutes," I reminded Killian softly.

He nodded. After a silent moment, he squinted and cocked his head to the side.

"You okay, man?" Dax asked, concern flashing across his confused face.

"It's so loud," Killian said with a groan. "I can almost hear, but not quite."

"I said, are you okay?" Dax repeated more loudly.

It was difficult not to chuckle, because I was pretty sure Killian meant he was trying to hear someone's thoughts—probably Dax's. He was going to use the singer's thoughts against him. I almost felt bad, but I quickly remembered the stakes. Killian's mom, my sister, and my friends counted on us. The thought reminded me that saving them would likely be dangerous for many other people. Maybe we didn't need the necklace, after all.

Not that again, Killian's voice said in my head. *We decided, together, that we would go through with this.*

He seemed to hear well now, though that could be because I was physically close to him. I still wasn't exactly sure how his magic worked.

Killian cleared his throat. "I know the necklace is magical, Dax. I know it helps you do... this," he said, his arms spread to indicate the chaos around us.

Dax's eyes widened. "I just bought it last night. Haven't even tried it out yet. Although, I can already tell it's going to be powerful." He eyed Killian suspiciously. "How did you know that?"

Killian showed him a sly smile. "The same way I know that you're terrified of going back to the way things were before. When you were just a... crappy singer who was holding the rest of the band back." His voice inflected almost to a question by the end of the sentence. Reading Dax's thoughts must have been challenging, judging by the strain on Killian's face.

Dax paled. "You're reading my mind," he whispered. He stared for a moment, then continued. "I've never really told anyone that before. But it's true." He hung his head.

His shame tugged at my heart. "It looks like you've made something of yourself, though. That lawn is packed with people waiting for you."

Dax clutched the pendant in his fist and shook his head. "They're not waiting for me, man. They're waiting for a guy I created by using magical artifacts until they dried up, constantly chasing the next item that would hide the fact that I'm just a mediocre singer of a college garage band. My buddies were better off without me, but I'm the one who discovered the magic." His dark eyes clouded as he turned to me. "I left them in the dust. The friends who stuck with me when I was no one. The girl of my dreams. For what?"

Killian clapped him on the shoulder. "I think anyone would jump at the chance to be a rock star. Don't be so hard on yourself."

Dax continued to stare at me, but he didn't respond.

I smiled at him, though I didn't feel any joy. His story illustrated one of the problems with magic that made people like my sister distrust and dislike it. And his confession didn't exactly endear me to him. Though I appreciated his honesty. I wondered if we could have gotten the truth out of him if Killian hadn't showcased his ability.

The silence in our small space seemed louder than the surrounding bedlam. It was certainly less comfortable. I broke eye contact with Dax and turned my attention to my shoes.

Finally, Dax spoke again, softly. "This necklace is said to be very powerful. I bought it hoping I wouldn't have to keep finding new items to, uh, enhance my voice." He winced at the words but continued. "I want to help you guys, especially if your problem is as serious as you say it is. But I can't go back now; I'm in too deep. I can't just walk back into my buddy's garage and announce I'm back to be the lead singer of Thursday Rain, which no one has ever heard of, or ever will hear of. Can you imagine me tracking down Izzy, begging her to take me back after I bounced five years ago? I broke her heart. We'd been together since–"

"Tenth grade," Killian interjected.

"That's creepy, dude," Dax said. "Plus, there's no need to read my mind when I'm literally telling you what's on it." Annoyance crossed his face, and he took a deep breath in.

Killian shook his head. "I'm not reading your mind."

"Then how did you know that? I've never talked about her to the press."

I glanced between them. Dax's annoyance was turning to

frustration, but Killian appeared to be pleased with himself. What was going on?

Killian turned to me with a grin that told me he thought he'd just sealed the deal. Then he turned his back to us and motioned toward the entrance we had come through moments before.

What the hell are you doing? I thought, hoping he could hear me.

He could. *Just watch.*

I hated when he was cryptic. It reminded me of Bram. And, if I was being honest, my mother. Cora James was the queen of cagey mixed messages. Still, I made the split-second decision to trust Killian. After all, I'd trusted him this far. Well, kind of.

"Isabel Taylor was in your math class freshman year, but you didn't talk to her until you were sophomores. She sat next to you in 2D art, and you shared a colored pencil case."

The confusion on Dax's face mirrored how I felt. Before either of us could question what was going on, Killian continued.

"She knew you were it from that very first day. Just thinking about it makes her emotional."

"Okay, man, I have to know what the hell you're doing." One of Dax's fists was clenched at his side. Killian had definitely hit a nerve.

I sure hoped he was right about this game he was playing without me.

Killian turned back to Dax with a gleam in his green eyes. "Izzy has attended every one of your concerts over the last five years within a driving distance—and some that weren't. Including this one."

Chills ran up my spine. Killian had been reading Izzy's mind, which had to mean she was nearby. And he'd pointed toward the entrance, so there was a great chance she was waiting for one of the V.I.P. experiences after ours. I knew what Killian was doing, and I had a feeling it was going to work.

Dax's hand relaxed and his eyes brimmed with tears. "You can hear her? She's here?"

The assistant who had taken our picture appeared behind Killian. "You guys need to get going. We still have another person left to meet Dax, and we're on a schedule."

Dax's face lit up, followed by an expression of fear. He made a shooing motion to his assistant, then grabbed Killian's shoulders with both hands. "Why is she here, in the V.I.P. line?"

Killian's eyes squinted, and he listened silently. "This is the last stop of your tour, right?"

Dax nodded.

"She wants to tell you she loves you. She wants to ask you to… I'm not sure. It's all jumbled." He scrunched up his face apologetically.

"Ask her yourself," I said, nudging Dax with my elbow. When he turned to me, I inclined my head toward the entrance, where a pretty blonde woman had appeared.

Dax's hands dropped to his sides, and he gazed at Izzy as she walked toward us timidly.

His assistant, who was walking her over, cast a pointed glance at Dax as she neared.

"They can stay," he told her, not taking his eyes off Izzy. "For a minute, anyhow."

She shrugged. "If you say so, boss. Want a picture with this one?"

"In a minute," he said with a wave of his hand.

Killian and I stepped aside so Izzy could be closer to Dax, but she stood in place, staring at him as intently as he did to her.

After an awkward silence, Killian cleared his throat. "Guys, seriously. I'm standing right here."

I chuckled, wondering what they had been thinking to make

Killian blush.

"Izzy," Dax said finally, reaching for her hands.

She grasped his fingers in hers. "Danny."

"Danny?" I asked, as Killian appeared to be ready to do the same.

Dax shrugged, glancing at me. "Daniel Jackson Smith. Pretty boring for a rock star, right? So, I changed it up a little."

Made sense. "Look, Dax, uh, Danny... whatever. We want to get out of your hair, but we need to talk about–"

He shook his head. "Nah, man, we don't need to talk about it. If what your boy says is true, I'll give you the damn thing."

Killian and I exchanged surprised, relieved glances.

"If what's true?" Izzy asked, her voice soft and melodic.

"That you still love me."

Tears filled her eyes. "I never stopped. I tried to move on, but I just couldn't. Since tonight's the last stop of your tour, I flew here on a whim to tell you how I feel. I didn't know when I'd get another chance."

He pulled her in, and they embraced. Which was sweet, romantic, and uncomfortable as hell for me, and probably Killian, too.

Over her shoulder, Dax looked from Killian to me. "Can I use it one time, though? I can't disappoint the fans. They're already here, waiting for a show. I can announce tonight that I'm retiring, and you can have it right after."

Izzy reeled back. "Retiring? Why would you do that?"

Dax grinned like the love-struck twenty-something he was. "I thought I wanted this life, and it's cool in some ways, but I mostly just ended up with regret. I'd like to go back home and live a different life. With you. If you'll have me."

In response, Izzy stood on her tiptoes and kissed him passionately.

I turned away. It wasn't like they could have real privacy, but I didn't want to actively watch.

After a moment, Dax laughed. "You can look now."

I caught Killian's eye as we both turned back toward Dax and Izzy. He was trying not to laugh, but his cheeks were a little red, as well.

"Meet me back here after the show, guys. I'll give it to you then."

Izzy cocked her head to one side. "I don't understand."

Dax smiled sadly, fidgeting with the necklace. "This thing is magical. Before I go on stage, I'm going to say an incantation, and it's going to create the sound you hear when I sing. You know that's not my voice, Iz. You've heard me sing."

She blushed. "I thought you'd gotten lessons or something. It never occurred to me you were ch—using magic."

"You can say it," Dax said. "I was cheating. I am cheating. And I'm going to do it one more time. But that's it. Then it's you and me, baby."

She smiled up at him, and he leaned down to kiss her again.

Killian nodded toward the way we'd come in. He was right; we had our plan. There was no need to stay any longer. As we walked toward the exit, Killian held out his hand and I grasped it, lacing my fingers through his.

The hard part was done. We could enjoy the concert and put all thoughts of Bram and this plan behind us, at least for a little while.

TWENTY

THREE HOURS LATER, KILLIAN pulled me against the crowd toward the side of the stage, his clammy hand encasing mine. With his black jacket on, he looked both more dashing and intimidating. Feeling the coolness of the leather sleeves brush against my arm evoked images of my dad's jacket hanging useless in Marina's closet. It wasn't so much that I couldn't wear it—though it was super comfortable—but that I wanted to feel close to someone, in particular my father.

I sighed and pushed away the image that had begun to form in my mind. This was not the place to reminisce about someone long gone. I had a job to do.

We reached the barricade, which was a portable metal fence guarded by a twenty-something man in a black shirt that read *concert security*. "Dax is expecting us," Killian told him.

The man smirked. "Sure."

Killian grinned and waved his arm over his head until Dax's assistant walked over to us.

"They can come back," she told the man as she scooted a section of the fence out of our way.

"Whatever," he said with a shrug. Clearly, he took his job seriously.

The assistant turned to us as she rushed the stage. "I don't know what's so special about you guys, and I really don't care. The show's over, so I just have to make sure Dax gets on the tour bus in one piece." She motioned us forward and gestured to the barstools we sat on earlier.

It felt good to sit after being on my feet since we got here, so I wasn't bummed that Dax was nowhere to be found. But after a few minutes, anxiety crept in. Was he going to ditch us after promising to turn over the necklace?

Killian appeared to be at ease on his stool, no worry lines creasing his forehead. He took in the surroundings as if he hadn't been back here just a few hours ago. *Don't sweat it,* he said in my head. *He's nearby and focusing on giving us the necklace. It doesn't sound like he's thinking of backing out.*

That helped a little, but I wouldn't be completely at ease until the necklace was in our possession. Then I had to figure out how to sabotage Bram from the inside.

But first things first. Dax was heading toward us, holding Izzy's hand. He looked both wired and exhausted at the same time.

"Thanks for letting me use it," he said when he stood before us.

"You paid for it. We should be thanking you," I said.

"We *are* thanking you," Killian added. "With your help, my mom and her sister will be safe. Without it, they and many more people—including us—would be in danger."

Dax tilted his head as if he was intrigued by our story, but he didn't ask Killian to elaborate. Instead, he reached behind his neck and unfastened the necklace. He stared at it wistfully before extending his hand toward us. "At least I got to go out on my own terms."

I let Killian grab the necklace, which he placed in his jacket pocket. After I was confident it was safe, I turned back to Dax. "This doesn't have to be the end, though."

He flashed a sad smile. "Yes, it does. I don't want to spend all my time chasing the next magical item like some kind of addict or pretending to be someone I'm not. I'm not Dax Jaxon—rock-star with an amazing voice and the ability to shred a guitar with the greats. Even though the magic improved my abilities, this lifestyle is hard. I had been thinking about it before I even met you guys, which is why it was so easy for me to turn it over once I knew there was a life worth living outside of music."

He was right. It was exhausting pretending to be someone I wasn't. I was pretending to be okay with Grey marrying my sister, which was still tearing me up inside. I wasn't so much pretending to go along with Bram as I was doing so begrudgingly. But the life I wanted to live was simpler than this. It involved teaching at the university, coming home to my love every night, and my sister being my best friend. Instead, I got a poor memory, no lover, and a sister who worked for the Department that wanted to regulate the magic I didn't even ask to have.

I closed my eyes and took in a deep breath, mulling over Dax's words. I wondered if it was that easy to walk away from this magical world, like he was doing from music. If I could just get a mundane job and my own apartment, forget about my sister's suspicious involvement with the Department, and move on with my love life. I stole a glance at Killian's profile and let my mind wander, imagining him waiting on me at home instead of Grey, his arms around me, his body against mine.

Killian's cheeks turned red and his eyebrows raised. *So that's what you're thinking about when you forget I can hear you.*

It was my turn to blush. I didn't respond to him directly, instead focusing on what Dax was saying. I had missed the first part, though, so was lost as he told a story about his old band.

Finally, his story ended, and he reached to shake Killian's hand. "I hope it works out for you, whatever it is."

"Me too," Killian said.

"Thanks," I added.

Dax and Izzy turned their backs to us and headed toward their futures.

I ran my hands over the goosebumps on my arms. My shirt was long-sleeved but thin, because I hadn't wanted to get too hot with all the body heat of the crowd. "Let's get out of here. I'm getting cold."

He removed his jacket and placed it over my shoulders. "We have a bit of a walk back to the car. You look like you need this more than I do."

"Thanks." I stuck my arms through it and pulled it closed. "Now let's get that thing to Bram so we can figure out the rest of this."

Killian shook his head. "Tomorrow. We've done enough for tonight." He walked toward the exit. "It's later than I expected, so let's hit Pages and Potions tomorrow for the stone, too. That means tomorrow's a big day. Better rest up and be ready."

Unsure of how to respond, I just nodded. I didn't want to be doing any of this, but we had agreed. I kept in stride beside him until we made it to the car and sat silently while we waited for our chance to leave the parking lot. Knowing he could hear my thoughts, at least sometimes, I focused on non-Killian-related thoughts the best I could. Which unfortunately meant I thought about Grey, Marina, Bram, Bennett's book, and Ophelia. We couldn't let her realm merge with ours. We didn't really know what to expect if it happened, but it sounded dangerous.

After a mostly silent ride, Killian pulled his car in front of the door to Marina's apartment. He jumped out of the car before my seatbelt was even off and opened my door.

"You know you don't have to do that," I said as I stood.

"I know." He stood beside the open door, not moving to close it. He stared into my eyes, and before I knew it, he was somehow so close we could touch. "I wanted to," he said, barely above a whisper.

A lump formed in my throat. "You wanted what?"

The corners of his mouth turned upward. "This." He leaned forward until his lips touched mine so softly, I wasn't sure if I was imagining things.

I moved my mouth against his, testing the waters, and was welcomed with a deeper kiss. I definitely was not imagining this.

One of Killian's hands landed on my waist and the other moved to the back of my head, his fingers gently tugging at the base of my braid as they found their place.

We kissed until we pulled back simultaneously, both out of breath. "I wasn't expecting that," I whispered.

"No? You wanted it, though. I could hear it."

So, my attempt to keep those thoughts at bay hadn't worked; he could hear subconscious thoughts as well. Good to know. I shrugged. There was no point in refuting his claim, so I just smiled.

Killian stepped back, his hands leaving warm spots on my body. He closed the door and smiled back. "See you tomorrow, Tori."

I nodded, still barely believing what had just happened. "Yeah."

He walked around the front of the car and slid inside, but he waited until I had unlocked the front door before he left.

I stepped inside and exhaled deeply. Everything was happening so fast, and most of it was not good. But this—well, maybe this would be.

TWENTY-ONE

THE NEXT MORNING, I slept in until after Marina and Grey had left. We were out of milk, so I headed on foot to a bakery down the street. My legs felt pretty much normal, and the rest of my body was strong. If only my mind would catch up.

I ordered a bagel, a muffin, and coffee, and sat at a table by the window, intent on not thinking about Bram and his stupid plan until I absolutely had to. I read a book I'd downloaded onto my phone until my eyes were tired, and I decided to head home. Bram was waiting, and I couldn't put him off forever.

On the walk back, the sun shone brightly against a star-studded, cloudless sky. It was a beautiful fall day, with more leaves on the ground than on the trees and a crispness to the air that made me cross my arms as I walked. Since I knew he wasn't around to read my thoughts, I let them wander to Killian and the images I'd conjured yesterday before he had invaded my mind.

As I made my way up the sidewalk toward the apartment door, I replayed last night's kiss in my head. I wasn't sure what it meant. Maybe it was on a one-time thing. Maybe not. Did I really want to get involved with someone so soon after Grey?

I chuckled at that thought. Grey had moved on years ago—it wasn't soon. If anything, I was late to getting back into the dating game.

I took out my keys and moved to unlock the front door but stopped with my hand in mid-air, my breath caught in my throat.

It was already ajar.

I cautiously pushed the door in to get a view of the living room. It was an absolute mess. The furniture was mostly upright, save for a kitchen chair and an end table. But everything else was in heavy disarray. Papers were strewn across the desk under the window, some littering the floor. Most of the desk drawers were askew. A lamp lay on the ground alongside framed pictures that had rested on tables and counters. The bedding I had folded up next to the couch was thrown all over the furniture and floor.

I took a few timid steps into the apartment, unsure whether I should continue. If the intruder was still nearby, I didn't want to be alone with them, magic or not. For all I knew, the intruder had magic that was stronger than mine. After a few seconds of debate, I stepped back outside and dialed the only number I knew would be helpful.

Killian answered on the third ring. "I was just thinking about you."

"Someone broke into the apartment," I answered him.

"Are you hurt?" he asked, concern lining his voice.

"No," I assured him. "I came home to find the aftermath. I'm afraid to go inside, though."

"Be there in five," he said. "Wait outside." The line went dead.

True to his word, Killian's car sped into the parking lot a few minutes later. He flung his door open and jogged to where I waited on the front patio. "You sure you're okay?"

I nodded. "Fine, I promise."

"Good. Let's check it out." He led the way through the door, walking carefully. He let out a low whistle at the sight. "This is a mess. Look around; was anything taken?"

"It's hard to tell," I said, walking toward the kitchen. Some of the cabinets were open, and the broken dishes scattered across the floor. Past the kitchen was the bedroom, and I was afraid of what I'd find in there. At least Marina and Grey were at work.

The bedroom door was open, and I peeked in. More mess. Bedding everywhere, blinds dangling off the windows at odd angles, more drawers open, and clothes thrown around the room. Someone was looking for something small, something that could fit into a drawer or cabinet. It was impossible to tell if anything had been taken, and I had no idea what anyone could possibly want from my sister or Grey.

Killian was inspecting the living room when I returned. "Hey, my jacket." He bent to retrieve the leather jacket that I had hung on a hook on the wall last night but was now in a heap on the floor. He picked it up and slung it over his shoulder, then turned to me, his eyes wide. "Oh, Tori."

I frowned. "What?"

He tossed the jacket onto the back of the couch and patted it down, his movements becoming more frantic with each passing second. Finally, his eyes met mine.

Realization dawned just as he opened his mouth to speak. "The necklace."

Killian closed his eyes for a moment. When he opened them, they were no longer an emerald shade. They had darkened to a forest green, a hue that declared *rage.*

"I'm sorry," I stammered.

He shook his head. After a pregnant silence, he spoke. "It's not your fault; I'm not mad at you."

I crossed the room to stand beside him, reaching for the jacket, which he handed to me. Though I believed him, I had to see for myself. The necklace wasn't there. My eyes brimmed with tears. "What are we going to do?"

Killian punched the door. "Damnit!" He paced away from me, hands on his hips.

I remembered the pain in his voice when I'd overheard him talking to his mother. I wasn't sure what was wrong with her, but she seemed to be more vulnerable than Marina.

He took his hands off his hips and turned to me, defeated. "She's cursed. It's eating her mind. Doctors can't stop it or slow it down, even with all the magic they use nowadays. And her body... it's like she's decades older than she really is. I can't let her go down that road. Especially when...."

"When what?"

"It doesn't matter. Nothing matters right now other than getting that necklace back."

I agreed. If Marina's life was in danger, I needed the necklace, too. I wondered if there was a way we could both benefit from it. But we'd have to find it again first.

"I knew it was too easy," Killian muttered.

I chuckled. "Easy, really? Do you know how hard that was on me? I'm still drained."

He nodded and peered around the room again. "Let's clean this up while we plan our next move. We can probably get it done before your sister gets home."

We set to work, silence a third partner in our effort to straighten the mess someone else had made. Neither of us knew what to say; it wasn't like we were friends.

"That bastard," I heard from behind the kitchen island, followed by the sound of dish fragments hitting the bottom of the trash can.

I peeked my head over the couch, where I had been on my knees straightening the bedding.

"Johnny fucking Boston," he replied through gritted teeth. "It couldn't have been a coincidence that we ran into him at the auction. Who else would track me down like that?"

It made sense, but I wasn't convinced. "Couldn't anyone who

wanted it put a locator spell on it or something? That would mean it didn't have to be Johnny."

"It's possible, yeah," he mumbled.

"And you said Johnny is noble," I reminded him.

He flashed a wry smile. "Unless we were after the same item."

Oh, yeah. He had said that.

"I'm going to find him. If he doesn't have it, we can move on. But we don't have any other leads to start with." He picked up the broom he had rested against the refrigerator. "Just as soon as we finish this."

I closed my eyes and let in a big breath. We would make this work; we had to. Killian would find Johnny, and hopefully, the necklace, and we would get it to Bram. I exhaled slowly. I would much rather Killian use the necklace than Bram, though I wasn't sure how we would get out of giving it to Bram.

"If I can find the necklace," Killian said, interrupting my thoughts, "I can use it and tell Bram we couldn't get it back. But you have to understand, Tori—he won't stop. If it's not this necklace, it will be something else. If it's not you, it will be someone else."

I frowned at him, but there wasn't much to say in reply. After a moment, I sighed. "Let's get this done and find the damn thing, then." I returned to tidying the bedding on the couch.

IT TOOK US TWO hours, but by the time we finished, the apartment looked better than it had before. It was minus a few dishes, and I hoped the papers on the desk weren't too important, because they direly needed organizing. But on the surface, everything was perfect. And Marina and Grey wouldn't be home for a while, so we had beaten the clock.

I eyed the couch warily. I really wanted a nap, but it seemed there was no time. We had to find Johnny, and hopefully the necklace, and then figure out how to get around Bram's plan so Killian could use the necklace for himself. And keep everyone safe in the process. Just thinking about it made me even more tired.

"Is there a map around here?" Killian asked as he walked toward me from the bathroom.

"I didn't see one when I was cleaning. Do you need it to find out where Johnny is?"

He ran his hand through his short hair. "Yeah. I need a crystal and a map."

"I have a couple of crystals in my purse, but I don't think we'll find an old-fashioned map."

He cursed.

"How about a map on my phone?" I asked while heading for the hook by the door, where my purse hung. While he contemplated, I rummaged through it and came up with an opaque white crystal shard. I couldn't remember what it was called, but Bennett had said it was good for "catch-all magic," so I figured it might work here.

"It's worth a shot," he said. He stretched out his hand and I placed the crystal in it, then opened a map of the city on my phone.

Killian stared at the phone, dangling the crystal over it, silent.

"Are you going to–"

"Shh."

I complied and didn't finish my question. I guessed he was reciting a spell in his head. It amazed me what people with experience could do with few resources and mental power. Bennett had to speak his spells aloud and use various items to power them. I had kept myself and Killian invisible at the auction through mental power, but I had also been holding herbs that magnified my powers.

Before I could finish thinking about that, the crystal twitched. "What?"

"Shh," Killian grunted.

The crystal swung like a pendulum and then moved in a circle. Killian held just the tip between his finger and thumb, and it threatened to jump out of his grasp.

Beads of sweat appeared on his forehead. Whatever he was doing was working, but taking its toll.

The crystal stopped moving.

Killian lowered it slowly to the screen until it hovered just above it. "There," he said finally. "Let's zoom the map in on that section and try again."

We zoomed and tried three more times until we came up with a one-block radius. "Good enough for me," Killian said. He handed me the phone and crystal. "Let's go."

We headed for the door. Marina and Grey would be home soon, and we needed to be gone when they arrived. Plus, we had a lot to accomplish before breaking into my sister's store tonight to steal some spirit stones.

TWENTY-TWO

KILLIAN SPED THROUGH THE city streets without speaking, coming to a sudden stop in front of an old motel. "We're in the middle of the perimeter the crystal outlined. I'd imagine this is the place." He craned his neck to peer down the road. "I don't think there's anywhere else here he would be."

I didn't know the area well enough to have an opinion. We had driven almost twenty minutes across town, and I hadn't been here since my coma. The buildings weren't new, like Marina's apartment, but they were just as nice. Even the motel we parked in front of was well kept. "If you say so," I told Killian. "But now what? There are easily thirty rooms in this place. Do we do more magic to find Johnny's?"

He smirked. "This is where my location spell ends, and we do it the old-fashioned way." He grabbed a wallet out of his back pocket and pulled out several bills.

"You're going to bribe someone?" Well, that was one way to do it.

"Sure am. Let's go." He stepped out of his car and headed toward the main office, not bothering to open my door or wait for me.

I jogged across the parking lot to catch up with his long strides. My legs were tired but not sore. Physical therapy and time were helping me heal.

Killian held the door and ushered me inside, ringing the bell impatiently until a frazzled young woman stepped behind the counter.

"Is there a problem?" she asked.

Killian flashed her a sparkling grin. "I hope you can help me. My dad's memory has failed him a bit, and I need help finding him."

She frowned. "And you think he's here?"

He nodded. "His phone told us he's in this area, but I don't know for sure. If you could just tell me if you've seen him—"

"I'm sorry, sir." She held her hands up, halting Killian's lies. "I can't tell you if someone is staying here."

His features hardened. He slammed his other hand on the counter, leaving cash in its wake when he removed it. "How about now?"

The woman's eyes widened. "Oh, sir, I don't know," she stammered.

"Look," Killian said, urgency creeping into his voice. "It is imperative we find him. Immediately. It's a matter of life or death."

"Oh," she said, her eyes growing even bigger. "Really?"

"Would I lie about life and death?"

Technically, he was being truthful. There are multiple lives that could be affected by Bram not getting that necklace, not to mention Killian's mother's life, if Bram got it instead of him. This was becoming complicated.

Killian's voice entered my mind. *You don't know the half of it.*

I hated when he did that. I didn't think it would ever seem normal.

The woman seemed to contemplate his words. "Okay, fine. What does he look like?"

Killian described him while I stood back, observing. He was a smooth talker, and his good looks didn't hurt his case. I half expected him to mentally thank me for the thought, but he didn't. Instead, he concentrated on the woman, who was taking in his description with concern in her eyes.

"I think I've seen him," she said finally. "But if it's the right guy, he's not here. He left this morning."

Killian's eyes flashed a darker shade of green. "What?"

She smiled sympathetically. "Sorry. He took a late check-out and left around noon, I'd say. I remember because he was especially charming when he brought his room key back. But that's all I know." She shrugged.

Killian glanced at me. "I don't know how we were wrong. He's supposed to be here."

"Why would it be wrong?" I wasn't sure if I should reference the magic or not, so I was purposely vague. I had discovered in my short time awake that not everyone took easily to those who practiced it.

He shook his head. "I don't know." He turned back to the woman. "Is there a chance he stayed back somehow?"

"He turned in his key. I don't see how he could have. Plus, I don't see his car in the lot anymore."

"His car. What kind of car was it?" I asked.

"How is that helpful?" Killian grumbled.

"It might be." I turned back to the woman expectedly.

"Um, silver. Convertible. Newer."

"Thanks," I told her. I grabbed Killian's arm and headed for the door.

As we walked back to his car, he continued to grumble. "I don't know why it didn't work. And my magic only goes so far. I don't know how to find him. Knowing the color of his car does nothing." He opened my car door and waited.

I slid into the car and pondered. "I don't have a solution, Killian. We can try again. Or... is there someone you know who specializes in location spells?"

"Not that I know of." He slammed my door and walked around to his. As he sat down, he said, "I tend to keep to myself. This little team Bram formed is the first time I've worked with anyone in a while. I only know Johnny because we've run into each other a few times while I've been looking for the necklace. He never let on he was looking for it, too. But then again, I didn't tell him I was, either. I wonder what he wants it for," he mused.

"What does it do, anyhow?"

He sighed. "A lot. It's said to be a powerful medium for magic, amplifying whatever spell is being done. Especially when you combine it with another item, like–"

"Like a spirit stone," I finished. "I remember there was a nook in the pendant. Can the stone fit into it?"

He nodded. "I don't know how big the stone is, but yeah, I'd imagine so."

The stones I had seen were way too big for the pendant, so I wasn't sure how they would be combined, but Bram seemed hell-bent on having both items. I assumed they would work together somehow. Speaking of spirit stones...

"How about we head to Pages and potions now? It's earlier than we had planned, but Marina should be gone by now."

He grunted. "I guess we can do that and try to figure out our next move. I don't like not having that necklace, though." He started the car. "I can't believe we had it and it slipped through our fingers. Fucking Johnny Boston."

I stared out the window, my stomach churning. The necklace had been in my home and now it was gone. It was my fault. I just hoped we got it back and stop Bram from bringing forth the Realm of Lost Souls.

<h1>TWENTY-THREE</h1>

THE PARKING LOT WAS empty, which wasn't surprising. The psychic was by appointment only, according to the sign, and Pages and Potions closed at six. It was almost seven, which meant Marina would already be home. We could slip in and out without her ever knowing we were there, as long as my magic could get us in without breaking the lock.

Still, we were quiet as we made our way to the front door. I wrapped my fingers around the doorknob and imagined it unlocking in my mind, repeating the word for *open* in both Latin and Greek, for good measure. With a soft click, the knob turned, and the door swung open.

I smiled, pleased at the ease with which that worked, and stepped inside.

And stood eye to eye with Grey.

"Tori?"

I stammered, unable to come up with coherent words. Obviously, anything I said now was going to sound like a lie.

"And you brought Pretty Boy with you? The magician?" He spat the word.

"Hey now," Killian said, showing his palms. "We don't want any trouble."

"It's a little late for that, my friend," Grey glared at Killian. "I bet you're with Grandpa, aren't you?"

I frowned, glancing between the men. "Grandpa?"

Grey made an exasperated sound. "The dude I just caught inside. White hair, big smile?"

"Johnny," Killian muttered.

"So, you know him," Grey accused, his eyebrows knitting together in an expression I'd only seen a few times before—and never aimed at me.

I squirmed under his gaze, then found my bearings and stepped between them. "Grey, we're not with him. We were just looking for him. Where is he, anyway?" I craned my neck to see past him.

He shook his head. "Tori, I don't know what's gotten into you lately, but I won't get caught up in your lies. Your friend broke in the back door a few minutes ago and tried to steal some stupid rocks from the shelves."

"He's not my friend," I said through gritted teeth.

"Whatever. He's here to steal something, and you guys show up a few minutes later. An hour after the store closed. How do you think that looks?" He crossed his arms over his chest. His body filled my view.

Wherever Johnny was, I couldn't see him. I stared at Grey, hoping to send the message that I was serious. Unfortunately, I probably made my case a little worse. I wanted to apologize, but he was right; we were there to steal something. We just weren't in cahoots with Johnny Boston.

"Where is he?" I asked again, ignoring Grey's question. I knew how this looked. It looked exactly like what it was. But I didn't have time to play around right now. We needed to find Johnny and the necklace, and somehow get around Grey and find the spirit stone.

He glared back at me silently, the stern expression returning, marring his handsome face.

Fine. We'd do this the hard way. Putting my hands on my hips,

I stood firm. "I need to show you something."

Killian held his arm out in front of me. "Tori, no."

I didn't take my eyes off Grey. "It's the only way."

"Show me what, Tor?" Grey sighed and tapped his foot.

I closed my eyes and tried to concentrate, but I couldn't with the sound of Grey's foot against the hard floor. "I'm having a hard time," I confessed.

"With what?" Impatience seeped from his voice.

I didn't want to freak him out with an invisibility spell. Plus, I needed to keep that one a secret in case I had to use it inside. So, I did the next best thing. I put my hands in front of myself, about a foot apart, palms facing each other. I said the Latin words for *fire* and *ball*, and a small flame simmered between my hands. It grew into the size of a softball. I watched Grey's face, unsure of what to expect.

His eyes were wide. He stepped back quickly, catching himself on the doorframe to keep from falling over. "You. You're one of them," he sputtered, his tone filled with hatred.

It sounded like I was a monster. Tears threatened my vision, and I found myself upset that his opinion still meant so much to me.

Grey stretched his hands in front of himself, as if warding off something evil. Me.

"I'm a magician, Grey," I whispered. When he didn't respond, I continued. "I've had this magic ever since the Unveiling, and we think my coma had to do with it."

He shook his head. "I don't want to know, Tori."

Killian placed a hand on my arm, his touch warm and light.

It was a welcome gesture, though it didn't soothe the anger pulsing through my veins. I stared into Grey's hazel eyes, pleading with my expression for him to hear me out. "I'm not a witch; I'm not using my magic to harm people." I wanted to tell him

I was actually trying to help someone important to both of us, but I couldn't bring myself to share that snippet. It had been made clear to me that no one was supposed to know about my involvement with Bram's crazy scheme, and it wasn't a good idea to test his words with my sister's life at stake.

"Does Marina know?" Grey asked.

I shook my head. "I don't think she'd take it as ... well ... as you are."

Grey laughed. But it wasn't his normal warm, throaty laugh, the one I used to find so sexy. It was nervous and accusatory. "Oh, you think I'm taking this well?"

"You haven't called the Department yet, so I'm taking that as a good sign."

He crossed his arms over his chest. "You know I can't trust you now."

My whole body tingled. I wasn't sure if it was because of the anger rising in my chest, or a magical reaction to Grey's statement. I remained silent for a moment, not trusting myself to speak. Instead, I glared at him, breathing deeply through my nose. Finally, I spoke, my voice low and even. "But why, Grey? I'm still the same Tori I was when you saw me this morning, the same girl you trusted years ago. I'm not any different."

"Well...." Killian said.

I punched him in the arm. So much for a calming presence.

"You're not the same, Tori. You're magical. One of them," Grey said.

"One of who? Someone who happened to be granted magical abilities? I didn't ask for this, you know."

He nodded. "But you have it all the same."

Killian made a confused sound. When we both turned to him, his face matched the noise he'd just made. "Dude, you own a magic shop. What's your problem with Tori using the very thing your shop endorses?"

Grey winced. "To be honest, I hate it. I don't trust anyone who comes into this store." He stared pointedly at Killian, and then turned to me. "I especially don't trust people who lie about their magic."

"That's why Marina works the shop, and you just manage the books." I nodded slowly.

His scowl softened. "It was a bookstore, Tori. It was her dream since she was a kid."

"Don't tell me about Marina's dream. I've known her a hell of a lot longer than you have."

His expression hardened again. "I didn't want her to add magic to the store. But she didn't feel she could keep her dream unless she compromised with society."

Killian cleared his throat. "I hate to interrupt this argument, but we need to stop Johnny from stealing the spirit stone."

He had a point. While we stood here glaring at each other, Johnny could be slipping out the back door.

My shoulders slumped. As if being persecuted by my former lover wasn't bad enough, I still had to deal with a thieving con artist. "What do you want me to do?" I asked Grey.

He dragged a hand across his face. "I don't know. I guess we can start with you telling me why you're here, though. Seriously."

"Sorry. The less you know, the better." I put my hand on his arm, and he flinched, jumping back. The action stung, maybe even more than his accusing words, but I didn't have time to dwell on it. "We need to find Johnny. He took something important, and we need to get it back."

He shook his head. "Absolutely not. I can't trust you, Tori. Not anymore."

I sighed. His words made my face burn, but I couldn't focus on that. Instead, I did the only thing I knew to do. I made myself invisible and slipped past him into the store.

"Tori!" Grey called behind me.

Ignoring him, I ran toward the magic summoning me until I stood in front of the clear case at the back of the store. The stones sat inside, just as they had the last time I was here. Their magic threatened to cancel out my own. It was so strong. And I had no idea which one to take. All I knew was that the other famous *lapis*—the *lazuli*—was blue. But that didn't mean the *manalis* was as well. Still, it was a place to start.

Unsure how to get into the case while still invisible, I held my breath. Grey would likely find me in a few seconds. Quickly, I summoned all the intent I could into one phrase, using the Latin words for *hand* and *through.* My hand that was atop the case sunk through the plastic, and I lurched forward, slamming into it. Still, I couldn't see my hand. How was I maintaining invisibility and moving through plastic at the same time?

I touched a stone and felt a surge of electricity through my fingertips. I touched the other, and my arm felt warm and tingly. I had no way of knowing how Ophelia's stone was supposed to make me feel.

After a mental struggle, I scooped all five stones up and tossed them into the pockets of my hoodie. They weighed me down a little, but I kept my head clear and concentrated on my Latin phrases.

Instead of heading back to the men, I made my way through the store quietly. Johnny was here somewhere, probably hiding. Unless Grey had thrown him out already. I hoped like hell that wasn't the case.

A sound grabbed my attention from behind the counter. The stockroom.

I hurried toward it, maintaining my invisibility. If I could sneak up on him, I might be able to grab the necklace before a fight ensued.

"Hi, girly." His voice cut through the silence, the words making my skin crawl.

Did he sense me somehow? Was his magic that strong, or was mine wearing off? Since I no longer had the element of surprise, I responded. "Johnny." As I did so, my hands reappeared in front of me. I couldn't sustain the spell while I spoke. I wondered why I could use two spells at once just moments ago, but couldn't use one and speak now.

"Tori!" Grey called from the front of the store. "Stay right there."

Apparently, I was fully visible again. This was getting better and better.

I ignored him and focused my attention on the man in front of me.

Johnny leaned against the doorframe leading to the stockroom, a large silver necklace in his hand. "You have the spirit stone."

"Do I?"

A smile spread across his face. He would have been a handsome older gentleman if he hadn't been such a jerk. I doubted he was a gentleman, either. "You're out of your league. You won't know what to do with that much power."

I glared at him. "What do you want the stone for, Johnny?" I clenched my fist around the stones in my pocket. I didn't know which one was special, so I couldn't risk him grabbing any of them.

Footsteps pounded behind me, and Grey appeared at my side. "Why do any of you want any of this?"

Johnny threw his head back and laughed. "I'm not here for the stone. But your girl is probably going to use it for something nasty. I wouldn't let her get away with it." He tightened his grip on the necklace. "I just need this jewelry and a few other things, and I'll be on my way."

Killian stepped beside me. "You're not leaving with the necklace, Johnny."

Johnny's smile widened. "Watch me, son." He stood upright and squared his stance. He was ready to fight.

Killian inched forward until Johnny took a step backward into the stockroom. If he forced Johnny back farther, he would be trapped. *Exactly my plan*, Killian said in my head. *You have to help me, though. Your magic is stronger than mine.*

I glanced at Grey, who still wanted answers, but wasn't going to get them. "I'm sorry you got involved in this." Before he could respond, I thought the necessary Latin words and flickered out of sight, moving to stand beside Killian. I touched his arm so he would know I was there.

He didn't respond, instead walking closer to Johnny, who took another step back.

"Where did she go this time?" Johnny's voice betrayed his confidence. He wasn't afraid at all. What did he know that we didn't?

Killian's voice entered my head in a whisper. *I'll distract him. You—*

What? I asked mentally. *I what?*

He didn't respond.

I turned to see confusion across his face. Now was not a good time for him to glitch. I would have to go it alone.

I edged past Killian and into the stockroom.

Johnny was standing in the center, surrounded by boxes on all sides. He smiled at Killian eerily.

It was now or never. I couldn't hold this spell all night.

I took a big step toward Johnny, trying to be quiet. My plan didn't work, however, and I tripped over a box, kicking it with a thud.

"There she is," Johnny said, laziness spread through his voice.

In seconds, his arms were around me.

In my shock, I stopped concentrating. My body became visible again, Johnny's strong arms holding mine at my sides.

"Tori!" Grey shouted.

I was surprised he cared, given his anger toward me moments ago. But I didn't have time to ponder what that meant. I needed to get out of Johnny's clutches and steal the necklace back.

First things first. I stepped on Johnny's foot, hoping to distract him, but his grip on my arms tightened.

"You're not going anywhere, sweets," he said in my ear. "And your friends here aren't going to be much help. See, I know Killian. His power is weak and uncontrollable, and useless in this situation anyhow. And this guy," he said, indicating Grey with his chin, "well he isn't magical at all, is he? The best he can do is call the Department, and I'll be gone before they get here."

Grey sputtered but didn't argue.

Killian grimaced. Johnny was right, and he knew it. His magic was mostly limited to mind reading, which wasn't going to be helpful here. He could perform basic magic such as conjuring a fireball, but he couldn't hit Johnny without getting me, too.

I writhed in Johnny's grasp. "All this over a stupid necklace?" I asked.

He howled in laughter. "Stupid necklace? Oh, my girl. This necklace is worth far more than your life."

Suddenly, in a blur of movement, Killian launched himself at the old man, tackling him to the ground. "How's that for useless?" he asked as Johnny wriggled beneath him.

I grabbed the necklace from his grasp and shoved it into my pocket with the stones.

Johnny bucked, and Killian almost fell to the floor. Instead, he punched the old man in the face, and Johnny's head thudded against the ground. He moaned, and Killian repositioned himself over him. "Call the Department," he said.

I stared at him. That didn't seem like a great idea, even if Johnny was a threat. If he could hear my thoughts, he didn't mention it, and he wasn't speaking to me in my head. We just stared, like two normal people stuck at an impasse.

Finally, Grey spoke. "I'll call. I won't tell them about you, Tori, but you need to get far away from here." He reached for his phone and dialed. Within seconds, he spouted off an address and hung up. "They'll be here soon."

Killian rose from Johnny's unconscious body with a grunt. "We can't stay." He grabbed my arm, attempting to pull me toward the exit.

Not moving, I glanced at him, then to Grey, who watched Johnny with his phone still in his hand. "Look, we'll get out of here, okay? Just forget you ever saw us tonight. And please, please, please don't tell Marina."

Grey shook his head but didn't look away from Johnny. "You know I can't do that, Tori. This is something I can't keep from her. I'm sorry."

I reached for Grey's shoulder, not removing my hand even when he visibly recoiled. "Grey. If there is any part of you that ever loved me, I need you to keep this secret."

He turned to look at me over his shoulder. "You know I ... did." His face flushed as he stammered. He sucked in a deep breath and tried again. "I'm marrying Marina, Tori. I can't keep this from her."

I moved my hands and wiped at the corner of my eye. "Fine. Just give me a couple of days so I can line up a place to live. Can you do that for me?"

Something flashed across his eyes that I hoped was empathy.

"You have one day."

That seemed to be as good as it would get. One day to figure out pretty much every detail of my life. Unfortunately, a place to live and a phone of my own ranked lower on my list of priorities than stopping Bram from raising Ophelia. I needed to consult the only people I could trust now.

But first, I needed to avoid the Department and get out of there before Grey changed his mind. "Fine. Let's go." I let Killian lead me through the dark building and out the front door.

TWENTY-FOUR

AFTER I BUCKLED INTO Killian's sports car, I passed him the neck-lace. Last time I'd hung onto it, it was stolen. I didn't want to be responsible for it anymore. I already had the stones weighing my pocket down, anyhow.

"Was it there?" Killian asked as he drove off the parking lot.

My gaze was already fixed out the window as I contemplated our situation. "Maybe. I'm not sure."

"Was there a stone there or not, Tori?" He was irritated, and I didn't blame him.

I turned toward him. The streetlamps cast unnerving shadows across his face as we passed them, and I wondered how much I could trust him. Or should trust him. I wasn't naïve enough to think one kiss and a few instances of teamwork meant we were in this together.

"Yes, Killian, there were stones. But I can't tell if any of them are Ophelia's or not." I turned back to the window and stared at the night sky.

He sat in silence, likely contemplating what this meant for Bram's plan, and consequently, for us. Finally, he sighed. "I can imagine you don't want to go back to Grey's place right now. Where can I take you?"

I gave him the address and texted Bennett, hoping he was okay with me stopping by. He was both agreeing and concerned, but I didn't elaborate.

"Is this that mage I saw you with?" Killian asked, turning the car away from downtown.

I hesitated, then realized he might tell from my thoughts, so I answered honestly.

"He has the book you were telling me about," Killian surmised. "He can help you find the stone?"

I nodded.

"We should be there in ten minutes," he responded.

We drove in silence until we were almost there. "I'm sorry," he said.

I turned to him, unsure what he meant.

"That everything is going south with your sister. I know you two are close. Hey, maybe she'll forgive you for keeping a secret and you two can make up." His voice held a hopeful tone I didn't feel.

"It's not the fact that I kept a secret that she's going to have a problem with." I watched the houses passing by. The sun was setting, casting an eerie glow over the world. With the exception of the extra stars in the sky, it looked like a typical late October evening. I wished that was the case.

After another minute, we turned into Bennett's neighborhood. Killian pulled up to the curb. "Is this it?"

"Yep," I answered. "I'll get a hold of you tomorrow, and we can figure out where to go from here." I opened the car door and placed my foot on the ground. But instead of getting out, I glanced over my shoulder at him. "I don't know how we're going to get out of this, Killian."

His lips pursed into a line. He nodded wordlessly.

We stared at one another for a moment, possibilities lingering in the air. Not all of them were good, and some were definitely better left unspoken. I missed the old days where such a stare was a sign of sexual tension, rather than apprehension over the potential end of life as we knew it. Hell, I still wasn't used to this life yet.

Finally, he broke the silence. "Have a good night, Tori. We'll talk tomorrow."

The front door opened, and Casey appeared in the doorway, clad in a gray T-shirt and plaid pajama pants despite the early hour.

"Hey, Casey," I said as he moved back so I could step into the foyer. "Were you heading to bed?

He smiled. "Nah. Just getting comfy. But enough about that; Bennett says you need some help?"

"I said maybe," Bennett said from the kitchen. He held up a mug. "I thought I might need this if we're going to be up for a while."

"Have a seat in the living room," Casey told me. "I'll bring us some drinks."

"Water's fine. Thanks, guys." I headed for the living room. The stones in my pockets felt heavier with each step.

Sitting on the coffee table was the brown leather-bound book of magic. I wondered what it would have to say, if anything, about the five stones in my pockets. I also wondered where the sixth one was, and if that mattered.

"So, Tori, what's up?" Bennett called from the kitchen.

I grimaced. Telling them about Bram was not an option, but I needed their help figuring out which stone in my pocket was special. "Well." I paused, unsure how to continue.

Casey came into the living room, frowning. "Is it that bad?"

Wordlessly, I took each stone out of my pocket and laid them on the coffee table. As more and more stones came out, Casey's face contorted in deeper confusion.

"What's with the rocks?"

I sighed. "There's a reason I wanted to know about spirit

stones the other day. And I think one of these might be one. But there's too much power in that shop. I don't know how magicians can go in there, to be honest. I can't distinguish these stones apart. One of them—or more of them, I guess—is powerful, but I can't tell which. For all I know, they're powerful for other reasons and none of them are what we're looking for."

"What you're looking for," Casey corrected.

I looked up, stones still in my hands. "Huh?"

He smiled a little, but it wasn't because he was happy. "You haven't told us why this spirit stone is so important. And it feels like you're hiding something on purpose."

"Hon, don't badger her," Bennett called. "I'm sure she has a good reason for keeping us in the dark. You know, her only real friends, since her sister doesn't know about her magic," he added pointedly as he entered the living room.

"Guys, I–"

He held up the hand not holding a coffee mug. "It's fine, Tori. I trust that you know what you're doing. Or at least, that you're doing what you think is right."

My stomach knotted. Was I doing the right thing? Should I have let Bennett in from the beginning, given him the chance to get the hell out of dodge if he wanted? It was too late for that now. I was knee-deep in this mess, and only Killian knew the whole story. The less Bennett and Casey knew, the better.

I hoped.

I returned my attention back to the stones, feeling each one with my fingertip for a moment before moving to the next. A surge of energy went through my hand with each, though they all felt different from the previous one. "This one, I think... it feels very strong." I picked up a dark blue smooth stone and put it to my cheek. "It's like a surge of electricity, whereas others are more soothing."

Casey nodded. "Possibly. Babe?"

"We can do a spell, I'm sure. We'll figure it out," Bennett said.

I cupped my hands around the stone, feeling its energy course through me. It was powerful, but I didn't know what the *lapis manalis* was supposed to feel like. For all I knew, it was supposed to feel warm and fuzzy, not strong and powerful.

Casey sat in the chair again, observing with interest.

Bennett took a sip of his coffee, then sat down next to me. "Close your eyes.".

I did as he asked.

"Concentrate on what you know about the stone you're looking for, or why you want it."

I didn't know much, so I focused on Ophelia's name and on the phrase *lost souls*. I even translated the phrase into Latin in my mind, chanting it with her name repeatedly.

"Good. Keep it up." Bennett chanted out loud, a combination of Latin and modern English. He was asking for the truth to be revealed, for the owner to present herself.

After a moment, the stone felt hot. I opened my eyes and saw it was emitting a faint blue glow. Its magic multiplied exponentially as the glow increased, along with its heat. I dropped the stone, but the magic flowed through me. I inhaled sharply and put a hand on my chest. The magic was strong, palpable.

"Can you guys feel that?" I asked.

Casey nodded, and Bennett said, "I'm sure it's not as strong as it is for you, but it's there."

I closed my eyes briefly and concentrated on dispersing the magic into the air. Within a minute, the power wasn't as overwhelming, though it was still strong.

"So, it is the one?" Bennett asked, reaching to pick it up. He turned it over in his hands. "It's hot. And still glowing," he said, holding it up for both of us to see.

I touched it with a finger and got a mental glimpse of what could only be Ophelia. She was asleep, or dormant, or somehow inactive. But her energy was still very alive. I could even see her, somewhat. Ophelia had dark, curly hair falling to her mid-back. Her eyes were dark and violet. She was beautiful, enchanting... and lethal. I wasn't sure how I knew that, but I did. She was not a happy keeper of lost souls.

"This is it," I whispered, my eyes still closed.

"Great," Casey said. "So, now what?"

"If we knew," Bennett interjected, touching Casey's arm, "we probably wouldn't have agreed to help her learn about them. I can't imagine much good coming from using this spirit stone."

I nodded. I felt tears well in my eyes and tried to blink them away. "I can't tell you guys. I want to, but it might put you in danger."

Bennett nodded slowly. "You're easy prey; powerful magic and very little knowledge of how to use it. Hell, you don't know much about the world post-Unveiling at all. You might be the most vulnerable magician out there. I'm not surprised someone has tapped you to do something you don't want to do."

I looked at him, letting the tears flow. "How did you...?"

He shrugged. "Your expression says it all. I don't know what you were threatened with, but I imagine you are using this stone for something dangerous, and against your will, too."

I nodded again. "I don't know what to do, Bennett. I feel so helpless."

He clasped a hand over my forearm again, leaving it there. "Whatever you need, we're here for you. Even if you can't tell us what you're into. We understand."

Casey nodded. "Anything you need, Tori."

I attempted a tense smile. "Thanks, guys. You were right, you know. You're about the only real friends I have right now."

Confusion crossed both handsome faces.

"What about your sister?" Casey asked.

Bennett chimed in. "And Grey? Aren't you guys on good terms, despite... everything? I was joking earlier. Kind of."

I sighed heavily. The tears flowed faster, and a sob welled up in my chest. It escaped, and I felt my shoulders heave.

Casey stood up, grabbed a nearby tissue box, and sat next to me on the arm of the couch. After handing me the box, he put his arm around my shoulders. "It can't be that bad."

"I showed Grey my magic."

Bennett gasped. "But he hates innate magic."

"I didn't have a choice. He caught me sneaking into Pages and Potions—"

Casey pulled back to stare at me. "Why were you sneaking in? To get these stones?"

I nodded, sniffling. "I couldn't tell them what's going on, so I snuck in. Grey was there, and..." I couldn't tell them about Johnny without telling them everything else. But they waited patiently for me to finish, so I sucked in a deep breath and said, "and I stole the stones."

Bennett tilted his head to the side. "I'm not understanding this whole thing, Tori. But I'm not going to ask questions if you can't give me answers."

Pinching my nose with a tissue, I squeaked out, "Thanks."

"So," Casey said, standing and facing us. "What do we do now?"

I thought for a moment and then answered. "I hide this stone so no one can find it. It's necessary for a spell that will bring its owner and her realm here. We definitely don't want that."

Casey furrowed his eyebrows. "The owner's realm? What about the soul of the keeper, like you said before?"

I sighed and told them what I had discovered about the improper translation, leaving out everything about Bram, Killian, and blackmail.

"Wow," Casey said when I finished.

"Not good," Bennett confirmed.

Restless, I stood and paced the length of the room. After a few laps, I stopped. "Help me hide it."

Bennett and Casey started speaking together, each stammering their excuses.

I fixed each of them with a raised eyebrow.

Bennett stood. "Tori, we want to help you. But if you're saying this is dangerous, then maybe we shouldn't know where the stone is hidden."

It made sense. But I didn't know how to hide an object magically on my own. My powers may have been strong, but they were in their infancy. I couldn't bank on my knowledge of Latin to make up chants that would work every time.

When I told them so, Bennett nodded. He reached for Casey's hand and squeezed it. "Babe, she's right," he said. "To secure an item like that, she needs a specific spell. Chanting *hide the stone* in Latin probably won't cover it."

Casey closed his eyes for a couple of seconds, then opened them and watched Bennett. "This sounds like a dangerous situation. You're probably already in trouble because of training her in public. I don't want you to help her hide this and get blackmailed into doing something horrible, too. Or worse. It's too risky."

Bennett opened his mouth to speak at the same time I started to protest. But Casey cut both of us off. "Which is why I'll do it. But you can't know where we hide it or how to uncover it, Bennett."

Bennett shook his head. "No."

Casey took Bennett's other hand and held them both. I stood

in the middle of the room, clenching and unclenching my fists in anticipation. "Yes. You said yourself her chants won't cover it. She needs a mage who can help her with a secure spell. But it can't be you. No," he said, letting go of Bennett's hands and putting his own in front of his chest in protest, "don't argue. I'm going to do this because I love you. And if you're not cooperative, I'll wipe your memory when I'm done. So, hush up."

Bennett stared at his lover in awe. Finally, he nodded slowly. "Okay. You do this. But be safe about it." He looked at me. "He'd better come back in one piece, Tori."

I nodded. "I'll do my best. So, where do we start?" I asked Casey.

He stood up, grabbing the book. "Garage."

I flashed Bennett an apologetic look and followed Casey to the garage. "He's going to kill you," I told him once the door was shut behind us.

"Only if this doesn't first," he answered solemnly.

"Um, Casey? Is this spell dangerous?" I twisted my ring around my middle finger.

He set the book on a workbench and turned to me. "It sounds like whatever you're into is dangerous, and you're asking for help. So I'm going to help you."

"But Bennett seems to think—"

He smiled, showing me straight white teeth. "Bennett is a worrywart. This spell itself isn't dangerous. He just doesn't want me getting involved with whatever you've gotten into."

I chewed on my lip, unsure of what to say. He was right that it was dangerous, yet here he was doing it—for me, someone he had just met.

"Let's get started, okay? Give me the stone."

I handed him the stone, its power seeping into my hands even after it left them.

Bennett opened a wooden box on the workbench and took out a piece of cheesecloth. He carefully wrapped the stone in the cloth and set it back down. Immediately, the magic in the air diminished.

"What the hell was that?" I asked.

"Enchanted cloth. It's a magic dampener. It will help us keep anyone from picking up the magic scent while we transport it, or later, when it's hidden."

I nodded. "Okay. So, we've dampened the magic. We have a spell book. Are we going to, what, bury it in the woods or something?"

Casey stood and took a step toward me, smiling. "Something like that. Close your eyes."

I did, and then Casey was gone. Everything was gone, and I was once again in the dark.

TWENTY-FIVE

"WHAT THE HELL?" I asked, sitting up and sputtering.

"Casey's a trip, huh?" Bennett asked, handing me a bottle of water.

I peered around—I was in Bennett's living room, on his couch. I snatched the bottle out of his hands but didn't open it. "Trip doesn't quite cover it. He ambushed me! What happened?"

Bennett sat on the coffee table across from me, a wry smile on his face. "He decided not to tell you where he was hiding the stone. He thought it would be better that way. Now no one can read your mind or force the truth out of you."

I shook my head. "How did he... you...?"

"He called me a few minutes ago and told me you were in the garage, passed out. You're lucky he didn't take your memories. He just knocked you out long enough to get out of there."

I felt my head for a knot.

"Magically. He didn't touch you."

I gulped. There was so much magic could do that I had no idea about. I was living my own personal Harry Potter story—which I had always thought would be cool, in theory. In reality, it was more frightening than anything.

"So, what do we do now?" I asked.

Bennett steepled his fingers. "We wait."

"Are we supposed to, like, play Parcheesi and pretend nothing is happening?"

He laughed. "I don't own Parcheesi, but I think that's the general gist."

"This isn't cool. We have to find him." I stood, knocking my knees into Bennett's. "Can't you track the GPS on his phone or something? Oh, I learned a spell for finding people. All we need is a map and ..."

He took my hands in his and stood so we were almost eye to eye. "I'm not going to do either of those things, Tori. I trust Casey. He had a good reason to do what he did."

I shook my hands out of his. "Bennett–"

My phone vibrated in my pocket. It was Grey. Oh, great, the last person I wanted to talk to right now.

"Yeah?" I answered, not bothering to be polite. I knew he was calling to chew me out about earlier.

"Tori? Someone took Marina!"

TWENTY–SIX

BENNETT AND I PULLED up to Grey's apartment in record time. Bennett had assured me teleportation wasn't a real thing, at least in his knowledge, so I resigned to sitting shotgun in his Jeep. As soon as he stopped the car, I flung open my door and ran across the small yard. I burst through the front door without knocking; I did still live here, at least until tomorrow.

Grey was sitting at the breakfast bar, his head in his hands and his shoulders shaking.

I squeezed his shoulder. "Tell me everything." I didn't even bother sitting down. I had too much energy inside me to confine it to a bar stool. "You may remember Bennett," I added as he walked through the door I had left open.

Grey nodded in Bennett's direction but said nothing. "I don't know anything I didn't already tell you. I stayed at Pages and Potions after the Department left, and then I did a quick inventory on some of the more valuable items." He stared pointedly at me, so I knew he was doing inventory because of my visit. And possibly so I would feel guilty that he wasn't here to save Marina. Whether or not that was his intention, it was the result. "When I came home, I assumed she was in bed, so I didn't check on her. Why would I check on a twenty-six-year-old, Tori? What have you gotten into that makes me have to check on a grown woman to make sure she hasn't been kidnapped?"

I took a step backwards. "Grey."

He stood abruptly. "No. Don't. You are into something, you and your new *friends*."

Bennett spoke up. "Hey, man, I get you're upset–"

"I don't even know you. Why are you here?" Grey spat.

Before Bennett could speak again, I interjected, raising my hands in defense. "Bennett drove me, Grey. He's my friend. And he's not involved with any of this, so leave him out of it."

Grey crossed his arms over his chest and glared. "Any of what, Tori? Whatever it is, it got Marina taken while I was at the shop, and you were off gallivanting around town doing God-knows-what." He took a breath, and I thought he might be done. But he was just gearing up to be even angrier. "Where's the Tori I used to know, huh? You've changed. You never would have pulled this shit when we were–"

"When we were together? You mean before you hooked up with my sister?" I interrupted with a scoff. "You're right, Grey. I'm not the same person I was. I've changed because I discovered my last four-and-a-half years had been a lie—they never actually existed. The man I thought was my fiancé is engaged to my sister. Magic is real. Oh, and I have it. That's right, Grey." I balled my hands into fists and glared at him. "I've known since the ride home from the hospital. I have been meeting with Bennett every day to learn how to hone my magic so I don't hurt anyone. I've met necromancers, mind-readers, people who want to use magic for evil. I've been blackmailed into helping these people, which I've only done to avoid my sister being hurt."

I angrily wiped tears from my eyes. "That didn't work. But I did everything I could."

Bennett put a hand on my arm from behind me. I was too upset to be soothed, but didn't bother to shake it off.

"The Tori you used to know is gone, Grey. This is me now."

He stared at me silently and then nodded. "So, since you've been working with these people, you know how to find Marina."

I gaped at him for a moment. That's what he took out of that whole spiel? "Yes, Grey. I can call Killian and see if he knows anything."

He didn't respond, so I turned away and dialed with trembling hands. Part of me hoped Killian knew where Marina was, but if he knew and hadn't called me yet... well, that signaled I couldn't trust him, after all.

The phone rang in my ear. And rang. Finally, a nondescript voicemail introduction played, and I hung up without leaving a message. "He's not picking up," I said, not turning to face Grey. I didn't want to see the anger and disappointment on his face.

Grey cursed and it sounded like he hit the counter or wall with a fist.

I flinched. I had never seen him become violent in all our time together. Though, that time was much shorter than I thought it was. Still, this was a side of Grey I didn't expect.

It wasn't that I didn't also feel angry or worried. My stomach was in knots over Marina's disappearance. But Grey's verbal attack had made me focus on him rather than her, at least for a few minutes. I turned to Bennett, tears threatening to spill.

He offered a sympathetic expression and pulled his own cell phone out. "Casey will help us look. Maybe with more people, we can find her."

"More magic, you mean," Grey snarled.

"That too," Bennett responded.

"Don't you think magic has done enough in this situation?" Grey asked, running a shaky hand through his hair.

For a brief, inappropriate moment, I had a memory of running my own hands through his hair, which he used to love so much. But I shook the thought off and put my hands on my hips.

"Marina wasn't taken by magic, Grey. She was taken by a person who wants my help to do something horrible. I've been helping him to keep Marina—and the rest of you—safe, but I'm trying to come up with a way to stop him before it gets too far."

"I'd say it's gone too far."

Grey had a point. This situation was surprising, especially since Killian and I had just spent the twenty-four hours obtaining the objects Bram desired. But Halloween was tomorrow, so he was probably getting restless that we hadn't brought him the necklace and spirit stone yet. This was likely his way to ensure we followed through rather than trying to sabotage his plan. Bram—one, Tori—zero.

I sighed, letting my hands fall to my sides. "It has, you're right. But I think I know where Marina is. Let's go. Bennett, call Casey from the road." I spun toward the door.

Grey's keys jingled. "I'll follow you. Once we find Marina, I want as far away from all of this as possible."

I wasn't surprised this sealed my fate as far as Grey was concerned. I just hoped he had given me time to get my meager belongings out of his apartment before I was shut out of their lives.

As we pulled up to Bram's house, Bennett whistled. "This is where your blackmailer lives? I'm not sure whether to be disgusted or impressed. Surely someone with this kind of money can just buy whatever he wants, right?"

"It's a little more complicated than that."

A car door slammed, and Grey appeared at my car door. "Let's go," he ordered as I opened it. He began to run up the long driveway, but Bennett and I each grabbed an arm.

"We have to be cautious," I told him. "There are only three of us, and we haven't been able to reach Killian or Casey. We could be outnumbered as soon as we walk in."

He looked at me like I had three heads. "That's my fiancée in there."

"And my sister." I squeezed his arm. "We have to be careful. Have a plan."

"The plan is, we charge in there and get Marina back. I'm not arguing about this." Grey wrestled out of our grips and stalked up the driveway. He peered over his shoulder. "You can stay there, or you can come with me. After all, she is your sister."

Bennett and I exchanged a glance and followed Grey. I wanted to warn Grey who he was dealing with, but I didn't think it would matter at this point. Instead, I followed him silently with Bennett behind me.

Just as we reached the porch, the door creaked open.

"I've been expecting you," Bram said, his voice low and quiet.

I edged between the guys and stood directly in front of Bram. He was about an inch shorter than me, so I made a show of looking down at him. "I want my sister. Unharmed. I'm not fucking with you anymore, Bram."

He smiled mischievously but didn't respond.

I moved to push past him, but he stepped aside and let me through. With Grey and Bennett close behind me, I searched the great room, kitchen, and hallway between to no avail. By the time I found the dining room, I was too angry to cry. My body tingled with magic that threatened to explode. "Bram!"

He entered the room and leaned against the wall. "Do you really think I'd kidnap someone and leave her in the dining room?"

"I don't know how evil masterminds think."

Grey, towering over Bram, grabbed him by the neck and slammed his head against the wall he was already leaning against. "Where is my fiancée?"

Bennett stepped toward Grey, a hand outstretched like he wanted to intervene. "Do you know who that is?"

"I don't care," Grey growled.

Bram made a gurgling sound, his hands clawing at Grey's arms.

"You're choking the governor," Bennett said with a mixture of fear and awe. "The fucking governor is a blackmailer. Oh gods, Tori, what have you gotten into?" He whipped his head around to face me.

"Does it really matter right now?" Grey asked through gritted teeth. He leaned in until he could have kissed Bram had he wanted to. "Where. Is. She?"

Bram's eyes bulged. He gurgled a few sounds until Grey released his grip. "Not here."

"Then where?" Grey emphasized the last word by smashing Bram against the wall again. He had showed more concern for Marina in the last minute than he ever had in our relationship. Then again, I'd never been kidnapped by the governor for an evil plan.

As the sound of the second thud resonated around the large room, footsteps approached quickly. Bram's hired men. The enforcers.

"You have to let him go, Grey," I said firmly. When he didn't respond, I touched his arm, not moving when he tried to shake off my hand. "As much as I want this bastard to die, we might not find Marina if he can't talk."

Grey's shoulders slumped as he weighed my words. Finally, he let go of Bram's throat and the man slumped to the floor.

"Stop!" a voice called from behind us.

We turned to find two tall, bulky men blocking the doorway

we had entered through. The other doorway was filled with two more men, hands on the weapons at their sides.

At least they spoke first and didn't just go straight for the violence. Though I wasn't sure we'd get out of this situation without an incident.

"It's okay," Bram said from the floor. When everyone turned to him, he motioned the men off with his hand. "Stand watch, but don't engage."

I was thankful for the moment, but we weren't out of the woods yet.

"Where's my sister?" I asked Bram again, stepping close enough I could kick him.

"Where's the stone?"

My body deflated. "I don't know."

"Then I don't know where your sister is."

Grey stepped forward, but Bennett held him back with a hand on his chest. "Not worth it, man. Look at all the muscle in this room."

Grey growled but stayed where he was.

I straightened my back, trying to portray a confidence I didn't feel. We were in deep, and I had messed up royally. "Bram, I honestly don't know where the stone is. It was hidden, and I wasn't told where."

"And why would you do such a stupid thing?" he asked.

In response, I glared silently.

"Bring in Killian," Bram said to the men in the doorway. He slowly stood and wiped his hands on his pants, as if there was dirt on them.

Killian? My heart raced even more than it already was until the pounding in my ears was almost unbearable. I hadn't been sure if I trusted him fully or not, and now I was even more confused. Was he working willingly for Bram, his story a ruse to make me more vulnerable?

He shuffled in as I examined memories we had shared for a sign of deception. He stopped a few feet away from us, his eyes cast downward. An expression of guilt.

I shook my head, unsure how to process what I was seeing. Had it all been a lie? Was I so naïve that I let myself be suckered by someone with a sob story and a handsome face?

"Tori," Killian began. He stopped abruptly with a glance at Bram.

"Tell me what she knows," Bram ordered.

Killian raised his eyes to peer into mine. He was silent, his face unreadable. After a moment, he said, "She's not thinking about the stone."

Which was true. I had been thinking about how stupid I had been to trust a man I'd barely known, who I'd met as part of a blackmailing scheme.

I never lied to you.

I frowned. He had spoken in my mind after hearing my true thoughts. I had forgotten he could do that, and no one seemed the wiser about it.

I just discovered this part of my power with you, remember? At the auction.

Images of the auction night flooded my brain. Killian in his tuxedo, the twinkling lights, the necklace sparkling on the table.

Do you know where the stone is?

No, I responded. Damn, now he got me thinking about the stone. It was time to find out who he was playing—me or Bram.

"Well? Surely, she's thinking about it now," Bram said.

"She doesn't know where it is." Killian's glance lingered on me before he looked at Bram. "She's being honest."

Bram's voice indicated his patience was wearing thin. "Then who does know where the spirit stone is?"

"Someone who's not here," I answered quickly, so no one else could give away Casey's identity. "And we haven't been able to reach him."

"Oh, well, that won't do. It sounds like we need your friend. If we're going to find the stone, then. If Mr. Costa is telling the truth about what he hears in your head, that is."

Killian grimaced but didn't respond.

"Yes, we need him. And we don't know where he is."

A sly smile spread across Bram's face. "I might be able to help with that."

Bennett's eyes widened. "You—do you have him? Did you take him?"

Killian's brows furrowed. He genuinely didn't seem to know who we were talking about.

Maybe I had judged him too harshly. It was still possible he was being honest and was only going along with Bram for his mother's sake. Maybe.

Bram eyed Bennett carefully. "My men followed him to a cemetery, but they lost him for a while. He had to have hidden the stone during that time. Find it and you can have him back."

"Unharmed," I insisted.

"Unharmed." Bram turned to me with the grin of a madman. "Who do you take me for, Tori?"

"Someone who threatened me and my loved ones more than once."

Bennett touched my arm. "He wants us to search the whole graveyard? There's no way we can find one stone in such a big place."

"If you want your lover and your sister back, you will," Bram said. He strode across the room, his bodyguards stepping aside for him to exit into the hallway. "Midtown Cemetery," he called as he walked out. "Midnight's coming up, so get a move on."

Midnight—the beginning of the day we called Halloween. The anniversary of the Unveiling. The day when the veil between our world and the other unknown ones would be the thinnest and merging them would be the easiest. Once midnight hit, we had twenty-four hours to push Bram's plan off course.

Did Marina and Casey have that much time?

TWENTY-SEVEN

WE STARED AT EACH other after he left, speechless. I rubbed the hem of my shirt between my thumb and forefinger, a nervous habit. Grey paced the room, scowling. Bennett, still stunned, stared into the air with his hands on his head. Only Killian appeared unfazed.

"I didn't know about this," he told me in a small voice. "Any of it."

I shook my head. There was too much stimulation, even within the silence. I couldn't deal with my thoughts about Killian right now. Not only were my nerves wrecked and my body tired, but I tingled from head to toe. I needed to perform magic, quickly, before it let itself out in unpredictable ways.

Killian reached for my arm, but I pulled away. He sighed. "You need to release your magic."

Grey and Bennett turned to me, both wide-eyed. The remaining two henchmen—one at each entryway—backed up a few steps but maintained watchful eyes over the room.

"I saw what happened before when you got worked up, and your magic came out on its own. You don't want to put anyone in danger, do you?"

Grey's expression hardened, but he didn't say anything. He didn't have to. His look said *you'd better not hurt me, too, like you've already gotten your sister hurt.*

He was right; they both were. I needed to release this energy before I made the room shake—or worse. Closing my eyes, I cupped my hands together to prepare a simple ball of magic.

"Wait," Bennett said suddenly.

I opened my eyes.

"There's a spell to return someone's memory to them, but it needs power behind it. If you're about to spend your magic reserve anyhow, we should try the spell. You may remember where Casey was going to put the spirit stone." His eyes expressed a hope his shaky words didn't.

"We need to do it fast," Killian said.

Bennett nodded. He began patting his pockets, producing items from both his jacket and jeans—a crystal and two pieces of chalk. "I'll need you, too," he told Killian as he kneeled on the floor.

Rather than question or argue, Killian nodded and kneeled with Bennett.

I wasn't sure if I should kneel, as well. No one was being very forthcoming about the plan.

Killian chuckled. "Just wait there and keep your magic from spilling out." He took the piece of black chalk Bennett passed to him.

Bennett muttered something about a memory sigil, then emptied the rest of pockets onto the ground. He had a small vial of liquid, a sachet of yellow herbs, and some white powder.

"Cocaine?" Grey asked from across the room. "Anthrax?" It was hard to tell how much he was joking. Surely, he was, but his voice didn't betray any whimsy.

Killian groaned. "Hush up, pretty boy." He stretched his arms as far forward as he could and drew on the expensive tile floor with the chalk.

Grey's face paled. "You're just going to do it—here, now?"

"Would you rather we wait and see if Bram lets Marina and

Casey go without getting what he wants?" Killian asked, not looking up from the sigil he was drawing.

"You call him *Bram*?" Bennett asked.

"Not the point here," I grumbled.

Grey huffed. "You do whatever is necessary to keep her safe. This wouldn't have happened without you here."

Grey, who used to want my safety—who used to love me—was now unconcerned with what was good for me, or the world. Marina was all that mattered anymore.

Pain stabbed at my chest, so I focused on the symbol forming on the floor. It was unfamiliar, like most magical emblems still were to me.

Working quickly, Bennett was outlining Killian's black sigil with a white circle.

I didn't know if the color made a difference or not, because Bennett hadn't taught me anything about chalk.

Killian responded to my thoughts. "We don't need chalk for much. It helps mages since they don't have magic of their own."

"But we're using my magic, right?"

Bennett glanced over his shoulder. "Yes, but I only know how to do the spell this way." He shrugged. "I'm just a mage, remember?"

Killian stopped drawing and sat back on his knees, wiping his hands. "And I don't do much ornate magic. I can't help but read people's minds, but beyond the basics, I don't really care about it."

Bennett returned to his circle on the floor.

"What kind of basic magic?" I asked Killian while we waited.

"You know—housework, refilling my coffee, that kind of stuff. I didn't ask for this power, you know," he added, his voice softer. He stole a glance toward Grey, who stood silently against the wall, arms crossed. "And it's made my life horrible. Why would

I want to learn more about it?"

"Done," Bennett said, rocking back onto his knees and dusting his hands off.

I stared at the drawing on the floor, the sigil within the circle. It looked like something you'd see in a horror movie. I was in disbelief that this was a real symbol in my life now.

"I need you to come here," Bennett said, reaching for my hand.

Taking it, I lowered to the ground outside the chalk circle, kneeling with Killian and Bennett on each of my sides.

Bennett took my hand and added a couple drops from the vial onto my wrist. It smelled floral, like perfume. He closed his eyes as he rubbed the liquid into my skin, and I figured he was saying an incantation in his head. When he opened his eyes, he guided my hand to the center of the sigil. "Don't chant anything, don't use any words. Just focus on the blank space in your memory—what you remember before and after, and home in on the hole Casey left." His voice cracked as he said his partner's name.

Wanting to reassure him, but not sure how, I invested my energy into following his instructions. Within seconds, I became distracted. "What's with the other stuff you set out?"

"Focus," Bennett said.

I nodded. "I can do this." Closing my eyes, I planted my hand firmly on the ground and strained mentally. When the distracting thoughts resurfaced, I sucked in a deep breath, hoping all that meditating I did in yoga classes would help me now.

Someone's hand touched my shoulder, probably for good vibes or reassurance.

My mind's eye clouded, a rolling fog filling my view. From far away, I heard voices, but couldn't make out the words. I strained further, reaching into the haze until they came closer, louder.

"If I do this, you'll help me find what I need to save her?" The voice was familiar, but sounded like it was in a tunnel.

"I'm a man of my word." Was that Bram's voice?

A figure appeared, silhouetted in the fog. I knew instinctively it was a man, and he was close enough for conversation but too far away to be intimate. His features were cloudy, as if I were seeing him in a dream. Which this kind of was, I guessed.

The voices were silent, seconds stretching into what seemed like several minutes. I wondered if I had lost my connection to them, and what I was hearing in the first place. This wasn't my memory, I was certain.

Finally, the familiar voice spoke again from somewhere nearby. "You say that, but how do I know I can trust you?"

The shorter silhouette laughed, and I recognized the sound. Bram. "Son, you're going to have to trust me if you want to help her. You've been trying for... how long now?"

"Years," the other voice said, crystal clear this time. Killian.

"Exactly. You haven't gotten any closer to finding magic powerful enough to rid your mother of her curse in all that time. You simply don't have the resources." Bram's face shifted into focus, his smug expression filling my view.

Killian grunted, a sound I'd come to recognize. But where was he? Why couldn't I see him?

I looked around, the answer becoming apparent within seconds. In this vision, I *was* Killian. What the hell was happening?

Seemingly oblivious to my confusion, Bram continued. "I have the reach to find what you need, and you know it."

"Then why do you need me?" Killian's voice asked. It was very strange to know it was coming from me, but not.

Bram laughed again.

I hated that laugh.

"Do you think I can be seen doing the dirty work? I'm the

fucking governor, Killian. My men aren't innate like you, and I can't just ask a random magician off the street to help me." He paused. "Well, maybe I could. It's amazing what people will believe when an authority figure tells them." He waved his hand to dismiss the thought. "But you have something those random people don't have—desperation."

I couldn't feel Killian's body or his emotions, but his head turned in a gesture I recognized as shame. His voice said, "I love my mother, Bram. And she doesn't deserve the fate that befell her. If anyone should be cursed, it should be me."

"But dear, sweet Mom couldn't bear to see her son in such pain, so she demanded to be cursed in your place," Bram added.

Killian was silent for a good minute. Finally, he said, "I won't hurt anyone. Don't ask me to."

"I have people for that, if it comes to it," Bram said with no emotion.

Killian sighed heavily. "Just tell me what I have to do."

In an instant, the fog disappeared, Bram along with it. I opened my eyes and stared into Killian's green ones, which were wide and scared.

"What the fuck just happened?" he asked, his voice a mixture of anger and fear.

Bennett jumped back from where he had been standing next to me. "Did it not work?"

"Oh, something worked, all right. But I don't think that was supposed to happen," Killian said.

Grey unfolded his arms and took a couple steps toward us. "What happened? Did you remember?"

I felt a little bad that I couldn't tell him the answer to finding Marina, but his demanding voice made it difficult to feel genuine sympathy. "No, I didn't remember... my memories, at least."

Bennett and Grey stared at me, confused. Confusion also

clouded Killian's face, but I had a feeling he had a similar experience to me. That would be my first line of action—figuring out what he had seen.

I turned back to him expectantly. "I was in *your* memory. Bram was there. I think you were agreeing to work with him." I lowered my voice. "He said your mom took on a curse that was meant for you—is that true?"

Killian nodded and wiped a hand down his face. "My biggest regret. So, you didn't see it happen. You just heard Bram mention it?"

"Correct. Why didn't you tell me? I could tell there was more to the story—to your guilt—than you let on."

"We're practically strangers, Tori."

Admittedly, that stung a little. It was technically true, but we had been through a lot together in the short time I'd known him. And after seeing his memory, I was pretty sure I could trust him. He was just trying to save his mother. But I tried to keep any emotion off my face and focused on my next question. "You saw something too, didn't you?"

His green eyes flitted to Grey and back to me. "It wasn't one coherent memory, like yours seemed to be. More like a montage of moments. Your hair was shorter, and you were with him in all of them." He glanced at Grey again.

"You saw my memories with Grey?" Why would he see that?

He shrugged. "Your sister was there, too, sometimes. I saw you guys moving into an apartment and him proposing. It just seemed like a lot of happy times. Was that what you were thinking of when you touched the sigil?"

"Not at all," I said, shaking my head. "I was remembering everything I could about being with Casey right before the hole in my memory."

Bennett clicked his tongue. "I'm sorry, guys. I don't know what happened." His face crumpled. "If you can't remember, we're never going to find Casey."

"Or Marina," Grey added, though his voice wasn't as haughty as before.

I took a breath and counted to five as I let it out. "We'll find them, guys. First, we need to address the spell. Killian, you said you saw all those memories, but they didn't actually happen."

"What do you mean? What did I see then?"

I began to speak, but Bennett cut in. "I've been thinking about your coma, Tori. I think we can say with a fair degree of certainty that it was magically induced. We still don't know why it happened, but there were more like you. Some of them still haven't woken up."

"What does this have to do with the pseudo-memories Killian saw?" Grey asked. He stepped closer to us and stood on the other side of the magical circle.

"To Tori's mind, that time she spent in the coma *was* a memory. It wasn't just a dream she had to pass the time. She was, in some sense, living that time out. It was a part of her life. So, I think when she focused on the hole in her memory, that was the memory that came up."

"Why did we see each other's memories, though?" I asked.

Killian's lips settled into a thin line. "I touched your shoulder, remember? It was a gesture of support, but I should have known not to do that when you were performing magic. Somehow that physical connection caused us to get into each other's minds. Creepy," he added with a shudder.

"That's never happened before," Bennett said, shaking his head.

"Well..." I looked at Killian, who seemed unsure what I was going to say. I just blurted it out. "Killian and I can talk to each other in our minds."

"What?" Bennett asked incredulously.

"You can do that?" Grey exclaimed.

Killian shrugged. "I've always been able to read minds—well, since the Unveiling, you know. But Tori's the first person I could talk to mentally. Maybe that connection allowed us to switch memories."

Bennett put his hand on his chin and nodded softly. "Could be." He pondered in silence.

We all glanced at each other, unsure how to proceed.

"Are you still seeing each other's memories?" Bennett asked.

Killian and I both shook our heads. That was a relief, at least. Bennett nodded and continued to think.

"Like I said earlier, I try to avoid complex magic," Killian said. "So, I'm not much help in figuring out what went wrong."

"What if nothing went wrong?" I said, thinking aloud. "It's possible I really don't know where the stone is."

"So, your mind filled in the blank with another memory," Bennett added. "Could be. It's also likely Casey didn't tell you where he was putting the stone in the first place, so we couldn't retrieve the memory. Damnit, Casey." Bennett's face scrunched up, like he was trying to avoid crying.

I put a hand on his shoulder. "We'll find him, Bennett. And Marina too," I said with a quick glance to Grey. It was hard to look at him, knowing that Killian had seen us in my memories, especially since I didn't know all the memories he saw. Hopefully, it wasn't anything I wouldn't want someone else to see.

Killian laughed. "No worries. I promise."

Would I ever be able to have a secret thought around this guy?

"Sure. My magic is unpredictable, remember?"

I tilted my head toward my shoulder. "You've had it for five years and you still can't control it. Why is that?"

He shrugged.

"Doesn't the Department come after people who can't control their magic?"

"Only if something happens. No chaos has ever come from me reading someone's mind—or not. Or maybe I'm on a list somewhere. I don't really know."

Grey scoffed.

We turned to him, but he didn't elaborate.

It dawned on me that Killian could very well be on a list somewhere, thanks to my sister's reports to the Department. I hoped he didn't hear that thought.

If he did, he didn't let on.

"Guys," I said slowly, hating what was about to come out of my mouth. "We're going to have to search that cemetery. Could magic help us?"

The group sighed collectively. It was going to be a long night.

TWENTY-EIGHT

AFTER AN HOUR OF searching Midtown Cemetery in the dark, I turned to the guys with me and sighed. "None of our magic has found the spirit stone yet. And this place is huge. We're not going to find it."

"Maybe that's a good thing," Killian said softly. "Without it, Bram can't complete his plan."

"Then we won't find Marina," Grey snipped. "Or Casey, either."

"He's right. We need to convince Bram to give us Casey so we can get the stone."

Everyone grumbled, but we all knew it was our only option.

Killian pulled out his phone. Someone answered quickly after he dialed. "It's me. No, we haven't found it. Yes, we're at the damn cemetery, Bram. Ask your men—two of them are trailing us."

We all turned to see two of the men from Bram's house standing beside their car at the edge of the grass. They stared at us, stone-faced.

"We need Casey, Bram. Yes, I'm sure. We won't get to the stone without him, especially if you want to do the spell before the sun rises." Killian grimaced as he said the last part. "Yes, yes, fine. Just tell me—okay. Thanks." He hung up. "You won't believe this, guys."

"Is he okay?" Bennett asked, his words rushed.

"As far as I know. He's in the groundskeeper's building. At this cemetery."

"I think we passed it on the way in," Grey said.

"He's been this close the whole time?" Bennett seemed both happy and angry.

"Let's go get him," I said, putting a hand on his arm.

It didn't take long to walk to the building. It was near the edge of the cemetery, but on the backside, opposite where most people would enter the graveyard. We had entered that way to avoid being seen from the road. Which was probably why Bram picked the building to hold his hostage.

"Do you think Marina's there with him?" Grey asked.

"I hope so," I answered honestly. She was not going to be happy with me, but I needed to know she was safe.

We walked most of the way in silence. Occasionally, we heard the crunching of leaves behind us, signaling that the goons still followed us. Finally, we reached the building. The door was locked, of course, but Killian made haste with picking it. He opened the door and motioned for us to be quiet as he stepped in first. We followed suit, treading lightly.

The main room was filled with items I'd expected—shovels, pruning shears, tarps, and the like. A commercial lawn mower sat on one side. But there was no Casey.

I shivered and rubbed my hands on my arms. It had been cold outside, and it wasn't any better inside. I guessed they didn't really need heat in this overgrown storage shed.

"Over here," Killian whispered. He pointed to a closed door on the side of the room. Opening it, we discovered a flight of stairs. A basement. Of course, Bram would keep hostages in a basement.

It was difficult to descend quietly, but it didn't matter. Two of Bram's men stood at the base of the staircase, waiting for us.

Their stern expressions didn't waver as they watched us, but they stepped aside to let us into the room.

I gulped, hoping we weren't about to be trapped as well. As I entered the room, I took in my surroundings. The basement looked like the perfect one to hold hostages in—a single light in the ceiling, dust everywhere, and a mess of clutter against the far wall. But what made it even more realistic were the two metal chairs in the middle of the room.

Casey and Marina each sat on a chair, hands behind their backs, rags tied around their mouths.

Grey and Bennett flew forward, only to be stopped by one of Bram's men. "Wait here." He motioned toward Casey, and the other man walked toward him.

Bennett's eyes widened.

The man bent and took the tie out of Casey's mouth.

"Bennett! What are you doing here?" he asked, coughing.

"What do you think? Saving you." Bennett wiped at his eyes.

I smiled even though I couldn't muster much happiness. Casey and Marina were alive and seemingly alright, albeit a little dirty. And was that a bruise on Marina's cheek? But even though we'd found them, we weren't out of this mess yet.

Marina glanced at me, then to Grey, as if unsure where to focus her attention. She tried to speak but was muffled by the fabric in her mouth.

I turned away, unable to see her like that. Knowing it was my fault. I wondered if she knew it was my fault. Well, if she didn't already, she certainly would soon.

"You shouldn't have come," Casey said.

"How could I not?" Bennett asked, his voice soft. "I love you. I'll always find you."

"You plan on this kind of thing happening again?" Casey asked.

No one laughed at his attempt at humor.

The henchman worked the ties behind Casey, and in a moment, they fell free.

His feet hadn't been tied, so he stood up, rubbing a wrist with his other hand. He stepped forward timidly, as if waiting for permission. When no one stopped him, Casey lunged at Bennett, embracing him tightly.

From my new view of Casey, I could see a trail of blood trickling from his hairline over his eye. I closed my eyes to block out the view of my friend hurt—because of me.

"Why am I free? And what about her?" Casey asked as he pulled away from Bennett.

Bennett didn't respond immediately, as if weighing how he wanted to break the news to his partner. Yes, he was free, but only to help Bram with a task that would change the world. Again.

Casey looked from Bennett to me, and finally to Killian. "Someone tell me."

When no one spoke up, Killian cleared his throat. "We can't find the spirit stone. Bram is letting you bring us to it." He glanced at his shoes after he spoke.

"I won't." Casey said, stepping back from Bennett.

Bennett reached up to wipe away blood that threatened to fall into Casey's eyes. "We tried to restore Tori's memories when we couldn't find you, but it didn't work."

"Yeah, someone knocked me out without telling me where he was going first," I said dryly.

Casey blinked as a stray drop of blood reached his eyelid. "I thought it best if no one knew where it was. Tori made it sound pretty bad if the stone got into the wrong hands. I mean, look at us now. I still say it was the right move."

The first henchman took a step toward us. "It won't be right for you if you don't figure out where it is. I'm sure your partner here would like you to come home after this is over."

Bennett's face crumbled. "Oh, Casey."

Casey flashed him a heroic smile. "It'll be okay, babe. If it's not okay, it's not over yet."

"It's not okay, *and* it's not over yet. Bram wants the stone. And I've been instructed to give her a less than pleasant stay if he doesn't get it soon," the henchman said, indicating Marina with his hand.

His partner was still standing behind Casey's chair. He walked around to be in front of Marina and bent down until he was eye level with her. He reared a clenched fist back like he was going to hit her.

Casey jumped in front of him. The blow landed solidly in his gut, and he doubled over in pain.

Bennett screamed, and Marina wailed.

"Guys," I said, my voice raised to be heard over the ruckus. "I get why we don't want to give Bram the stone. I do. But maybe we need to give in."

All eyes turned to me. Grey, who was watching Marina intently, seemed on board with the idea. Marina was too scared to have much of a reaction besides continuing to cry. But Bennett and Casey showed their disdain. "We can't," Casey said, clutching his abdomen as he stood.

Bennett rubbed his back. "I agree that it's not a good idea, but neither is dying over it."

Killian turned to me, staring straight into my eyes. "I agree. And I wouldn't suggest you try what your blond friend is thinking."

Frowning, I turned to Bennett.

He stared past me at Killian. "There are five of us, and only two of them." He nodded toward Bram's men, his hands balled into fists at his sides.

I knew then what he was thinking, and I couldn't say I didn't agree. Our little group had two magicians and two mages, and we didn't know if Bram's thugs had magic at all.

Some of them do, Killian told me in my mind. *And don't forget the two that were following us.*

He was right. The odds in our favor were drastically decreasing. Two mages—one of which was injured—and two magicians—one of which only practiced basic magic, and the other was new to magic altogether—were probably not a match for four hired henchmen, magical or not. And Grey would be absolutely no help on our side.

"It's not worth it, guys," I said with a sigh. "Bram may not seem like much, but we don't know what kind of power his men have. He has a necromancer with him, at least. I'm not sure what all he can do, but I don't want death magic turned on me."

Grey folded his arms again. "So, we're going to take this dude's word instead of trying to get out of here? You guys can't be serious." He stared at Marina as he spoke.

I turned toward the nearest security guard. "Can we let everyone go, and I'll figure this out on my own? Bram wants me, not them. He only took Casey and Marina to get me to do what he wants. I'll do it. Just let them go."

The man looked like he wanted to laugh at me. Before he could deny me, though, Casey spoke up. "You can't."

I held my hand up to silence him.

"No, I mean you can't. Not without my memories." He shook out of Bennett's reach and stepped toward me. "I don't like this, Tori. But I don't want to cause harm to everyone else. So, I'll get my memories back."

I glanced at my sister, who turned her head toward the wall. There was no sense trying to shield her from magic at this point.

She was going to know everything soon enough. I nodded.

Bennett reached into his pockets and grabbed the same items as before. He handed Casey a piece of chalk and squatted to draw the memory sigil in black chalk, not saying a word.

Casey drew the white circle, and they both kneeled beside the drawing. He took the vial Bennett handed him, dripping liquid onto his wrist and rubbing it in, just like I had. He stuck out his tongue, and Bennett placed some of the yellow herb on it.

I guessed I didn't need the herb when I did it, since my magic was innate. But I wasn't going to interrupt their ritual to ask. And I certainly wouldn't be touching Casey while he performed this magic.

Bennett rocked back to sit on his heels. "Just forget everyone else is here, babe. Concentrate on the hole in your memory."

Casey nodded and leaned forward onto all fours so he could touch the center of the sigil. He closed his eyes and breathed in deeply. He sat like that for several minutes.

I wasn't sure if he was waiting longer than I was or not, because for me the memory came and went quickly. When he had been silent for a few minutes, I fidgeted, shifting from one foot to the other.

Finally, Casey opened his eyes and sat up on his knees. "I know where it is." His voice showcased his hesitation and pride in being able to remember. He and Bennett stood up and turned to face me and Killian. "Let's go get the stone."

"One thing first," I said. I turned to the nearest henchman. "Let her talk." I knew better than to assume they would let her go with us.

He looked at his colleague, who shrugged. Within seconds, Marina's mouth was free. "Oh, my god." She coughed. "What, what just happened?" Marina choked out. Her voice was hoarse, and I wondered if she had been choked or if her throat was simply dry.

My guilt was so strong I almost couldn't look at her. But she deserved an explanation. Too bad I didn't have time to give her one. "Magic," I said curtly, before turning to Grey. "Wait here with her."

He didn't need to be told twice. "Of course." The pain in his hazel eyes was evident; he couldn't hold or comfort his fiancée. Who wasn't me.

"You guys will be okay," I assured them, hoping I sounded more confident than I felt. "We'll be back. When this is done, we'll get you out of here."

I looked at the three men who were going with me. "Ready?"

We headed up the stairs, through the main room, and out the door in silence. As the door closed behind us, Killian took my arm. "I can't go with you."

We all stared at him. He had been this far with us. Was he really going to turn on us now?

He shook his head. "Bram made it clear to me that my mom is still in danger. He sees the fact that he had to have Marina kidnapped as meaning I failed him. I need to get to her before his men do." He gazed into the darkness for a moment, then looked into my eyes. "And if this goes Bram's way, I don't want her anywhere around here."

I nodded. I didn't like it, but I understood. If I could have left town with Marina, I would have. "Go. Take care of her. I hope you find what you need for her." Indecision caused me to lean in for a hug and then lean back and stick my hand out for a shake.

Killian grinned, likely amused by my uncertainty, and leaned forward for a hug. He held me tightly for a few seconds, his scent lingering in the air after he pulled back. "Be careful," he whispered, placing a quick peck on my cheek.

"You too," I said as I released him. The thought of kissing him ran through me, but before I could decide whether to act on it, Killian turned and walked toward the road, where his, Grey's, and Bennett's cars were parked. And then there were only three of us.

TWENTY-NINE

CASEY LED THE WAY, bringing us to a section far away from where we had looked earlier. We never would have found the stone at the rate we were going.

We stayed silent as we trudged across the graveyard. I'd never walked through one in the dark until tonight. It was kind of creepy, especially knowing that magic existed. What else could exist that we'd run into in a cemetery? I pondered Ophelia's Realm of Lost Souls—was it full of ghosts? If so, were they Casper ghosts or horror movie ones? I had so many questions, but no one would know the answers until Ophelia and her realm arrived. If we couldn't find a way to stop it, that was.

After several minutes, Casey stopped before the door to a mausoleum. It appeared to be very old, the stone weathered and needing a power-wash.

My mind conjured images from my favorite vampire show, which frequently saw the heroine searching or battling the undead in such buildings. And here we were, heading inside for a dark, magical purpose. I half expected a vampire to jump out when we opened the door.

Instead, three bats flew out when we opened it, escaping the dark building. They weren't vampires, but they were close enough.

I shuddered as they flew over our heads and into the night sky. "Could you have picked a creepier place?"

Casey chuckled. "This mausoleum is in the back corner of an old cemetery that's seen better days in terms of up-keep. I figured it'd be safe here for a while. I truly had hoped we wouldn't be retrieving it anytime soon." He looked over his shoulder at me as he stepped inside. "You really stepped in it this time, huh, Tori?"

He didn't even know the half it.

I entered the mausoleum a moment later, realizing that Casey and Bennett truly didn't know most of what was going on. Casey might bear the scars from tonight's adventures, judging by the look of the gash on his forehead. He deserved to know why he had been kidnapped.

The structure was small, dark, and very dusty inside. I coughed into a cold hand as I used the other to hold Grey's phone, its flashlight illuminating the stone walls. "Where did you put it?"

Casey shone his phone flashlight around, the light bouncing off the walls. "In the urn," he said, letting the light shine on an empty vase perched inside a crevice in the wall. It probably wasn't an urn—this was a mausoleum, not a columbarium—but correcting him would be silly at this point.

I walked to the pot and reached into it. A spider crawled up my hand and I screamed, jumping back. Spiders and bats. Just how I wanted to spend my night.

The guys laughed, the hollow sound echoing off the walls.

I picked up the large pot, smacked it down onto the spider, then peered into it with my flashlight. There were several stones inside. Only one, however, was blue.

When I grabbed the stone, its magic flowed through me, hot and intense. This was it, for sure. I could see Ophelia more clearly than before. She was still asleep, but she was strong.

"I wish we didn't have to give this to Bram," I said, holding it up. "But my sister's life is at stake."

Casey nodded. "We know you don't have a choice. I would do it too, for my sister."

Bennett put an arm around Casey's shoulders. "I would do it for you." He leaned over for a kiss, and I averted my gaze.

Finally, we were ready to go. I put the stone into my pocket, and we headed back across the cemetery toward the groundskeeper's building. We had a few minutes of walking ahead of us, so I used the time to illuminate my new friends on what they were now involved with.

They listened with rapt attention as I rushed through Bram's plan and how Killian and I had been enacting it. At one point, Casey stopped with his hands on his head and stared at the sky silently.

I couldn't blame him for being angry, or scared, or over-whelmed. I was all those things.

Just before we reached the building, I finished. "I could try to flub the spell," I said.

Bennett shook his head. "Don't you have someone else work-ing the spell with you? The necromancer?"

Shit, I had forgotten about Poe. "I could pretend it's an acci-dent?"

"And you'll just have to keep redoing it until you get it right," Casey said.

He was right, of course. I gritted my teeth and opened the door in front of us. "I don't know how to stop this, guys."

They followed me inside silently. It seemed as if no one had a way to stop Bram's plan without Marina getting hurt. I could only hope Killian would fare well with his mother.

"Do you want to go back in there?" Bennett asked Casey as we crossed the floor of the main room.

"I'm not waiting out here on my own. This place has bad

vibes."

I couldn't tell if he was joking or serious, but I was surprised he wanted to return to the basement, where he had been held hostage not too long ago.

We clomped loudly down the steps, and I stood as tall as I could before both guards. I assumed the other two were around somewhere, having followed us from a distance as we collected the stone. Holding the spirit stone in one hand, I ordered, "Now let my sister go."

Bram's goon smiled at me. "Do you really think it's that easy?"

I lifted my chin and stared down my nose at him, despite him being a little taller than me. It was necessary to use all the bravado I could muster. Now was not the time to cower in fear. "Get Bram on the phone. Tell him we brought the stone, and he needs to let Marina walk."

From across the room, Marina whimpered. Her arms were still tied behind her back, but her mouth was free.

Grey sat on the floor in front of her, his hands on her knees, comforting her. At least he was allowed to do that.

The man in front of me grabbed his cell and hit one button. "She's back. With the stone." He held the phone out between with the speakerphone on.

Bram's voice boomed through the speaker. "Good. I knew she'd come around."

"What do you want us to do with the sister?"

Bram hesitated.

I clenched my fists at my sides. If he didn't let Marina go, I didn't know if I could control my anger enough to keep my magic at bay.

"Bring the sister upstairs," Bram said finally. "She's going to watch."

I protested, but Bram cut me off. "It's not over yet, Tori. Try to double-cross me, and your sister will be more intimately involved than she already is."

"When and where?" I asked him, my voice shaking.

Poe's New England drawl filled the air. "It's after midnight, so we can do it now."

"We'll be there soon," Bram said. "Oh, Tori? Happy Halloween."

THIRTY

WE ALL WAITED OUTSIDE the groundskeeper's building for Bram and Poe to arrive. Why we couldn't wait inside, where it was warmer, I didn't know. Marina was freed from the chair, but each guard had a strong grip on one of her arms. She wasn't going anywhere.

An old car pulled into the cemetery and parked in front of us. Poe got out of the driver's side, and Bram from the passenger side.

"Everyone ready?" Bram asked, clapping his hands together once.

I glared at him.

"Oh, Tori. Where's your sense of fun?" he asked. He motioned me forward and began walking into the grass.

I turned to my sister. "I'm sorry. I didn't want any of this—"

She turned her head, the only recourse she had to get away from my apology.

"Not now, Tori," Grey said.

We didn't know how this was going to go. If not now, then when? But his face showed his resolve, and Marina had made it clear she didn't want to talk to me. I wondered how much Grey had told her about the situation. Probably everything, including the secret I'd kept from her.

Sighing, I put a hand on each of Bennett's and Casey's shoulders. "You two stay here." I shook my head at their arguments.

"Someone needs to stay safe to help Marina and Grey if I can't."

Bennett cast his eyes downward. He had to know I was right; even though he had been studying as a mage for five years, he wouldn't be a match for a demi-goddess from another realm. If it came to it, I needed to know Marina could get away safely.

"Good luck," Casey whispered.

I nodded and walked away. As I stepped away from the shelter of the building, the crisp October air nipped at my skin. My jacket was already zipped up, and I didn't want to waste any magic trying to stay warm. While the thought had crossed my mind, I didn't know how Bram would take it if I ran out of energy too soon. With a deep breath, I trudged ahead.

A few minutes later, I sat cross-legged on the cold ground across from Poe, two large tombstones flanking us. Nearby, Bram leaned against a tall headstone, watching us silently. This might have been his scheme, but he didn't have any magic. The only way he could participate was by making sure I didn't run away. Though the two men who had been following us were also nearby, not to mention the two holding onto Marina. Suffice it to say, I couldn't go anywhere.

On the ground between me and Poe, we had three candles, the necklace, and the spirit stone. The air was heavy with magic, not just from the artifacts before us, but from the world. All Hallows Eve was the day when the veils thinned and magic from other realms could be felt, at least by those of us who had magic in our veins already.

Poe picked up the stone and fitted one end of it into the crevice of the necklace. The stone itself was bigger than the jewelry, but it locked into place as if both pieces were magnetic. He looked at me expectantly.

I nodded and frowned in concentration. It was my job to recite the difficult chant. It was more complex than normal, combining the Greek Poe used for his magic with the oldest version of Sanskrit I could reliably translate. I scanned the phrases I had written on a piece of paper once and then read aloud slowly.

Poe joined in, his pronunciation awkward and his voice shaky. I secretly hoped he fudged the words and instead of raising Ophelia, we'd create a flock of birds or fill the cemetery with fluffy kittens.

I was unlucky. After stammering through the first iteration, Poe's voice became louder with confidence. We said the words in unison, asking for the sleeping goddess Ophelia to hear our plea and grace us with her soul, her realm.

After four turns of the phrase, the air around us dropped several degrees. I shivered and tugged my jacket closer to my body, careful not to mess up the chant.

I added a phrase asking Ophelia to come to us, and Poe lit a candle. A blue flame shot through the air several feet high before condensing into a normal-sized flame. It was still black, though, which was enough to make me stutter over a routine Latin word.

Poe glowered at me.

I collected myself and continued. Another new phrase, another candle lit, and another tall blue flame. This time, I was ready for it.

The temperature dropped again, and the wind picked up around us. The flames danced as if we were indoors, but my hair was blowing into my face.

Goosebumps decorated my skin. As I said the last new phrase, Poe lit the last candle. I prepared myself for the tall blue flame, but not for the vortex of swirling wind around us. The paper in my hands flew away, and I gasped. My hair whipped around, stinging my skin when it made contact.

From memory, I recited the chant again, and soon, it was so cold I could see my breath. It hadn't been warm to start with, and I had dressed appropriately for the cool autumn night. It didn't feel like fall anymore, though; this was winter weather. I looked at the sky, but no snowflakes fell. I sucked in a breath, my throat and lungs cold. When I let out, I almost choked on it.

Across from me, Poe was rubbing his hands together to warm them. He continued to recite the words for the tenth time now by memory, as I was. We watched each other and when I was ready, I nodded. Together, we grabbed the necklace which held the *lapis manalis*. Immediately, a surge of energy flowed through the necklace and into my hands and arms. My eyes widened and teared up, and my breath came in involuntary short, quick bursts. Poe's was the same. I couldn't see or hear Bram to know how wide the vortex and temperature change spread.

With the wind so heavy, I couldn't hear my own words, let alone Poe's. I shouted the chant, and Poe followed suit. We shouted into the wind, louder and louder as it became stronger. We each used our second hand to grab onto the necklace, which swayed in the wind despite the weight of the stone. The necklace was hot, burning my hands, but I didn't let go.

Against the howling of the wind, a new sound appeared. It was a cacophony of shrieks and bellows coming from all sides. Around us, apparitions formed in various shapes, all shades of gray.

And then she appeared.

Ophelia, her skin olive-toned and her hair thick and curly, hovered beside us, a few feet from Bram. She was not completely corporeal, but her violet eyes glowed. She was beautiful in a way so close to perfect it was almost frightening. Her mouth was set into a thin line.

You'd think she would be happier that we woke her up from her magical slumber. But maybe interdimensional travel was unpleasant.

She spread her arms, the belled sleeves of her cream-colored dress flowing. She opened her hands, light emitting from her fingertips. The apparitions nearest her slowed to a stop and stared at her. Within moments, Ophelia's ghostly figure turned solid, and her feet touched the ground.

She spoke in something that sounded like Classical Sanskrit, but slightly different. She might have said, "You have freed me." Despite the whirlwind around us, I could hear her clearly, as if she was whispering in my ear.

I dropped the sizzling necklace and collapsed onto the ground, panting.

Poe's movements matched my own. The spell had taken a toll on both of us. "Does she speak English?" he shouted to me.

I looked up at Ophelia for an answer.

She lowered her hands, and the wind died down. The night was calm again, except for the crickets and owls and other regular night sounds. Fog formed around us. "I can speak however you wish," she answered. Her accent was thick, and hard to place. "Is this better?"

"It is, thank you," I said. I was unsure how to proceed. Should I bow? Kneel? I was already on the ground, and that didn't seem appropriate either. Her magic pulled me to her, and I stood and walked toward her.

She waited for me to rise and then said, "Good. Tell me, magician. Why have you awakened me?" She glared as she spoke, but wasn't incensed, as I had originally surmised. She seemed more annoyed than anything.

Still, I stammered through a response. "Were you not a prisoner to be freed?"

She closed her eyes for a moment and gave a curt nod. "I was given to sleep several centuries ago. Many have tried, I imagine, to rouse me. How is it the two of you have succeeded where others have failed?"

I looked to Poe and then behind me, at Bram. I really didn't know.

A small smile formed on her beautiful face as she took in our artifacts. "You have found my spirit stone." She beheld the figures around us, gesturing widely with both arms. "Therefore, my realm is merging with yours."

"Yeah," I retorted. I had nothing profound to say to that. Bram's murderous desires brought a world of undead beings with it. I figured we'd probably spend years clearing this realm out, if it was even possible. "We have no need of your spirits," I told her. "Can we have an audience with you without the realms merging?"

She laughed, and I knew my answer.

I turned to Bram, my heart pounding. "Look at what you've done."

A smile tugged on his lips. He stepped over the necklace—still glowing red-hot—and candles to stand before Ophelia. "Lady Ophelia," he said, bowing slightly.

Ophelia's eyebrows raised in amusement. She waited silently for him to continue.

He stood and gazed into her violet eyes. "I have a request, one that should be simple to someone of your immense power."

"Go ahead, mortal." Ophelia arched an eyebrow at Bram and waited.

"My family," he started. His voice cracked. "My wife, my little girl. My unborn son."

Ophelia nodded. "Continue."

"What has come of them?"

She smiled warmly. "Their souls are not lost."

Bram did a double take. "You know them? My babies?"

Ophelia put a hand on his shoulder and stared into his eyes. "I know of whom you speak, mortal. But they do not roam my land. I cannot bring them to you."

He shook his head. "No. No, you are the keeper of souls. You guard the gate to the underworld." He dropped to his knees. "Why can you not bring them back to me?"

Ophelia's features warmed. "Because I am the keeper of *lost* souls, my dear. Your family is not lost. Your family was loved beyond measure and had what they needed to move on to a higher plane."

I raised an eyebrow. It was difficult to imagine anyone in Bram's life being *loved beyond measure*. But maybe their death had created the horrible man I knew. "How do you know them, then?" I asked Ophelia.

She turned her attention to me. "Everyone passes through my realm on their way to their ultimate resting place. I assess what you would call their soul, and sort them accordingly. Many remain with me, as they have ... unfinished business ... and their souls cannot move on."

I shook my head. "Wait, so you're saying your Realm of Lost Souls is, like, purgatory?"

She frowned. "In some senses of the word, yes. In others, no."

Oh, that cleared it up.

Bram reached a hand forward and grasped Ophelia's leg.

She didn't jump, but her expression was less sympathetic than it had been.

"Can I see them just once?"

Ophelia shook her head. "They are not in my realm any longer. This man," she said, indicating Poe, "can bring them to you, but not in the form you'd like."

He wiped at his eyes with his free hand. "There must be a way."

"I feel your grief. I understand your pain. I had a mortal family as well, and losing them was confusing for me, and painful. But as keeper of lost souls, I cannot bring to you souls who are not lost."

"Then how can you be a goddess, a keeper of a realm, if you have so little power?" he goaded her, rising to his feet until he stood eye to eye with her.

Ophelia's features cooled again. "I am keeper of the realm by birthright, but I am also half human. My powers are greater than your mortal mind can understand, but they are not unlimited. Especially outside my home realm."

Bram's hands clenched at his sides. He took a step toward her and raised onto tip toes until he was taller than Ophelia. "If I cannot see my family again, I don't wish to live further."

Ophelia put hands on both of his shoulders. "I will not grant what you seek. I will not fight you to appease your broken heart."

He hung his head in contemplation. When he raised it again, his eyes were dull. "Poe, dear friend. We have served each other well, have we not?"

Poe smiled and reached his hands out for Bram, who stepped away. "We have, since childhood. But I'm not sure what you're doing here, friend. We'll try another way to speak to your family."

A slow, sad smile spread across Bram's face. "I've exhausted all my options. I've hurt people for this cause. If Lady Ophelia cannot help, there is no help for me." He paused and stared into the night sky. "Tell Killian he's off the hook, will you?"

Moving more quickly than I expected, given his grief, Bram pulled a knife from the sleeve of his jacket and plunged it into his stomach. His eyes widened as he sank to his knees again, blood pooling onto his shirt.

Poe rushed forward. "What the hell, Bram?" Poe shouted. He put his hands atop of Bram's, which kept the knife in his gut.

"I can't live without them," Bram said softly. "I won't."

The moment seemed to pass in slow motion, giving me ample time to hope Bram's act would be successful because he was an asshole, and then change my mind as I thought about the pain that drew him to his actions. They were still undeserved, and people had suffered due to his greed, but I couldn't watch him die. I wasn't heartless. I wasn't him.

I stared at Ophelia, who still stood behind Bram, her beautiful face twisted into an expression of sadness. "Can you do anything for him?"

Ophelia shook her head. "It's not his time, not yet. The wound will not kill him."

Bram tried to remove the knife, but Poe wouldn't let him. I assumed Bram was planning on stabbing himself again after hearing Ophelia's words.

"Can't you do anything?" I asked Ophelia. "He's hurting."

"He brought the wound on himself," she reminded me. "As well as others, for people other than himself. You know that well." She turned her head toward the cabin where Grey and Marina stood, her still in the arms of Bram's henchmen.

I followed her gaze. Marina's eyes were wide in horror, and Grey's face was ashen. I knew in my gut they wouldn't forgive me for getting them into this mess, at least for some time. I sighed and looked back at Ophelia. "Everyone deserves to be forgiven." I meant it more for myself than for Bram.

Ophelia's expression softened just a little. "If you can forgive him enough to ask for this, I will see what I can do." She closed her eyes and cupped her hands together as if she was holding water in them. She mumbled something I couldn't hear.

The spirits around us moved in synchronicity, and a faint murmur overcame them. In the distance, they multiplied, some dark and hooded and some light and wispy. I couldn't think about the hooded figures, though, because the murmuring increased to a significant din. Then suddenly it stopped.

Poe gasped, and I turned around.

Standing over Bram was the willowy figure of a small girl, probably about six or seven years old. Her brown hair was in pigtails. She was smiling, as if unbothered by the knife in Bram's belly.

"Don't cry, Daddy," she whispered. Her voice was soothing and clear. "I'm not lost."

Bram looked up, tears filling his eyes. "Baby girl."

She touched his hair, running her little fingers through it. "Don't you want to be with us, Daddy?"

He nodded. "More than anything, sweetheart." He released his hold on the knife and put his arms around the ghost. Despite her near-translucency, his arms did not go through her as I imagined they would. He held her and cried as he peered up at her.

"You can't right now," she told him, continuing to touch his hair. "You haven't been a good man since we left. If you were to leave now, you wouldn't be with us." She touched his face with a small hand. "I want you to be with us forever, Daddy."

He stared up at Ophelia. "Is this true?"

She nodded. "Your soul would be weighed, and it currently would not be found in favor of the plane on which your family resides."

He turned back to his daughter. "Honey, Daddy will do everything I can to change that. So that one day, when my soul is weighed, I can come to be with you and Mommy and Bubby."

She smiled a sweet child's grin. "You promise?"

He nodded. Then he reached to his head and plucked a piece of hair. "I don't think this will really work without your real hair, but this is how we make a promise now." He took her hand in his and wound his hair through their fingertips. "I promise you I will make amends for my actions, and I will wait until it is my time to leave this earth, and I will see you all again."

She squeezed his hand. "Thank you, Daddy." She glanced at Ophelia quickly, then back to Bram. "I have to go now."

"No!" he yelled. "Don't leave me. Not again." He clutched her to him, his head resting on her stomach as he pulled her tightly against him.

"I'm sorry," she said. Her voice was lighter, fainter. And then, just as suddenly as she appeared, her ghostly figure dissipated. "I love you, Daddy."

She was gone.

Snot and tears fell onto the cold earth as Bram stayed there, on all fours, crying like he probably cried the night she died.

Poe embraced his friend with tears in his eyes.

I dabbed at my own eyes. I still couldn't excuse Bram's actions, but I could understand them a little more now. If I could have brought my dad back, or at least gotten more time with him, at age thirteen, I would have done it, maybe even hurting people I didn't care about in the process.

Ophelia continued to watch Bram, a peaceful expression on her face. Over her shoulder, the horde of spirits closed in on us. Some hovered, transparent and light gray. Some were more human-shaped and a medium gray color, and they walked toward us slowly. At least they weren't shuffling like zombies.

Then there were the dark gray, almost black ones, hooded and scary. All they needed were scythes to be the grim reaper. As one drew closer, I could see under the hood. There was nothing, black air. I sucked in a deep breath. "Lady Ophelia? What are those, the ones with the hoods?" I asked, pointing.

She kept her eyes on me the entire time. "Those, my dear, are wraiths."

THIRTY-ONE

I HAD HEARD OF wraiths, but only in media, where they were portrayed differently depending on the writer. "They look... angry," I said, concerned.

"Oh, they are," Ophelia assured me. "Wraiths were once human beings, who were killed both magically and malevolently. They are perpetually tortured, and the longer they exist as wraiths, the more tortured and enraged they become."

That sounded dandy. I was facing half a dozen wraiths, interspersed with other specters and beings. It was a horror movie coming to life, and Bram was still oblivious to his surroundings. Poe kneeled beside his friend, trying to soothe him with words. Was I the only person who noticed what was going on?

"What do we do about all this?" I waved my hands toward the horde of undead beings.

Her eyebrows knitted together in confusion. "About what, mortal?"

"All these spirits flying around. And the wraiths!"

"My dear, you summoned my soul and my realm, did you not?"

I groaned. Technically, that was true, but I didn't want to do it.

"This is now the Realm of Lost Souls. These souls," she said, gesturing with her arms wide, "are simply doing what they do every day—wandering. Most will not harm you."

I raised an eyebrow. "Most?"

"Well... some wraiths are particularly tormented. They will not try to kill you, but their essence will harm mere mortals. It's full of magical energy."

"Malicious magic," I added, thinking back to what she had just told me about them.

She nodded. "As for the others... a ghost is simply the spirit of a dead human. They just wander aimlessly around for all time. They're easy to identify—they're very light in color and will ignore you. Now, shades." She smiled, as if thinking of her favorite pets. "You need to watch out for the shades. They were the spirits of non-humans, and some of them have retained their magical abilities even in death. I imagine it may irritate some of them to be dead."

I frowned. "So, a shade is worse than a wraith?"

She shook her head. "My dear. Nothing is worse than a wraith."

As if on cue, the hair on my arms and neck stood on end. Something was close. Something magical, and mad. I turned away from Ophelia to face the wraith that now hovered near Bram, its hollow visage pointed toward him.

Bram was my least favorite person right now, but he was a person. And I did just witness a heartwarming promise made to a dead girl, so something told me his days of being a bastard were behind him.

I sighed. My magic was weak from using so much to raise Ophelia, but I still felt it coursing through my body. I hoped Ophelia was messing with me, and it wouldn't be as bad as she'd implied. Did goddesses joke around with humans? I made a mental note to find out later. First, I needed to make sure this wraith didn't hurt anyone.

Stepping toward Bram, I waved my arms, trying to get his attention.

He saw me and nudged Poe, and they both stood to face the dark presence that glided toward them.

It didn't take long for me to arrive beside them.

"Wraith," I said, as if that explained everything.

"This is bad, isn't it?" Bram's voice quivered as he spoke.

"I think so," I said honestly.

Before we could discuss further, the figure turned toward me, and I felt lured toward it. It was stronger than the spirit stone, but not as strong as the pull toward Ophelia. It was, however, darker. Soulless.

Dark energy consumed me until I felt nothing—not fear nor hatred, but empty, hollow.

Beside me, Bram's visage changed. His eyes narrowed into a glare, his features hardening. He clenched his fists at his sides and a growl escaped his throat.

The wraith was bad news, alright. If Bram was already experiencing the anguish of its presence, I figured me and Poe weren't far behind. Our magic must have slowed the process, but I could feel my energy slipping away with each passing second. We had to act, and fast.

Mustering the rest of my strength, I used the wraith's magic to summon my own, my fingers tingling. Within seconds, a bright orange orb appeared in my hand, dancing on my fingertips. The wraith was too close to throw the orb, but it was the first weapon I could think of — a fireball.

The wraith glided toward me, its energy field strengthening until I was choking on its magic. Malicious magic.

My hand trembled beneath my fireball, but I kept it alive. Darkness crept into my bones. I was seconds from succumbing to the creature's power.

"Tori!" someone shouted behind me.

I snapped my attention away from the soulless figure to see

Bennett running toward me.

"I can't believe this," he said, huffing and puffing.

My body wanted more than anything to turn back to the wraith, to surrender to its magic. Gluing my eyes to Bennett took strength I didn't know I had. "Help me," I pleaded.

Confusion clouded his face, but after a moment, he grabbed my arm, and Poe's, and dragged us a few feet away, reaching back for Bram once we were out of the wraith's aura.

Slowly, the void inside me filled with positive energy, tingling and warm. I turned to the others, whose faces showed that the same thing was happening to them.

Bram's features relaxed, and he unclenched his fists. "That was horrible." He choked on his words, as if hands had been around his neck. "I couldn't feel anything, and then I felt ... livid. Just angry at the world."

"Stay away from those things until we can figure out how to handle them," I told him. I turned to Poe and Bennett—the people who knew magic better than me. "Do we have to kill it? We can't exactly send it back where it came from."

Bennett rubbed his chin stubble. "Casey would probably know more than me."

I glanced around. "Where is he?"

"In the car. I think he has a concussion."

"Ugh, I'm sorry, Bennett. Do you think he should be alone—what if he falls asleep?"

He frowned. "I think that's mostly a myth, but now I'm worried."

"You can go," I told him, hoping he didn't take me up on it.

He shook his head. "You need help here. We'll take care of this quickly, and I'll get back to him."

"Okay. So, what now?" I eyed the wraith suspiciously.

It hovered in the same place it was before, not trying to come closer. Yet.

Bram grunted and clutched his stomach in pain. His wound wouldn't kill him—I could tell that even without Ophelia's confirmation—but that didn't mean it wouldn't hurt.

Poe wrapped an arm around his friend's waist. "I'm going to settle him, then I'll come back," he told us.

And we were alone, a mage and a baby magician, against a wraith.

I grabbed Bennett's arm and pulled him toward Ophelia, who was watching the scene with amusement.

Bennett gazed at the goddess with awe, not speaking.

Turning my attention away from the gawking human, I asked, "What do we do?"

"The best option is to let him take you," she said matter-of-factly.

"Take me? You said wraiths won't actually hurt me."

She smiled again, showing glistening white teeth. "Magician. I said they will not try to hurt you on purpose, but their magic *will* harm mere mortals."

"I have innate magic, so I'm not a *mere* mortal, though, correct?" When she nodded, I continued. "My magic is battling the wraith's; I can feel it. It's like it wants to suck me into darkness and despair. Is that what you mean by taking me?"

She nodded, folding her arms over her chest. "Anger consumes the wraith. It will feed off the emotions of others, leaving nothing in its wake. Not wrath, not guilt, not even confusion. Nothing. And in doing so, the wraith will become stronger."

I was impatient and grabbed Ophelia's arms. "How do I stop it?"

She shrugged. "You don't. No one stopped wraiths in my realm before. In their natural habitat, there are no mortals, only souls. But here ... here, they will grow strong."

I was getting nowhere with Ophelia. She was good at playing mind games, but not at giving actual answers.

"Bennett," I said, nudging him in the side. "Can we cast a spell to shield our emotions from the wraith, so it doesn't take them from us?"

He looked surprised but nodded carefully. "I think so. You're going to have to do it, though. I don't have much on me for a spell like that."

I sighed. "I don't really know what I'm doing."

"You can do this, Tori. Just concentrate and chant. Your magic is powerful enough to do this. I've seen it. And I think it's why Bram chose you, too—everyone who's woken up from a coma has had magic like you. You're stronger than you know."

The confidence boost was nice, though I wished I could be like Bram or Casey and avoid the whole thing. I glanced around to find the wraith, which had started circling us. I wondered if it was keeping its distance from Ophelia. Maybe standing near her was saving us, for a moment at least.

I took Bennett's hands in mine, trying to ignore the pull of the nearby wraith. It wasn't as strong as before since I wasn't as close to it. But I didn't want there to be a pull at all. Sucking in a deep breath, I focused on what I wanted to accomplish, then said it aloud in Latin. I didn't know if Bennett's mage powers could help me at all, but I held his hands anyhow—just in case.

I chanted the Latin statement again, louder.

Nothing happened.

Shaking my head, I dropped Bennett's hands. "I don't know what to do."

He offered a sympathetic smile, which somehow made me feel worse. Of the two of us, I was the one with real magic. Speaking of magic ... My gaze latched onto what—or rather, who—I needed. "Poe!"

He stood over Bram, who was sitting with his back against a headstone, clutching his stomach. Poe nodded and ran to me. Silently, he grabbed one of my hands and one of Bennett's, understanding he would have to perform a spell.

"The wraith. Death magic," I said, hoping he understood.

"Of course. My specialty." He gripped our hands even tighter and closed his eyes.

"What are we doing?" Bennett asked.

I eyed Poe, who was shifting his weight and rolling his shoulders, preparing for a major task. After the original spell we'd cast, I didn't think I had enough strength left for anything else. I hoped he did. "I don't know much about death magic; most of what I know, I learned from you. But wraiths were made from death magic. So, the death magic that created them needs to be undone."

Poe nodded. "It's a little more complicated than that, but you get it."

"So, how do we undo this death magic? We don't even know how old this guy is or anything," Bennett asked. Beads of sweat gathered on his face.

The wraith howled as it circled us, moving faster than it had before. Before Poe could answer, the wraith lunged.

We let go of one another's hands and jumped back separately.

The wraith moved through the spot we were just in, shrieking.

I glanced at Ophelia, who shrugged. "Is this amusing to you?" I shouted above the wraith's wails.

"Somewhat," she answered.

Poe stared at the creature and mumbled words I couldn't hear.

I grabbed Bennett's hand again, more for comfort than the spell. Poe was doing all the heavy lifting, anyhow; I didn't know that our presence helped at all. My palms itched with sweat, and my heartbeat pounded in my ears. I didn't think I'd ever been this afraid in my life.

After a moment, Poe's eyes glowed a dark amber color. He lifted his hands and shouted at the wraith in Greek. It wasn't as crisp as mine, but it was sufficient. He was telling the wraith to seek its body, to find substance and take up mass. He was making the spirit corporeal. We could conceivably kill it if we could touch it.

When he finished his chant, he clenched his opened hands into fists. Then everything stopped. The amber in his eyes flickered back to brown, and the world seemed quieter for just a moment.

I watched the wraith's charcoal body darken to black. Its hood was still up, like it was a part of its body rather than an item of clothing. But beneath the hood, I could see pale skin developing. It hid in shadow, so I couldn't make out any identifying features, but the wraith was taking on elements of the person it used to be.

The wraith was becoming humanoid again. It had a body, solid features we could punch and shoot and burn. And yet, the wraith expanded. It literally increased in size as we watched.

The magic in the air multiplied with the wraith's body. I clutched my chest as it overpowered me. After a moment, I fell to the ground, taking deep breaths.

The wraith, though corporeal, was growing stronger. How were we supposed to kill it when we couldn't get near it?

Bennett kneeled beside me. "Is it the magic?"

I nodded and leaned against him.

"I can feel it, but not like you. You have a stronger connection to magic than I've ever seen."

I stared at him for a moment, wanting to ask more about his thoughts on my magic and my coma. But now was not the time.

I watched Poe.

He was fiddling with his bracelet, which had a glowing amber stone on it. He gripped it and chanted again. In ancient Greek, he bound the now-corporeal wraith to a small perimeter so it couldn't move too far and infect us with its magic any more than it had.

"But now we can't touch it," Bennett said when we finished.

Poe shrugged. "It's a trade-off, yeah. We bind it, we can't touch it. But it gives us time to plan our attack before we un-bind it again and kill the son of a bitch."

It made perfect sense. Except one thing was nagging at me. I stood and wiped my hands on my knees. "It's stronger. Way stronger."

He nodded as he reached into his pocket. He pulled out a lighter and a lone cigarette. After taking a long drag on it, he looked at me and nodded again, slowly and deliberately. "Here's the thing. Making something corporeal involves inflaming the death magic–"

"Inflaming it? We purposely increased its power?" What the hell had Poe gotten us into?

He sucked on the cigarette again. "Think of a balloon, right? Someone made the balloon in the first place—the death magic, making a wraith. We came along and blew the balloon up real big."

"Enormous," Bennett added.

Poe glared at him. "We'll blow it up so big, in fact–"

I chimed in. "It'll pop."

"Beauty and brains," Poe said.

"What happens when it pops?" Bennett asked. He rubbed his cheek, his eyes wide with panic.

"Anyone in the blast range will be affected by the magic. Death magic," Poe added with emphasis.

Oh, my god. If we didn't kill this guy before the death magic reached its peak, we would all die. This wasn't a well-thought-out plan.

"I know what you're thinking," Poe said, his accent heavy. "But it's the best way. We have a few minutes to kill it, and I think it can be killed now. We just have to get around really powerful magic to do it."

"Alright," I said, clapping my hands. "Let's kill this sucker."

Bennett took a step toward the wraith, but Poe grabbed him back.

"One more thing. Very important."

We watched as he finished his cigarette and stomped it out with his boot. "Wraiths are made by violent magic, right? What's more violent than being attacked with intent to kill?"

I shook my head. "Wait, wait. What you're telling me is that if the wraith kills us, we will become wraiths ourselves."

Poe nodded. "The increased power in the wraith at this moment will result in a very empowered wraith being created, if that were the case."

I groaned. "Why do we have to be the ones to do this?"

From behind us, a thickly accented voice responded. "Because you're the ones who have a problem with my wraiths."

I turned to her and scowled. "Your wraiths will kill people if given the chance."

She shrugged, the movement effortless and graceful. She may not have been the vengeful demi-goddess I had feared, but she was going to be no help cleaning up this mess.

I looked at the wraith. Its magical field was visible now, it was so strong. I was farther away than I was before, but I could still feel it. How were we supposed to get close enough to kill it?

THIRTY-TWO

"THERE'S A GUN IN my car," Bram called. His voice sounded less labored than it had previously.

Poe shook his head. "Binding spells won't let anything out, but they won't let anything in, either."

"That would have been too easy," I said, shaking my head. I still had no clear vision of how this was going to go.

"I don't think we have much time, though," Poe said, his eyes showcasing his fear. "We need to do this now."

Bennett raised both his hands and closed his eyes. Soon, his hands held glowing blue orbs.

Poe nodded in approval and turned to me. "What about you?"

It only took me seconds to conjure a fireball this time. I was getting better; well, faster, at least.

Poe waved his hands in the air and began his chant. I recognized it as a similar version to what bound the wraith in the first place, but I didn't know it by heart. His eyes and bracelet blazed as he spoke in Greek.

As soon as Poe's words were done, we all began using our weapons simultaneously.

The wraith moved more quickly than before, as if it were running toward us, if one could run while hovering.

I flung fireballs at it, rapidly replenishing them, though I wasn't sure how long I could keep the pace up before I was too drained to create any.

The wraith stopped suddenly, its form twisting and writhing as it took direct hits from my fireballs, Bennett's orbs, and the white lightning-like flashes Poe was throwing. It howled in what I assumed was pain, though it could have been a war cry. Lurching forward, it continued its path to us, much more slowly than before.

I cast a glance toward Ophelia, who watched the scene play out with mild interest. This was probably the first battle she'd witnessed involving one of her lost souls. Amid the pounding in my chest and ears, a small pang clutched my chest. Whoever this wraith was, it used to be a person. And we were blasting it with whatever magical power we had, intending to decimate it.

Bennett dropped his hands, his head hanging in defeat. Being a mage meant he had less to work with than me and Poe, and it appeared he had exhausted his resources.

I wanted to tell him it was okay, that he had done everything he could, but I was too busy trying to avoid the wrath of a giant floating grim reaper. My energy stores depleting, I took a deep breath and glanced at Poe.

Sweat beaded on his face, which wore a grimace. He grunted and threw more lightning at the wraith.

Its shriek pierced my ears, and for a moment, I covered them with my palms. The wraith seemed to stumble backwards, dropping to the ground into a charcoal mass.

Poe edged closer to it.

"Poe! It's not dead!" I called. Though it was waning, I still felt its magic.

"I know," he said, turning back to me. "But the balloon's about to pop. We need to finish this." He thrust the wrist wearing the bracelet in front of him. A blaze of white emitted from his hand and flew toward the wraith.

And then reversed and flew right back at Poe.

He collapsed, clutching his chest. "Too strong," he stuttered.

We rushed to him, but the wraith's magic was too potent. I stumbled a few feet away. Poe was right; it was too strong. I reached for Bennett, but he wasn't as close as my eyes believed. I fell to the ground next to Poe. The magic in our bodies was betraying us, this close to the powerful wraith.

And the balloon was about to pop. We'd all be dead any minute now.

Behind the wraith, Bram ran toward us, his shirt stained with blood. As he neared, he raised his knife. "This is for my daughter." He plunged the knife into the mass and twisted it.

The magic in the air slowly became less overwhelming.

Bram rushed to Poe. "My friend."

Poe clutched his chest still. The color quickly drained from his face.

Bram took his hand and held it, tears falling down his cheeks.

Poe's lips were turning blue and his face white.

The wraith's magic was dissipating quickly, and I was able to sit up without its heavy weight on my chest. "Ophelia!"

She walked over like she was taking a leisurely stroll. "Magician?"

"You're a goddess. Can you help him?

She shook her head. "I can only weigh his soul once he is gone. Which will be any moment now."

I closed my eyes, letting tears spill. Poe wasn't a friend; hell, he was a bad guy when this whole thing started. But he would die trying to help us defend our realm. And he would die in vain, I realized, as I surveyed the rest of the world around us. Spirits still hovered against the black night sky. There were a couple more wraiths around here too, but none close enough to harm us currently. I'd worry about them later; I needed fresh magic and a new plan to deal with them.

All I could do in the moment was focus on the dying man before us. "Poe." I crawled to where he laid a few feet away.

His glassy eyes locked on mine. "It's too late. But take…" he coughed. "Bracelet."

I spotted the silver bracelet around his wrist, the glow in the amber stones fading. I didn't know if I could use it, since I wasn't a wizard and certainly not a necromancer. But I would honor the wishes of the man who gave his life against the wraith. I nodded and unclasped it. "Thank you," I whispered to him.

"And you," he whispered back.

And then he was gone.

THIRTY-THREE

The magic in the air had disappeared, making it easier to stand, though my body ached as if I'd been in a fight. Which I guess I had. I wiped my hands on my knees.

The others stood too, and we all gathered around our fallen comrade. Bennett put his arm around me and pulled me close.

Bram remained on the ground, cradling Poe's lifeless body in his arms. His shoulders shook as he cried, and my heart broke for him. To lose his family and then a close friend...

I could kind of relate, between the loss of my dad, my mother's coldness, and Grey moving on without me. Only one of those people was dead, but they were lost to me all the same. Who knows what I would be willing to do to reverse some of that loss?

My shoulders slumped. Other figures floated around the cemetery, and it was clear we weren't prepared to handle them.

Ophelia's voice cut through the darkness. "Magicians. Mage. Human," she added, almost as an afterthought. "I have never witnessed what I have just seen from you. You are all stronger and smarter than I expected." She glided toward us, ethereal and regal, stopping a few feet away. "I cannot bring back your friend, as I told you already. But when I weigh his soul momentarily, I will consider his bravery and his last attempt to save others from the wraith. They are monsters, the worst in my realm, and the sad thing is, they don't even try to be."

That didn't excuse anything. Just like Grey and Marina didn't plan to fall in love, and Killian's mom didn't want to become cursed until she had to save her son. Things happened outside our control, leaving others to pick up the pieces.

I leaned into Bennett's embrace, empty and exhausted. I still had to get back to Marina and Grey and sort out that aspect of my life.

Bram stared up at us, hiccupping through his tears. "I've known him since grade school. The only reason he agreed to do this was because of our friendship. I've betrayed him."

He wasn't wrong, so I wasn't sure how to respond. Luckily, he started speaking again.

"Your sister is free to go. You are all released."

That was the best news I'd heard in a while, maybe since I woke up from the coma. I could make things right with Marina, knowing I didn't have to look over my shoulder all the time. I could tell her the truth—all of it. She probably wouldn't handle it well, but I owed her that.

With a last glance at Bram, who still held Poe on the ground, I turned toward my sister and Grey. Bennett's arm was around my shoulder, and we held each other as we trudged across the grass.

Before we reached Marina, a dark sedan pulled into the cemetery and parked next to Bram's car. The door opened and one of Bram's men stood up, surveying the damage with wide eyes. He spotted Bram and headed toward his boss.

The car was between us and Marina, and I could see the silhouette of a figure in the back seat. Who could that be? Everyone was here but Killian.

Worried, I stopped beside the car and opened the door.

A middle-aged woman with dark skin and emerald eyes stared back at me.

We gaped at one another wordlessly.

After a moment, the woman's shoulders slumped, and tears welled in her eyes. "I don't know how I got here."

The shock wearing off, I could think more clearly. "You're Killian's mom, aren't you?"

When she smiled, there was no doubt in my mind they were related. "You know my son?"

"I do." My heart, which had slowed down somewhat after all the excitement, thudded in my ears again. If his mother was here, where was Killian? "Do you know where he is?"

She shook her head.

Apparently, he hadn't made it to get her to leave town. He wouldn't leave without her... would he? Everything I knew about Killian said no, but as he so kindly pointed out earlier, we were practically strangers.

"Don't worry. I'll find Killian," I told her, hoping I hadn't made a promise I couldn't keep.

"Who?"

I sighed. Killian had mentioned his mother's mind was getting worse. Not that I didn't believe him before, but seeing it now brought a new sympathy for him. Watching his mother go through this had to be difficult.

When I called him, he answered after the first ring. "She's not here," he said immediately. His voice was hoarse.

"She's here, and she's safe."

He heaved a sigh of relief.

I hesitated.

"But?" he asked.

"She doesn't remember you right now," I whispered.

"I'm not surprised. It comes and goes." He cleared his throat. "Are you okay? You don't sound right."

Killian sighed. "No, I'm not. But I'll be better once I get my mom and get out of here. How long do we have before the ritual?"

As I pondered how to break the news to him, I surveyed the surrounding landscape. It didn't appear the beings were drawn to humans, as they roamed in random patterns around the large cemetery. I wondered why the wraith that attacked us did so—perhaps once they became close enough, their magic could sense ours? Either way, we were safe for the moment. But nothing would ever be the same again.

He understood my silence. "It's done, isn't it?"

"Yes."

"How bad is it?"

I glanced around again. Bennett stood beside me, his face showing his exhaustion. Bram was composing himself over Poe's lifeless body. Ophelia watched her lost souls meander with an unreadable expression. Over the top of the car, I could see Marina, no longer held by Bram's men, cuddling into Grey's arms, burying her head into his chest. "Bad," I told him finally.

"Where are you? I'll come to you."

"Same place. Bram had us perform the spell in the cemetery." It was as good a place as any for the souls to roam, I guessed.

"Ten minutes." He hung up the call.

I relayed the message to Killian's mom, who didn't seem fazed. "Can you wait with her for a minute?" I asked Bennett. When he nodded, I walked around the back of the car toward Marina and Grey.

I stopped in front of them and cringed. What I hadn't seen a moment ago was Marina cradling her arm, wincing in pain.

"What happened?" I cried, turning to the man beside her. He had released her but was probably waiting for Bram to give him official permission to walk away.

"Superman here tried to start something," he said with a

smirk. "She got caught up in the crossfire."

"I think it's broken," Grey said softly.

My mind brought me back to the encounter at Pages and Potions, where Grey had yelled at me and stood by while Killian and I dealt with Johnny. Yet he had tried to take on two oversized thugs to save Marina. If his choice hadn't been obvious before, it definitely was now.

"Marina," I said, stepping forward. I ached to hug her, but she wouldn't even look at me. "Are you okay?" I asked instead, feeling slightly awkward. When she didn't answer, I glanced up at Grey, who wouldn't meet my eyes. "I just want to know you're alright."

"Go away, Tori," Grey said, finally looking at me. Purple bruises were forming outside his eye, dried blood caked over a gash peeking out from under the frame of his glasses. "We don't want to see you. You've done enough."

My eyes threatened to water, but I nodded and took a step back. I wanted to say I understood and that we'd deal with it once it's all over. But wraiths were wandering all over town. I was going to be homeless tomorrow. A demi-goddess had been unleashed on Earth, and we didn't know what that would mean. How would we define *over* now?

"No," I said, my voice soft. I straightened my back and narrowed my eyes at Grey, who still wasn't looking at me. When I spoke, my tone was harsh. "*I've* done enough? *You* don't want to see *me*?" I balled my fists at my sides.

"And what exactly did I do to you? Did I lie to you about having magic? Sure. But you know why I did that?" I paused and searched their expressions, but neither reacted, so I continued. "I lied because you two are so phobic of magic users that I thought you would disown me just weeks after I came out of a fucking coma."

Marina flinched but didn't look at me.

"Do you think I want to see you touching my sister, Grey? We loved each other. It's good to see that love had limits." I took a deep breath, willing my magic to remain at bay. Flipping out with uncontrolled magic would be the worst thing that could happen right now. But I was so tired and angry, I wasn't sure I could restrain it if it activated. My skin tingled, but I didn't know how much I had left in me for a magic show; my energy was tapped.

Neither responded.

"You know what? Fuck you guys. I'm not the bad guy here. If you can't see that, I don't know what to tell you."

I stomped away several steps, but stopped when Marina called my name. I didn't turn, instead letting her talk to my back.

"I need you..." she said, her voice pleading through her sobs.

The tingling of the magic calmed down. "What?"

"Turn around and come here."

Uncertain but hopeful, I slowly turned back around. My skin teemed with anger, but I tried to set it aside. I could at least see what she wanted. Maybe my outburst had made her apologetic.

"Closer," Marina said. She reached a shaky hand toward her head and pulled a couple strands of hair out with a flinch. Holding it, she stretched her arm toward me.

The gesture melted the last of my reservations, and I crossed the rest of the distance between us. Remembering the magical promise I'd made to her already, I pinched a piece of my hair out and clutched her hand with mine. "I love you, Marina. I don't want to fight over something I can't control. Just tell me what to do and I'll do it." Tears burned my eyes as I waited for her to respond.

Marina's expression was unreadable. She waited while I wrapped both sets of hair around our wrists. "Tori. I want you to promise ..." Her voice trailed off and her icy blue eyes pierced mine.

"Anything," I whispered.

Marina sucked in a deep breath, her gaze never leaving mine. "Promise to leave me alone."

"Wh-what?" My eyes watered and my breath caught in my throat.

Grey's eyes widened. "Marina!"

She paid him no mind and kept her cold stare focused on me. "Did you see what you did, Tori? What you're capable of? I don't want this in my life, and that means I don't want you in my life. I don't want to hear from you, or see you, or know what's going on with you. Promise to stay away from me. For good."

Tears spilled, yet I stood there with my wrist bound to hers. I couldn't do what she wanted. I wanted to give her everything she asked for, but I couldn't give her that.

"Tori." She turned her head. She couldn't even look at me anymore.

"Don't make me do this," I said between sniffles.

Grey interjected again. "Come on, honey. You're just upset–"

"I am not *just upset*," she said, cutting him off. "I am *tired*. Tired of being lied to. Tired of wondering when someone's magic will mess everything up—not just in my store, but in the world. I can't live like this, Tori. I won't."

"I can't," I said, pulling my hand away.

She reached her broken arm toward me and clutched our fingers together. Her face showed her pain, but she kept her grip on our hands.

So, this is what she really wanted. This is what would make my sister happy. I took a deep breath. "I promise... God, Marina, I can't!"

Hatred gleamed in her beautiful crystal blue eyes. I couldn't see anything past the hate. She wasn't my sister anymore; she was a stranger.

I sighed softly. When I spoke, my voice came out in a squeak. "I promise to stay away from you." I yanked my hand from her grip and flung the hair onto the ground. Then I turned my back on my sister and walked out of her life.

THIRTY-FOUR

I CRIED INTO BENNETT'S shoulder while waiting for Killian to arrive. True to his word, a set of headlights shone through the fog a few minutes later. He parked beside us.

Killian flung open his door without killing the engine first. "Where is she?" He rushed toward me.

I stepped aside and gestured to the back seat.

The woman's face lit up when she saw her son. She spoke to him in a rush of words that were foreign to my ears.

Killian responded in the same language and leaned in for an embrace. "Are you okay, Mama?" he asked in English. "Did they hurt you?"

She shook her head. "I'm just scared."

He stood back up but kept his hand on her shoulder. When he turned to me, I got a better look at him—his face was swelling in places and purple in others. Blood dried along his left cheek.

"What happened?" I cried.

He removed his hand from his mother's shoulder and turned his back to her as if he didn't want her to hear. "Bram's men had already taken her and were waiting for me at her house. They made it clear my allegiance to him wasn't over yet, and I shouldn't leave town." He gingerly touched the cut on his cheek and winced.

"Oh, man." I wasn't sure how to respond.

"But she's alright, so I will be, too," he said. He attempted a smile, which emphasized the swelling in his cheek. He glanced around, taking in his surroundings for the first time. "Well, hopefully."

"Bram released us," I offered.

He frowned. "So, he got what he wanted?"

I shook my head. "Not exactly. But I think he's going to be a different person from now on." I wasn't sure what his politics were prior to this event, but I figured they'd be more altruistic afterward. He had to make up for his misdeeds to see his family again, after all.

Killian's face showed he didn't quite understand, and how could he? He hadn't been here for the chaos. Then his eyes widened, as if he had a new thought. "Where's the necklace?"

I pointed in the general direction. From here, I could see the candles, but the jewelry wasn't glowing anymore. It must have cooled down.

He stared for a moment. "Will you stay with her another minute? I'm hoping there's enough magic left we can fix her right here and now."

"Of course." I turned to Bennett as Killian ran toward the site of the ritual. "Go check on Casey. I'm fine here."

Bennett walked down the road toward his car, slower than normal.

I hoped the drain on him wasn't permanent. But I really didn't know how all this worked, and I didn't think he did, either. After another glance at his mom, I turned back to watch Killian sprint across the grass, dodging headstones and stray bouquets of flowers until he slowed to a stop.

Killian stared at the ground for a moment. Then he shouted, "Where is it?"

I frowned. "It's there, with the candles," I yelled. When he didn't respond, I ran toward him, leaving his mother alone.

"What are you shouting—Oh." The candles had fallen, their flames out. In the center of the triangle they created was a pile of ash, with a blue stone setting atop it. The necklace hadn't just gotten hot; it had burned up.

"I don't understand." His voice cracked.

An ache shot across my chest. His mother didn't deserve her fate. I didn't know what Killian had done to cause the curse, but no one deserved that. I hoped he could find another way to save her, one that didn't involve me. "I'm sorry. I didn't know."

He kicked at the ground silently. When his eyes raised again, they locked onto Ophelia. "Why?" He'd skipped the shock and awe at seeing a demi-goddess and gone straight to demands. If he wasn't careful, it could end badly.

Ophelia floated toward us. She peered at the ash and back up at him. "Moving an entire realm is powerful magic. It must have been too much."

Killian shook his head. "Now what do I do?"

Ophelia's face displayed sympathy. "If it is a conduit for magic you seek, I'm sure there are more."

"I've tried so many things, and none of them work. This was my last hope." His head hung and his shoulders shook.

I reached for his hand, grasping it in mine. "I'm sure you'll find something, Killian."

"I don't have information about anything else that might help her." He stared at the ground. "I'm going to lose her," he whispered.

Damnit. Not only did I pity him, but I empathized with him. I didn't know where Killian's father was, but I'd lost a parent—two, really—and my sister. Family wasn't just important; it was everything. I had none anymore, really, and I didn't know if Killian had anyone other than his mom.

"She's not lost yet," I told him. "There's still time."

He smiled meekly, as if he didn't believe me.

Hell, I wasn't sure if I believed myself.

"I need to get back to Mama," he said, releasing my hand. "See you around."

I nodded but stayed with Ophelia. I wondered what she was thinking of our world. What would happen next? For her, for me, for our city.

We sure as hell weren't going to fight another wraith. That one had nearly killed us all, and Poe didn't make it out alive. I fidgeted with his bracelet in my hands. The rest of the wraiths would have to wait until I figured out how to use Poe's magic or found someone who did. And we needed a better plan for the next one.

"Whoa," I said aloud, shaking my head. "Next one?" Was I really planning to take on more of these things? Who appointed me to be in charge of them?

Ophelia watched me with keen violet eyes. "I cannot remove them from your world, mortal, for your realm is now ours. However, I can bind them to your hallowed grounds so they may harm less of your kind." She closed her eyes and murmured a few words I couldn't make out. When she opened her eyes, she nodded slightly.

"Thank you." I gazed around, biting my lower lip. There had to be someone better suited to handle this turn of events than me. The rest of the world had been living with magic for five years, and I just woke up a few weeks ago. Maybe that was my next task—finding someone more qualified to handle this issue. But first, I needed to rest.

I bid Ophelia adieu and headed toward Bennett's Jeep. Part of me wanted to check on Bram, but I didn't have the energy to expend on him. Getting to Bennett and Casey was difficult enough.

"Hop in," Bennett said from the driver's seat.

I got in the back and leaned against the cushion behind me. I wanted to tell them about Killian's mom and Ophelia's binding. Instead, I closed my eyes and tilted my head back against the headrest. As Bennett pulled the car away, I wondered if it was only the wraiths who were bound to the hallowed ground, or if the rest of the undead beings would be too. And what would happen to Ophelia—where would she go now?

Where would I go? What would I do without my sister? I hadn't even gotten used to the idea of losing my fiancé, and now the only other family I had wanted me gone.

Tears trickled down my cheeks as the questions swirled around my mind. It felt like only seconds before I drifted to sleep, dreaming of lost souls and violet stars.

ACKNOWLEDGEMENTS

THIS BOOK PROBABLY WOULD have been finished without outside help. However, as with many (dare I say all?) creative endeavors, help and support from others has enhanced the final product. I would be remiss if I failed to acknowledge the impact these people have had on the creation of not only the singular novel you've just read, but also the entire Unveiled series.

Several people offered early critiques of *Revival*, but two stuck with it through all its iterations. Not only did they assist with word choice and errant commas, but they told me when a plot point was weak or contradictory, a character behaved inconsistently, or something simply did not make sense. These two fellow readers/writers became true critique partners, and I am forever grateful for their help. I also owe them each dozens of critiques. Jessica and Stacey – I couldn't have made it this far without you. Or, if I did, the result would have been lacking.

I didn't know the term "alpha reader" while this person was being one, so she had many unofficial titles. She read the (then) most recent draft in record time, offering feedback in statements that were much longer than I anticipated. She made references to characters like, "That's such a Bennett thing to say" in normal conversation, and was always ready to share ideas on the plot, characters, sequels, Kickstarter goodies, and even my author TikToks. She sacrificed her taste buds to test the teas (which she single-handedly designed) for the Kickstarter. Cheyanne –

your input elevated this journey, and the book itself. The entire series will bear the mark of your assistance.

Revival was made available to the public on 10/31/22 through Kindle Vella. That platform allowed me to introduce my work to people I wouldn't have offered it to, some of whom became sounding boards for sequel ideas or writing-related angst. It also showcased my typos to the world. My dear, loving, supportive aunt became the primary person to point these out. While that was at times annoying, it was immensely helpful. Don't be fooled – my aunt deserves acknowledgement for much more than this. But that's another story. Linda – what can I say? I love you.

The following people supported my Kickstarter campaign, helping provide funding to put the final product in your hands (or on your screen). Some of them were friends or family already, and provided emotional support throughout this adventure. All of them helped me reach my goal.

Jaeden Jarvis, Tammi L. Duis, Allison Wells, Sarah Riley, Amber Schmidt, Shannon J., Chele Cooke, Cate Dean, Kayla Ann, Adam Barnes, Haleigh Kirch, David Neth, Christine Kilner, Megan Astell, Brianna Welch-Martin, Natasha Rueschhoff, Sian Lloyd-Wiggins, W. Roongkham, Leslie, BeeGee, T.L. Ryder, R .L. Goodell, four anonymous backers, and others who were mentioned above – Kickstarter was a time-consuming pain, and your support made it worthwhile.

Thank you, thank you, thank you.

ABOUT THE AUTHOR

DEBBIE LYNN REMEMBERS SOME of her earliest fiction, written on lined paper with hand-drawn images in colored pencil. Over thirty years later, she can recall specific characters, plots, scenes, and even quotes, of these hilarious first attempts at authorship. Learning skills took practice, but imagination and passion for writing were present from childhood. Debbie studied some of those skills while earning a Bachelor's degree in English with a concentration in linguistics and a minor in creative writing. She also earned a Bachelor's degree in psychology and became a therapist, which she (half-jokingly) considers her back-up career until she can be a full-time author.

Debbie published two fantasy short stories, both in 2010, in anthologies with a small independent press. She has participated in National Novel Writing Month 13 times since 2006, which has generated 12 novels in various stages of revision, and one completed, edited, and ultimately published book (hint: you're reading it right now).

Learn more at www.debbielynnwrites.com.